T0208208

A LOST MAN

A LOST MAN

CLAY WADE, BOOK 3

ART CLEPPER

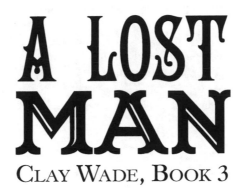
iUniverse®

A LOST MAN
CLAY WADE, BOOK 3

iUniverse books may be ordered through booksellers or by contacting:

iUniverse
1663 Liberty Drive
Bloomington, IN 47403
www.iuniverse.com
1-800-Authors (1-800-288-4677)

Cover by: ALLYSEN MILLER

ISBN: 978-1-5320-9234-3 (sc)
ISBN: 978-1-5320-9235-0 (e)

Library of Congress Control Number: 2020901573

Print information available on the last page.

iUniverse rev. date: 01/27/2020

CHAPTER

ONE

F or the last month, Clay Wade has ridden west, following his horse's ears, with not a care in the world where they led him. The sun is beating down so hot he feels like he is on fire, but he hardly notices. His hat is pulled low to shield his eyes, but the glare from the ground is almost unbearable. His horses plod along suffering from the same heat that he is. The little water in his canteen is almost too hot to drink, and he has only taken a couple of sips since leaving his camp early this morning. The horses had not had a drink since mid-day yesterday. He hasn't seen shade since the sun came up, and as far as he can see, there is no hope of finding any soon. He and his two horses seem to be the only living things in this barren country. Oh, he sees a lizard or scorpion occasionally, resting in whatever shade they can find, and far overhead, a buzzard sailed on the wind currents just waiting for something to die. Everything does sooner or later, and they have the patience to wait.

It's the hottest part of the day when he stopped to give his horses a little water from the small amount he has left. He dismounted, and

1

loosened the girth, poured a little water in his hat, and held it for each horse to get a few swallows. It wasn't much, but it was all he could do. They nudged him begging for more, and he felt terrible that he had none to give them. He put a small smooth stone in his mouth to try to get the saliva flowing. His mouth felt as dry as old shoe leather. After a few minutes, he switched the saddle and packs from one horse to the other. The horse he's riding is carrying much more weight than the one with the packs. When they have rested a few minutes, he took up the reins and lead rope and started walking, leading the horses. He walked until he begins to stagger, and then he mounted and continued toward the setting sun.

He rode with his eyes scanning the horizon, looking for any indication of shade and water. Indians from the Apache and Comanche tribes were known to frequent this area. So far, he hasn't seen any sign of them, but from what he has heard, by the time you see them, it's too late.

This whole west Texas appears to be perfectly flat with nothing to break the monotony. But he has learned as he rides that is not the case. Sudden dips and washes can hide an entire tribe that you won't see until you're right on top of it.

The sun went down, and the temperature dropped considerably. After a few more miles, Clay removed his coat from the back of his saddle and put it on. As hot as it gets during the day, the nights get cold enough for a fire and a blanket.

With no water for his horses, he saw no reason to stop for the night. They won't get any rest anyway, and knowing they are suffering wouldn't allow him to sleep either.

Long after the sun went down, and it was too dark to see more than thirty feet or so, the horses' heads came up, and they turned more to the north. They break into a trot and want to go faster, but he held them back. He can't see where they're going, but he trusts them not to fall off a cliff. After what must have been a half-mile or more, the ground took a sharp dip, and Clay heard the water splash when both horses bury their heads up to their eyes. He stepped down, dropped to his belly, and drank his fill. He didn't know what the water looked like, but it was wet, that's all that mattered for now. When his thirst was satisfied, he pulled the horses back from the water. He didn't want them drinking too much at once and get sick. He removed the saddle and packs and give each horse a cup of oats from his pack and staked them on a nearby patch of grass. It was too dark, and he was too tired to find wood for a fire, so he made a meal of jerky and water. Before he turned in, he led the horses to the water and let them have another good drink. He spread his blankets and bedroll on the sand near the water, removed his hat and boots, and lay down, hoping to get a good night's sleep, something he hadn't had in over three months. As soon as he closes his eyes, the picture of Ellen, with blood on her head, and their two-year-old son sitting by her side crying invaded his mind.

Since that day, he had been a man with only one thought, REVENGE. But there was no one to hold accountable.

From all the evidence at the scene, Ellen's horse spooked and threw her to the ground. Her head hit a rock, and she died instantly. Carter, their two-year-old son, was riding on the saddle in front of her when she was thrown, but he wasn't hurt.

Clay came upon the grisly scene as he was returning home. His first clue that something was wrong was when he saw Ellen's horse standing favoring her right front leg. As he rode closer, he saw Ellen lying on the ground with Baby Carter sitting by her side, crying. Clay jumped from his horse and took Ellen in his arms. He knew immediately she was dead. He sat holding her rocking back and forth, crying and cradling Carter in his arms. Carter didn't understand what was happening. He seemed to understand his mother was hurt, but that was all. After what must have been an hour or more, Clay finally got control of his emotions enough to lift Ellen onto his saddle, and mounted holding her in his arms, reached down and picked Carter up, and set him on his shoulders and slowly rode home.

When he rode into the barnyard Lefty, and the rest of the crew helped him down from his saddle. He carried Ellen in the house and laid her on their bed. Lefty entertained Carter in the bunkhouse while Matt saddled a horse and rode to Luke and Maddie's house.

Meanwhile, Gerald rode to Ed and Lisa's house to inform them. Ed was Ellen's brother.

When Maddie and Lisa arrived, Clay was sitting beside the bed, holding Ellen's hand.

They told him to go outside while they took care of Ellen. He walked out like a man in a trance and sat on the porch crying.

Willie rode to Cuero and informed the minister and Sheriff Helm. Word spread through Cuero like wildfire, and they were all there the next morning for the burial. She was laid to rest on the hill overlooking the house. Clay asked the undertaker to order a headstone, and place it where he could see it from the front porch. After the service, when everyone left, and Clay was alone, he sat by the grave late into the night.

Every day Clay went up the hill and sat by the grave until after dark. When he came down, he sat on the front porch and drank coffee. No one knew how long he sat there every night.

That was the second major blow in his life in the last six months. Their baby daughter had died during the winter from pneumonia. He and Ellen were just now getting over that loss, and now this happens. It was just more than he could stand right now.

Ed and Lisa took Carter to their house, and Clay seemed to forget he had a son.

Maddie tried talking to him, but he didn't appear to know she was there. He just sat and stared into space, and when Luke or any of the men tried talking to him, it was like he didn't hear them.

Work on the ranch went on as usual but without any input or help from Clay. He saddled his horse each morning and rode out, but no one knew where he went or what he did. When he came back, he unsaddled his horse and walked up the hill and sat beside Ellen's grave until after dark. They never saw a light in the house, morning or night. He sat on the porch until he went in and to bed without ever lighting a lamp. He ate his meals, when he ate, in the bunkhouse kitchen with the men, but never engaged in their conversations.

His hair grew long, and he seldom shaved or bathed. He lost weight and wore the same clothes for days.

That was the routine for over a month until one morning Clay didn't come out to saddle his horse. The men waited until long after the time he usually came out. When he didn't show, Lefty knocked on the door but got no answer. After knocking the third time, he opened the door and went in. No one was there, and it looked like no one had slept there the night before. He came out and informed Matt and Gerald. That started them looking around the barn where they discovered two of Clay's favorite horses were gone.

Further searching revealed a packsaddle, two panniers, and a large supply of food gone from the pantry in the house, and the kitchen in the bunkhouse. When Luke and Willie arrived a short time later, they discussed what they should do. Matt and Lefty decided to track him to see where he went. They had no trouble finding his trail where he left the ranch and crossed the Guadalupe River riding west.

They followed his trail all day until it was too dark to see. They made camp for the night, and returned home the next day, and informed Willie, Luke, Ed, and Gerald what they discovered, which wasn't much, just that Clay was headed west, and had not stopped for anything since leaving home.

The four men stood quietly, thinking, for a few minutes. Finally, Luke broke the silence, "Well, he has a lot to get straightened out. Maybe this is his way of handling it. We don't know what we would do. I hope we never have to find out."

Clay waited until midnight when he knew all the men were asleep. He had his saddlebags packed, and the food supplies he planned to take with him were laid out on the table. He went to the barn and got his pack saddle, and panniers, and packed them, and put them on the front porch. He then caught up his two favorite horses, Blue, and Socks. Socks were saddled, and the pack saddle strapped on Blue. They were brought around to the front of the house out of sight from the barn and bunkhouse. It only took Clay a few minutes to load everything. He made a final walk through the house and then walked up the hill to Ellen's grave. He spent a half-hour telling her goodbye. When he walked away, he didn't know if he would ever be back. There were just too many memories here. He had to get away. He was hoping a change of scenery would help ease the pain of losing Ellen. She had been his entire life for the last three years. All the plans they made and talked about for them and their children would never happen now. He felt like he had nothing to live for, just like when he returned from the war and found his parents had died, and his girlfriend married to another man.

These thoughts were all that was on his mind as he rode away.

The terrain ahead of him was the same as what he left behind. There was nothing as far as the eye could see except a few cacti, mesquite, and sagebrush from time to time. At every rise in the ground, he stopped to give his horses a breather while he scanned his surroundings. Even as distraught and grieving as he was, he never forgot to take care of his horses.

He was riding west in west Texas. He didn't know or care where he was or where he was going and had no plans for the future.

He rode all day, camped at night, and rode all the next day. The days all rolled into one, but the nights were something else. He felt like he wasn't getting any sleep. Every time he closed his eyes, he saw Ellen with blood on her head. She was there in his dreams every time he closed his eyes. He awoke each morning as tired as when he went to bed.

His horses were his only companions. He took to talking to them as if they were human.

He avoided all contact with people whenever possible. He avoided towns and ranches except when he needed supplies. He rode in, got what he needed, and rode out. If anyone tried to strike up a conversation, he just turned away and rode out of town. That almost got him in fights several times when men accused him of thinking he was too good to talk to them. He was dirty, unshaven, with hair down past his shoulders, and he was not in a good mood, ever. Most people took one look and stepped aside, giving him plenty of room.

He had just purchased supplies and was putting them in his packs on his horse when a big burly man made a sarcastic remark about his appearance. Clay kept packing his supplies, ignoring the man. After a couple of attempts to get a rise from Clay, the man grabbed Clay by the shirt and spun him around. His fist was drawn back prepared to hit Clay in the face when he felt the gun barrel in his stomach and heard the hammer click as it was pulled back to full cock. The man froze, looked down at the gun, and then saw the look in Clay's eyes. He lifted his hands above his shoulders and backed off. He continued to back away until he reached the boardwalk in front of the store and then walked away without taking his eyes off Clay. Clay watched the man until he was sure he was not going to cause any more trouble. He had mounted his horse and was turning him to ride out of town when the merchant came out the door of his store and started sweeping the porch. He called to Clay just loud enough for Clay to hear, "Say, fellow, you better watch your back. That was Bull Norton you just pulled your gun on. He thinks he's the bull of the woods around here. If I were a bettin' man, I would give some pretty good odds that he'll follow you out of town, and try to get even. He has three brothers and a daddy who is just as big and mean as he is. If they get their hands on you, I won't give two bits for your life."

Clay touched the brim of his hat in a two-finger salute and rode out of town, heading west.

As far as Clay could see, there didn't appear to be a hill, ravine, creek, tree, or anything else.

He knew he was in Indian Territory. The Comanche controlled most of this part of west Texas, but there were other tribes around also. He was as careful as he could be trying to spot trouble before it spotted him. He was continually watching for tracks of any kind, but so far, he had not seen any indication of Indians.

Clay kept a close watch over his shoulder just in case Bull Norton did decide to follow him. After about two miles, a small cloud of dust appeared on the trail behind him. After watching it for a minute and determined it was coming in his direction, he started looking for a place to make a stand. He wasn't looking for trouble, but if those men were, he was prepared to give them more than they could handle.

Every few minutes, he checked his back trail. The men were getting closer. Clay didn't try to outrun them. Even with two horses that were probably better than theirs, he knew they would eventually catch up, probably while he was sleeping. So he kept to a ground-eating trot while looking for a place that he could defend.

He checked all his weapons, made sure they were fully loaded, and in working condition.

Another look over his shoulder showed three men a half-mile back and coming fast. When they were three hundred yards back, he pulled his rifle, turned his horse sideways, dismounted, and laid the rifle over the seat of his saddle. By then, they were within one hundred fifty yards. He took careful aim and put a bullet in the ground in front of Bull's horse. Rocks and dirt flew up in the horse's face causing him to dart to the side, almost unseating his rider. They all came to a stop, and pulled their rifles from the boot, and sat looking in Clay's direction undecided what to do next. After sitting for several minutes, they moved back out of rifle range and talked it over.

Clay knew he could wait as long as they could, and he had no place to be, and no hurry to get there, so he got his canteen, and took a drink, poured some in his hat, and gave his horses some while keeping an eye on Bull, and his buddies.

After ten minutes or so, they split up. One man going left, another to the right. Bull stayed where he was. It was so simple what they were planning. Clay mounted his horse and galloped on up the trail, making sure they didn't get ahead of him while keeping Bull behind him.

He was probably a hundred yards ahead of the two on his flanks when a small dry creek showed up right in front of him. He rode to the bottom, and spurred his horse, and raced to get in front of the man on his right. When he figured he was about where the man would show up, he dropped from the saddle with his rifle at the ready. It was only a few seconds later when he heard the man slide his horse down the bank into the creek. Clay sprinted around the curve, where he saw the man dismounting with a rifle in his hand. "Hold it right there, and drop the gun." The man wasn't any smarter than Clay

8

thought he was. He tried to turn, and bring his rifle up for a shot while Clay was standing with his rifle already pointed at him.

Clay yelled again. "Hold it!" The man continued turning and lifting his rifle. Clay had no choice. His bullet hit the man in the chest, knocking him back against his horse, where he slowly slid to the ground.

Clay sprinted back the other way until he could see around the curve. The other flanker heard the shot and was racing down the creek toward Clay with a gun in his hand, so Clay didn't waste his breath with a warning. He shot him from his saddle without even aiming. After watching a few seconds, and saw no movement, he assumed the man was dead or at least out of action for the time being.

Now, where is Bull?

Clay listened but didn't hear anything. He waited a few minutes to see if Bull was going to make the first move. Many times the first to move is the first to die.

Clay was at a significant disadvantage being in the bottom of the creek with high banks on both sides. If Bull slipped up to the edge and looked down on Clay, and Clay happened to be looking in the opposite direction at that time, Bull could shoot him with no warning.

Clay saw what looked like a trail cut into the bank where animals had been crossing and quietly made his way to the trail. Carefully climbing to the edge and looked over right into the eyes of Bull Norton, not six feet away. It was a tossup as to which one was the most surprised. Both froze for a split second and then brought their guns up as fast as they could and got off a shot. Instinctively, Clay had dropped his head down behind the lip of the creek and fired two more shots at Bull. He heard a grunt and a moan, but he wasn't taking any chances. He slid to the bottom of the creek, and sprinted fifty feet before climbing to the top again, and looked over. This time he was more careful. When he saw Bull wasn't moving, he waited. Waiting doesn't cost anything; hurrying can cost you your life. He watched Bull for another minute or so then slowly climbed from the creek and, with his gun ready to fire, walked to where Bull was lying. He kicked the gun away and rolled him over with the toe of his boot. Clay saw two bullet holes in Bull's face and knew he was dead. He returned to the other two and found them dead also. Their horses were brought up, the bodies tied on, and sent back toward town. Clay thought about returning the bodies to the sheriff, but after what the grocer told him, he didn't want to be there when Bull's dad and brothers found Bull had gotten himself killed.

He caught up his horses and moved on down the trail. He rode until it was getting late in the day when he started looking for a place to camp for the night. Nothing seemed promising, so he kept riding. He had about decided he would have to make a dry camp out here on the open prairie when he topped out on a small rise and saw a patch of green in the distance. When he reached it, there was a small pool of water that looked good enough for the horses, but he would have to make do with what was in his canteen.

He got his fire going, had his coffee, and made a meal of beans and bacon and put out the fire and crawled into his blankets. As usual, it was a restless sleep filled with dreams of Ellen, and Carter, outlaws with guns trying to kill him, and big Mexicans with big knives. He was glad when morning came, but he was just about as tired as when he went to bed.

Later that day, he came to the Rio Grande River, and turned northwest, staying on the American side. He knew El Paso was up ahead somewhere, but he had no idea how far. He thought that would be his next best place to get supplies that he was going to need by then if he didn't run out before he got there.

Knowing there was a good chance some of the Norton's may be following him after Bull, and the other two showed up dead, he took every precaution he could think of to keep from being surprised. He also had to be aware that he was in Comanche territory.

He stopped before dark, prepared his meal, and extinguished his fire, and moved on for another hour. He made a cold camp and depended on his horses to alert him if anything came sneaking around during the night. As soon as he closed his eyes, that recurring dream of Ellen and Carter appeared. Some of his dreams were so vivid he awoke and looked around to see where they were. When he realized it was only a dream, it was all he could do to keep from crying. He was mad at the world and didn't care who knew it. That was one of the main reasons he avoided people as much as possible.

Four days later, he arrived on the outskirts of El Paso and sat on a hill looking down on the town. He was still a quarter-mile away, but he could hear the noise, and the smell turned his nose up and made him want to ride around the town, but he needed supplies.

He rode slowly down the main street, looking from side to side. He wasn't looking for anything in particular, but he had never seen a town this old. The population seemed to be mostly Mexicans. He had no problem with Mexicans as long as they didn't create the problem.

He stopped at the general store and bought his supplies. When he came out and had his purchases stashed on his horse, he saw a cantina across the street. It had been a month since he sat down to a meal other than what he cooked over a campfire.

He led his horses across the street, and wrapped their reins around the hitch rail, and walked in. Several men sat around, drinking and talking in Spanish. He understood some of it, but since it didn't concern him, he didn't pay them any attention. He ordered a beer, and whatever they had to eat. He ate his fill of enchiladas, rice, and beans, and was on his third beer when three men rode up outside. They dismounted and looked around. Clay noticed they were paying a lot of attention to his two horses standing next to theirs. One of them walked around them to look at the brand on the left shoulder and said something to the other two. Clay saw them remove the thong from the hammer on their revolvers. Until then, he wasn't giving them any thought, just watching. When he took a closer look, he saw they were all big, ugly, and looked like Bull Norton, and knew he was in trouble. With three of them, the odds were greatly in their favor. He quickly left money on the table for his meal and asked the man behind the bar if he could use the back door. The man just pointed, and Clay hurried out and went around the corner into the alley and walked to the front corner of the building. When he heard the men cross the porch and go through the batwing doors, he quickly untied

11

his horses and led them down the street until he was out of sight of the saloon, mounted, and galloped out of town. He kept a sharp watch on his back trail. He couldn't believe he got out of there without a shooting.

Just before it got completely dark, a grove of trees showed up to the left of the trail. He turned that way, and rode until he entered the tree line, and continued until he guessed it must be close to midnight when he made a cold camp and went to bed.

The next morning he rode until he came to a hill where he had a good view of his back trail. He staked his horses out behind the hill, took his rifle, and canteen, and took a position where he could watch the trail.

He chose this spot because there was a small dry creek bed running along about one hundred feet from and parallel to the trail.

After watching for over an hour, he saw riders about two miles back, he checked them out with his binoculars and confirmed it was the Norton's. Taking his rifle and canteen, he mounted his horse and leading the other, continued down the trail a hundred yards or so, and then angled off the side to the creek. When he found a place where the bank was not too steep, he eased his horses into the creek and turned back the way he came. He picked up the speed some and wasn't concerned about kicking up dust because the creek bottom was damp, but no standing water. When he had gone what he guessed was close to a mile, he stopped, dismounted, and waited for the Norton's to come down the trail. He stayed below the top edge of the creek until he heard the horses pass. He rose with his rifle pointed at the three men.

"Hold it right there." They quickly jerked their horses to a halt and looked in Clay's direction. The surprised look on their faces told him everything. They looked like a kid who just got caught with his hand in the cookie jar.

"Why are you following me?"

"Who says we're following you?"

"I do. Now answer my question before I shoot all of you on general principals."

"Mister, where we go, and what we do is none of your business, now put that gun down before we shoot you. If you ain't noticed, there's three of us and one of you. Do you think you can gun all of us before we get you?" The oldest of the group, who Clay assumed was Mr. Norton, was doing all the talking.

Clay asked, "Is your name Norton?"

"Yeah, and you're the murdering scoundrel who shot my son and two of my men, and we're gonna see you dead if it's the last thing we do."

Clay told them, "If you touch those guns, it will be the last thing you do. The first thing you're gonna do if you don't want to get shot is unbuckle your gun belts, and let them drop to the ground. Let the guns drop on this side of your horses. Do it now."

The old man said, "I'm not dropping my gun for any….."

Clay fired a shot that shattered the horn of Norton's saddle right in front of his crotch. The shock of the bullet hitting the saddle, and the unexpected shot, sent the horse into a wild bucking fit. It was all Norton could do to hang on. He finally got the horse settled down and turned toward Clay.

"What was that for?"

"Now do what I told you, or the next shot goes in your head. Drop those guns."

The two younger ones slowly lowered their guns to the ground.

"Now, get off your horse."

When the two young men were standing on the ground, Clay turned to the older man and said, "Now you," as he pointed his rifle at Daddy Norton, who still sat his horse staring at Clay.

"Your time is up, Norton. Drop the gun or draw. You can drop it, and live, or you can draw, and die. The decision is yours." Norton looked like he was going to die of a stroke, but he slowly unbuckled his gun belt and let it drop to the ground.

"That was a smart move. You could be dead now. Get off your horse." After more stalling, Norton finally stood on the ground. "Now, move away from the horses."

When they had dropped their reins and moved away, Clay fired three shots at the feet of the horses. The last they saw of them was a cloud of dust heading back from where they came.

"What did you do that for?" the younger one screamed.

"That's so you can enjoy your walk back home, and if I see any of you following me again, I will shoot you on sight."

"Mister, you just signed your death warrant. I'm gonna track you down, and when I get through with you, you'll wish I had shot you."

"Yeah, yeah, yeah, I've heard those threats before. Start walking before I make you remove your boots."

"Come on, Pa. We'll get him later." One of the boys said.

"Remember what I told you. I'll shoot you on sight the next time I see you. Now get moving."

Reluctantly they started walking. Clay knew it was going to be a gruesome trip for them. They had to be at least fifteen miles or more from the last town, and they had no water or food with them. Clay was glad he couldn't hear what they said about him.

After collecting all their guns, Clay mounted his horse and continued in a north-westerly direction.

He was guessing he was somewhere in New Mexico, but he had no way of knowing for sure, and it made no difference anyway. He wasn't going anywhere, just going, trying to ride away from the pain in his heart. So far, it hadn't helped any. The pain was still there and worse at night when he tried to sleep.

He rode as long as he could every day to postpone that misery as long as possible. Many nights he sat by his campfire staring into the flames, knowing that was a dangerous habit, but he didn't care anymore. He would just about as soon someone kill him, and get him out of his misery. The life he was living was no fun anymore, but for some reason, he kept going.

CHAPTER
TWO

H e awoke with the sun shining in his face. He rolled over and sat up. He was lying in an alley with a throbbing head, and his mouth tasted worse than the inside of his boot. His hat was lying next to him. He picked it up and put it on his head. For some reason, it didn't fit right. He felt of his head and discovered several knots and abrasions, one eye was swollen almost closed, and his lips were twice their normal size. It took him three tries to get to his feet and stand. He leaned against the building until the world stopped spinning. By holding on to the building, he made it to the street and saw a water trough. He staggered to it, and submerged his head, and held it under until he had to come up for air. Gasping, he looked around, trying to remember where he was. There was the saloon, he remembered going in there last night, but he couldn't remember anything after that. When he started walking toward the saloon, something didn't feel right. He stopped and felt around until he realized his gun and gun belt was missing, along with his wallet and money belt with all his money. He slowly walked back into the alley and looked around.

There was nothing there but empty cans, bottles, and lots, and lots of trash. He stood a few minutes, trying to digest what had happened and what, if anything, he could do about it. He went back to the water trough and dunked his head again to try to get it working. The pain was still shooting through his head, and lights were flashing behind his eyes. It was about all he could stand. He had never hurt so badly, even when he was shot while in the army, and later by Robert and then Charlie Thompson.

He felt through his pockets and found a dollar and a half in change. With that, he would have enough for coffee and breakfast. The thought of breakfast made him rush back into the alley and throw up. When he was sure he had nothing left, he threw up some more. Finally, when he was so weak he could hardly stand, he staggered to the saloon, pushed through the batwing doors, and found a seat at a table. The bartender brought him a cup of coffee and left the pot on the table for him to serve himself. After the third cup, he began to feel almost human. When the bartender came around to replace his empty coffee pot with a fresh one, Clay asked him, "What happened to me last night?"

The bartender looked at him a few seconds, laughed, and said, "I'm not surprised you don't remember. You were the main attraction last night."

"What do you mean? What did I do?"

"Well, first, you tried to drink the place dry. Then you tried to fight everyone in the place, and then you wanted to shoot everyone. That's when the Marshall took your guns."

"How did I end up in the alley?"

"I don't know. The last I saw, you were staggering out the door at closing time. I closed up and went home."

"Did you see anyone follow me out?"

"Two men left the same time you did. I didn't watch to see who went where. Why what happened?"

"Someone robbed me. All my money is gone, and my guns."

The bartender scratched his head thinking, "The Marshall has your guns. He took them when you wanted to shoot everyone in the place."

"Where's this Marshall's office?"

"He's across the street on the corner, down that way," as he pointed down the street.

Clay asked, "Do you know who it was that followed me out last night?"

"I don't know their names, but they've been in here the last couple nights playing cards."

"Thanks, do you have anything to eat, or do I need to go to the café?"

"I don't have anything ready. Café's next door, and they serve good food."

"Thanks, I'll check it out."

When he left the saloon headed for the Marshall's office, his head was throbbing, and his stomach felt like it wanted to be somewhere else and was making a good effort to get there in a hurry. He walked by a store window and saw his reflection, did a double-take, looked at his reflection again, and realized what a mess he was. He had not had a bath since he couldn't remember when; his hair was dirty and matted hanging down his back; he had not shaved since before he left home, so his whiskers were the same way, and he knew he must smell worse than a skunk.

He counted his money again and thought he had enough for a bath, shave, and haircut. He might have enough left over for breakfast, but he didn't want to go to the café looking like he did now. It never occurred to him to question why he felt that way now when he hasn't cared how he looked for the last four or five months. He went to the livery stable where his horses were boarded and got a change of clothes from his pack and rummaged through them until he found the money he had stashed away for emergencies.

When he left the barbershop wearing clean clothes, with a clean shave, and a short haircut, he felt like a new man. The thing that didn't change was the lost feeling and the ache in his heart. He felt like half his body was missing, and there was nothing he could do about it.

His head was still throbbing with every heartbeat, and the vision in on eye was slightly blurred, but he was steady on his feet as he walked into the Marshalls office. The Marshall was reared back in his chair, smoking a black cigar. He was a big burly man in his fifties with a well-trimmed beard and mustache.

"What's up, young fellow?"

"The bartender told me you took my guns last night. I'd like to have 'em back if you don't mind."

"That bartender must be mistaken. The only guns I took were from a dirty drunk who was trying to shoot up the bar and fight everybody."

"Well, from what the bartender told me that must have been me. I don't remember anything after walking into the bar last night. But, I do need to report that I got robbed after I left the bar. I woke up in the alley this morning. All my money is gone, and my guns. The bartender said you had my guns. Can I have 'em back now?"

The Marshall asked, "Are you gonna be trying to shoot anybody?"

"No, unless I find who robbed me, then I may be tempted."

"You don't strike me as the kind of man who would get drunk and cause such a ruckus. What happened that caused you to do that last night?"

Clay sat with his head down for a minute, trying to decide how to answer that question. After getting the lump out of his throat, he said, "Marshall, I've never done anything like that before, and I can guarantee you, the way I feel now, I'll never do it again."

"You wanna tell me about it? By the way, I'm Chester Greer."

"Glad to meet you, Mister Greer. I'm Clay Wade, formally from Tennessee, most recently from Cuero, Texas."

For the next half hour, Clay sat, and told Marshall Greer his life story. The Marshall listened and didn't interrupt. When Clay finished and sat with his head down with tears dripping on the floor at his feet, Marshall Greer cleared his throat and said, "Well, if anyone deserves a good drunk, you would be the one." They sat in silence for what seemed like several minutes, and then Marshall Greer asked, "Have you had anything to eat today?"

"No," Clay said, taking a deep breath and letting it out slowly, "that was going to be my next stop."

The Marshall reached behind him, and took Clays guns from a peg on the wall, and handed them to him.

Clay thanked him and strapped them on, checked to see that they were loaded, dropped them in their holsters, and stood to leave.

"Wait a minute, and I'll go with you if you don't mind."

They were sitting at the table drinking their coffee, and waiting for their breakfast to be brought to them when the Marshall asked Clay, "What are your plans now? Are you gonna go back home or keep on roaming?"

"I don't know, Marshall. I don't think I can face things at home yet, without Ellen there. I tried for two months or more, but everywhere I looked, I saw Ellen or remembered something she said or did. I couldn't stand it anymore. So, I guess I'll keep roaming, as you said. Maybe over time, things will get straightened out in my head, and I'll want to go home again."

"And you think that's the answer? You think it's gonna be any easier when you do decide to go back home?"

"I don't know, Marshall. I just don't know anything anymore."

Their meal came, and they ate in silence.

When they finished, and the Marshall paid for the meal, Clay thanked him and stood to leave.

"You gonna be around a while, Clay?"

"I'm gonna find a place to lay my head and try to get some sleep. Tonight I'll be back in that bar waiting for the two men who followed me out of there last night. If they are there, I'll find a way to find out if they are the ones who robbed me. If they are, I'll decide what to do then."

"Come and get me, and we'll decide together, ok?"

"Alright, I guess that'll be the best thing to do. See you tonight, and thanks for the meal."

Clay had not seen a hotel when he rode into town, and now he didn't have the money for one anyway, so he went to the livery, and asked the man if he could sack out in a stall or the hayloft for a few hours. He got permission to throw his bed down anywhere he could find a spot. He climbed to the hayloft, thinking it will be quieter than down here where all the activity is taking place. He didn't know if he would be able to sleep, what with his head pounding so, but he was surprised when he awoke, and it was dark. He fumbled around and found his hat and boots, put on his gun belt, and climbed down the ladder. After brushing the hay off his clothes, and out of his hair, he went to the watering trough and dunked his head again. When he came up this time, he realized his head wasn't hurting nearly as bad as when he went to bed. He shook the water from his head like a dog, ran his fingers through his hair, and put his hat on. He found his way to the café again, had a good meal, and returned to the saloon where he made such a mess of things last night. No one recognized him when he came in and took a seat at a table and ordered a beer. Several men were sitting around drinking and shooting the bull while others played cards. Clay sat watching until the bartender came by his table. Clay stopped him, and nodded toward the three men playing cards, and asked if that's the two who followed him out of the bar last night. The bartender looked at him and then did a double-take and looked again, "You're not the man who caused such a ruckus in here last night, are you?"

"I guess I am. Is that the ones?"

The bartender looked where Clay indicated, and said, "Yes, that's them. The third man is a local cowhand, now don't you start another fight. I'm don't wanna put this place back together two nights in a row. You just let it be or take it outside."

Clay thanked him, picked up his beer, and walked to the table where the three men were playing cards. "You got room for one more, mind if I sit in?"

"Sure, take a seat. I'm Will that's Jake, this gentleman," pointing to the cowboy, "is Roger."

"I'm Clay. What are we playing?"

"How does five-card stud suit you, dollar anti, pot limit?"

"Fine, I don't play much, I'm just looking for a way to kill time until I leave town tomorrow."

Clay saw the two men look at each other, and try to hide the smiles.

Clay didn't know a lot about cards, but he had played some while in the army, and knew some of the tricks that card sharks used.

The first thirty minutes or so went as you would expect with each player winning some and losing some. Everything looked normal until Clay noticed that every time Jake dealt the cards, Will seemed to have a good hand. That could be coincident, but Clay didn't think so. He started keeping a close watch to see if he could detect anything Jake was doing to help Will get those better cards.

The next time it was Jake's turn to deal, Clay was watching for any sign that he was doing anything wrong. As the cards were dealt to each player around the table, Clay didn't see anything to arouse suspicions until all the cards were dealt. The first card dealt to Clay was a king, the second, and third were aces, and the fourth card was another ace. He was feeling pretty good with three of a kind, but when the fifth card dealt was another ace, he was really surprised. So now he had four aces with a king. Only two hands will beat that, a royal flush, and a straight flush. Clay is holding all the aces, so that ruled out the royal flush, leaving only the straight flush that could beat the hand he is holding.

Everyone had anted up their dollar, Clay pitched in two dollars, and the man on Clays left, Will, raised five dollars, the cowboy folded, and the dealer matched the seven dollars, and raised another five, making it ten dollars to Clay. He scratched his head and looked at his cards again; finally, he put in the ten dollars, hesitated a moment, and raised it another ten. The two men look at each other and smiled. They each matched the ten and raised it another twenty to make it forty dollars to Clay. He knew he was going to raise the bet, but he wanted to make it look like he was sweating it. He fumbled with his money, looked at his cards again, started to fold, then changed his mind, and counted out the forty dollars, and called.

Will said, "Read 'em, and weep gentlemen," as he laid down his royal flush, and reached for the pot. Clay looked at the cards, and smiled, "Not so fast, Gentlemen, y'all didn't tell me we're playing with a deck that has five aces," as he laid down his hand of four aces and a king.

The dealer's mouth flew open, and his eyes bugged out. Clay said, "I wasn't supposed to get that last ace, was I? How many more do you have up your sleeve?"

"Are you accusing me of cheating?"

"It's pretty obvious. Where did you get the fifth ace? Jake dealt me the wrong card, didn't he?"

Jake and Will came to their feet, drawing their guns. Clay drew and shot Jake on his right while hitting Will in the face with his fist, and then swung his gun to the left, and shot Will. The punch in the face staggered him and threw his timing off just enough to give Clay time to do what he had to do. Both men were lying on the floor, groaning and holding their stomach and chest where the blood was pouring out. "Someone get the Marshall if you will, please." Clay picked up their guns and laid them on the table. When the Marshall came in, Clay told him what happened, and his story was backed up by a couple of other men who saw the whole thing. The Marshall went through their pockets and found a derringer and another ace up Will's sleeve and a money belt around his waist. Clay asked the Marshall to check the underside of the belt, "You'll find my initials, and the date 1866. That's when I bought the belt."

The Marshall found the initials and date and handed the belt to Clay. When he opened it and counted the money, it was all there. Clay considered himself lucky to get his money back and didn't have to take any lead to do it. He regretted having to shoot the men but figured they deserved it. He was pretty sure he was not the first person they had cheated.

Someone got word to the undertaker, and he came to collect the bodies. It turned out he was also the barber, the dentist, the veterinarian, and the only doctor in town. That made Clay even gladder he didn't get shot.

After collecting his money from the table, he bought the Marshall, the bartender, and himself a beer. While they were standing at the bar drinking, the Marshall told Clay, "I'll look through my pile of wanted posters, and see if I have anything on those two. If I do, you may pick up some reward money."

"That would be nice."

After one more beer, Clay returned to the livery, and took his bedroll to the hayloft and turned in. It had been a very long day.

While Clay was eating his breakfast the next morning, Marshall Greer came in with two wanted posters in his hand. "Look what I found, Clay."

The wanted posters described the gamblers to a tee. It also gave a good description of their method of operation which fit what happened last night, and offered five hundred dollars each for their capture, dead or alive.

"When the bank opens in a few minutes, we'll get your money."

Clay rode out of town with an extra one thousand dollars in his pocket, plus the winnings from the poker game.

CHAPTER

THREE

lay changed his direction back toward the south-east across New Mexico. The scenery was like nothing he had ever encountered before. There was nothing like this in Tennessee or Texas. There were canyons so deep it took him all day to work his way to the bottom and another day to work his way out. He saw mountains that looked like they were touching the sky. Towers of rock of every size and shape. Mountains and valleys covered with forest as far as the eye could see.

He rode all day and camped beside water when he could find it. When he needed meat, he shot it. He bought what few supplies he needed when he passed through a town or came to a trading post. Strange, he never encountered any Indians. He kept hearing about them in the vicinity and occasionally saw signs that may have been made by Indians.

He was gathering wood for his campfire beside a small stream late one evening when he came upon a place back from the water behind some bushes where someone had built a small fire. From the size and location, he assumed it was built by an Indian. A white man would have had a much larger fire, and it would have been closer to the water.

He gathered his wood, built his fire, made his coffee, and prepared his meager meal. As he sat eating and drinking, he was thinking about the fire and the tracks. He assumed, from the size and shape of the footprint, that the person who did it was a young boy, or maybe a woman, and they were not wearing shoes. The imprint was small and narrow, not flat, and spread wide like an older person's would be from walking on it for years.

The next morning as he saddled his horses and prepared to leave his camp, his curiosity was still eating at him. He took another walk around the area and found the tracks of the barefoot person as they crossed the small creek and headed north-west. He came back and went over the campsite, searching for any clue that would tell him more about this person. But there was nothing there, no food scraps, no sign of any other person or animal.

He rode out that morning following the tracks, but a barefoot doesn't leave much of a trail, so he took a sighting from where he saw the last tracks and headed in that direction. He tried to put himself in that person's place and went where he would go. Occasionally, he saw where the grass was mashed down, but could only assume the barefoot person made it.

He continued following what little sign there was all day. At each waterhole or creek, he found where the person had laid flat to drink. Now he knew this person had no way to carry water, but that he knew this country, and where the water was.

That night Clay camped beside a water hole at the same place his mystery person had camped probably the night before, or maybe two nights before. The fire was built the same every time, away from the water behind bushes. This time Clay found feathers and bones from a bird. That explained why he was camping away from the water. He was waiting for animals or birds to come to the water so he could kill it for his meal. But how did he kill it? There was no evidence that he had a gun, which would have been unlikely for a young Indian out here alone. Then he wondered why he was assuming this person was an Indian. There could be several reasons for the fire to be kept small. Upon close examination of the area, Clay found several small holes, maybe an inch in diameter, poked in the ground beside the barefoot prints. It took him a while to figure that out, but when he did, it answered some of his questions. Clay guessed the end of his bow made the small holes. As he stood or walked, he put the end of his bow on the ground, much like a cane. That also explained how he killed his food.

This cat and mouse game went on for two more days before there was any change. Clay knew he was gaining on the person because he was getting to the kid's campsites earlier every day.

Clay had no real reason to want to catch up with this person other than his curiosity, and he had nothing else to do, and this broke up the monotony and helped keep his mind off Ellen.

Clay found himself becoming fascinated with this person. The kid appeared to be very smart and was alone, as was Clay; they were going in the same direction, although they might not have been if Clay wasn't trying so hard to follow his trail.

Along about the fourth day, they were climbing out of the flatter grassy plains and into the rocky, hilly terrain approaching the Davis Mountains. The ground became harder, and Clay lost all trace of the trail he had been following. He kept following the easiest route, just because it was easier on the horses.

That night, before he turned in to try to sleep, he climbed to the top of a nearby hill to see what he could see. The wind was only a slow, gentle breeze blowing in his face. He picked up a faint smoke smell, but he couldn't see where it was coming from. He returned to his camp and brought his horses in close, so if anything came prowling in the night, they would alert him.

He left his camp earlier than usual the next morning, wanting to be in a position to see if someone was camped down there. He rode until he had a clear view for almost a mile ahead. He tied his horses in a grove of trees off the trail. He took his binoculars and found a spot that gave him a view of the trail ahead.

He saw just the smallest trail of smoke drifting up before it stopped completely. He thought the person had probably thrown dirt on it to smother it. A minute or so later, he saw movement farther down the trail. It looked like a small boy carrying a bow with a quiver of arrows, and a small pack on his back.

Clay waited until the kid was out of sight, then he went down to the campsite and gave it a close inspection. There were feathers and fowl bones nearby, so he had eaten, and he seemed always to know where the water holes and running creeks were. From all those signs, it became apparent the kid was no stranger to this country, and may not be as young as Clay had first thought. During his search of the camp, he came upon the spot where the kid had relieved himself. The soil was still damp, but something about it didn't look right to Clay. He couldn't put his finger on it, but it still bugged him. He spent another fifteen minutes going over the ground again but didn't find anything he had overlooked. He mounted up and took to the trail again. He was determined to catch up today and try to find out why this kid was out here alone so far from everything.

When Clay left the campsite, he was no more than an hour behind. By noon he should be within sight. From the top of a hill, Clay saw him walking a quarter-mile ahead. He had no idea what the kid would do when he discovered Clay on his trail but was determined to find out. He headed down the hill at a trot. The kid heard him and looked back. When he saw Clay, he darted into the dense brush and rocks.

When Clay got to where the kid left the trail, he stopped and called out, "Hey, Amigo, I am a friend. I want to talk." Then he tried the same thing in Spanish. "Oye, Amigo, I soy amigo. Sólo Quiero hablar."

He called a couple more times but got no answer, so he continued down the trail until he came to the next water, which was a small pool at the foot of a rock cliff. There was just enough water trickling out of the rock to keep the small pool full.

It was still early in the day, but Clay gathered wood, got a small fire going, and put his coffee pot on to boil. He was facing the trail that he had just come down, hoping to see the kid following him. He got some jerky out and put it in his small pot with water to heat so it would get soft enough to eat. The coffee smelled good, and the jerky was beginning to put off a pleasant aroma when it suddenly came to him what had been bothering him about the kid's last campsite. He stopped and sat there a moment to get his thoughts together. That one little clue was all he had, but he was sure he was right. From the position of the feet, and the wet spot on the ground, this had to be a girl. There was no other explanation. That is a young girl. She is either running from someone or trying to get to someplace that she is familiar with. Probably back to her family.

As he sat waiting for his coffee, he got that feeling of being watched. He couldn't see her, but he knew she was there, and watching to see what he was going to do. When the coffee had perked long enough, he poured a cup, and held it up as an offering to the girl, and sat it on a rock across the fire from him. He then put some jerky on a plate, and set it beside the coffee, and motioned for her to come on down.

He sat back, chewing on a stick of jerky, and waited.

Just as he was beginning to think she wasn't going to show, he saw movement in the brush. He waited to see what she would do. He was hoping she wouldn't put an arrow in his chest as he sat there trying to offer his help.

He saw her moving closer and continued waiting to give her time to look him over and decide if she should kill him or eat his food, or maybe both.

Either she hadn't made up her mind yet, or she needed to get closer to make sure her arrow went where she intended. Finally, she was standing ten feet away, watching his every move.

She wasn't as young as Clay had first thought. From her looks, she was probably in her late teens or early twenties, standing about five feet four, with a very attractive face and figure with black hair and dark eyes.

He motioned for her to eat, making eating motions with his hands. She had an arrow strung in the bow, and he was sure she could put that arrow in him before he could draw his gun.

Clay asked her, "Do you speak English?" and then again in Spanish. "¿Hablas inglés?»

She still just stood looking at him. Finally, she shocked him by asking in very good English, "Why you follow me?"

When he got over his surprise, he smiled and said, "Why not follow you? You know this country better than I do, and we're going in the same direction. Besides that, you know where all the water holes are, and I have food and coffee we can share. That way, we help each other. Come over here and sit. We can talk while we eat."

She finally reached over and took a strip of jerky off the plate, and put it in her mouth, and stepped back to where she was, about ten feet away.

She wasn't drinking the coffee, and it was getting cold sitting there, so Clay picked up the cup, and took a sip, and sat it back down across the fire from him. After a short time, she picked it up and took a sip. She made an ugly face, and Clay laughed. She smiled and took another sip and made another ugly face. He laughed again, and she laughed with him.

"Have you had coffee before?"

"Yes, but not so strong."

"Where did you learn to speak English so well?"

"At the missionary. The priest taught us English, Spanish, and other things. Most, I think not true."

Clay laughed at that, "I know what you mean. I've had that same thought at church. Come, sit, and eat. What is your name? What are you called? My name is Clay."

"I am called Morning Bird."

"Do you mind if I just call you Bird?"

"No, that ok."

She finally came and sat on the rock across the fire from him. He was careful not to make any sudden moves.

"What tribe are you from?"

"I am Comanche."

"Where is your village?"

She pointed west-north-west and held up five fingers and said, "Five suns."

"Why are you out here alone?"

"Bad men come where we staying and took me and my sister. They killed my mama, and papa, and little brother. We go many suns," she pointed south, "I run away after they killed my little sister. I been running and hiding many suns."

"Well," Clay said, "If you show the way, I'll help you get back home."

"Why you do that?"

Clay shrugged his shoulders and said, "I don't know. I guess it's because it's the right thing to do. I don't have anything else to do or any place else to be."

She didn't understand, but she didn't argue with him.

When they finished eating, Clay brought the horses up and loaded the cooking utensils, and put out the fire. When he motioned for her to climb up on top of the packs, she didn't understand that either, she just stood and looked at him. Finally, he told her, "Climb up here. It'll be faster and easier than walking."

He arranged the packs, blankets, and robes to make a comfortable seat for her, and they rode out headed north-west.

From time to time, she told him to turn here or there, and each time it took them to water, whether it was a creek, a water hole, or spring, the water was always good. They camped near water every night, and she usually killed something with her bow and arrows, so they had fresh meat almost every night.

The first night, as they were making camp by a water hole she had led them to, she was nervous and stayed across the fire from Clay and always had her bow with an arrow ready close by her side. After they had eaten, Clay took his bedroll, and laid it out close to the fire, and spread one of his buffalo robes on the opposite side of the fire from his, and said goodnight.

As they climbed higher into the mountains, the nights got colder. They built their fires out of sight as much as they could, and snuggled deep in the buffalo robes, and slept comfortably.

The higher they went, the colder it got. One morning when

they poked their heads out of their bedrolls, several inches of snow covered the ground and still coming down. Before they finished their breakfast, the wind had picked up and was almost gale force within an hour. They decided not to travel that day, so Clay put up the tarp to create a windbreak, and then set up his tent under the windbreak. The fire reflected into the tent and kept them reasonably warm. Clay covered both horses with buffalo robes, and Clay and Bird shared the other one. They kept the coffee hot, and the fire going all day. When night came, the snow was over a foot deep. They had been sharing the robe all day, so when night came, it was just natural for them to fall asleep under the same robe. Neither of them thought anything about it. The next morning when Clay awoke, he found himself wrapped in the girl's arms and legs to keep warm. She was still asleep, so he wiggled out of the robe, got the fire going, put the coffee pot on, and hurriedly crawled back in the bed and snuggling up to her to get warm.

Their camp was out of the wind with water and grass nearby, but they spent almost all of their time gathering wood for the fire and knocking snow off the grass for the horses.

Bird had no shoes, and walking in the snow was getting painful. She couldn't see what she was stepping on under the snow, and her feet soon had cuts, and bruises and her toes were beginning to show signs of frostbite. Clay told her to stay by the fire and keep her feet warm.

After he had gathered a sizable pile of wood, he asked Bird for the buffalo coat she was wearing. With his knife, he cut a one-foot wide strip off the bottom and laid it out on the ground. He had her place her foot on it and marked around it with the burned end of a stick from the fire. The rest of the day was spent building a pair of moccasins to fit her feet. He turned the hair to the inside, and when she put them on the first time, her face lit up like a child at Christmas

Clay spent a lot of the day kicking snow from the grass so the horses would have something to eat. They pawed the snow away as much as they could once they learned it was under there.

By the evening of the second day, they had used all the wood that was close to their camp. Clay was hunting farther and farther from camp to find wood when he came upon a place in the cliff across the stream from their camp where the wind and water had hollowed out a cave of sorts in the wall. It went back into the hill about twelve feet or so, was six feet high at the opening, and tapered down to three feet in the back, and was about ten feet wide at the front.

Clay gathered a big arm full of wood and got a fire started toward the back of the cutout. When it was burning good, he hurried back to their camp and told Bird what he had found. They broke camp and moved everything to the cave. With the aid of long poles and brush, Clay was able to hang his tarp in front of the opening, blocking the wind.

When he finally entered the cave, it was nice and warm. The creek was only a few feet away, so by breaking the ice, they had all the water they would ever need. The horses were moved every day to a new spot, and the snow was kicked away to expose what little grass was there.

The blizzard continued to blow for three more days. The horses were out of food, and grass, and were beginning to show the effects. Clay knew they would have to move on soon, regardless of the weather.

On the fourth day, they awoke to a day of bright sun and no wind. Snow still covered the ground, but Clay knew this was the best chance they were going to get, so they broke camp and continued west by north-west over and through the Davis Mountains. Bird told him her village was on the west side of the mountains in a valley by a creek. When they arrived there after a week of slow traveling due to the deep snow the first two days, there was no village. All the signs looked like it had been vacant for quite some time. She didn't know where they had gone. She thought maybe to their winter hunting ground far to the north, but she didn't know exactly where that was or how to get there. Clay scouted around and found faint signs of tracks where many animals and people had left going north. He pointed the tracks out to Bird, who, as it turned out, was a better tracker than he was. They followed the trail the rest of the day and camped on the banks of Carrizo Creek at the foot of Mount Doro. The snow had all melted except in the shade. The days were cold enough for a heavy coat, and at night the temperature dropped into the twenties.

The trail took them through the middle of Kiowa country, and Clay didn't know if they were friendly to the white man, and Comanche, but he was doing his best to stay out of sight. They spent a lot of time looking ahead and behind to try to see any unwanted company before it saw them. They remained in the trees and went around the open areas but always came back to the trail left by the Indians.

When they left their camp the next morning, the trail took a north-easterly direction and continued on that course as straight as the terrain would allow. Two days later, they saw the Rabbit Ear Mountains in the distance. The trail went around the west side of Rabbit Ear following a small creek. They camped beside it the next two nights as they continued following the trail of the Comanche as it wound around through the mountains. The third morning Bird pointed out a thin layer of smoke in the distance. "What do you think?" Clay asked.

Bird smiled and said, "My people."

"Are you sure?"

"No, but I think so. I remember being here when I was little."

"OK, let's go find out," Clay said as he led off, heading toward the smoke.

After traveling all day, they began seeing signs where people had gathered nuts and berries.

Bird was getting anxious and took the lead. She had her horse in a fast trot, and Clay was trying to keep up when they went around a curve in the trail and came face to face with a group of horsemen.

Bird was about fifty feet ahead of Clay when he heard excited voices ahead, and came around the curve, and saw a group of Indians surrounding Bird, talking excitedly. He didn't know what they were saying, but they looked happy to see Bird. When they saw him, they got excited and rushed to surround him before he knew what was happening. They all had their arrows, and spears pointed at him. He pulled his horse to a quick halt and reached for his gun, knowing it was a useless move and stopped his hand when Bird yelled, "NO."

He held his hands in the air while the group of horsemen surrounded him and began yelling in a language he didn't understand. Bird came riding back and pushed her horse in between them, yelling and waving her arms. All Clay could do was sit and wait, but his heart was pumping as if he had just run ten miles.

Bird was still talking and pointing. She put her hand on Clay's shoulder and held up her foot to show the moccasins he made for her. After a few more minutes of pointing and gesturing and speaking in that unknown language, the men began to smile and look at him with a new attitude. Each of them rode by and patted Clay on the shoulder and rode away, laughing.

Clay looked at Bird and saw she was smiling. "What's going on, Bird?"

"I told them you are my man, a great warrior, and you saved me from bad men who stole me and killed my family. They think we are, how you say, married?"

Clay moaned to himself, "Oh no, what have I gotten myself into?"

They followed the men to the Indian's camp about a mile away. Clay saw two dozen teepees along Beaver Creek, and a horse herd was farther downstream. It looked like a hundred or more with three teenage boys watching them. Clay was thinking there must be a good horse thief in this tribe.

There was quite a bit of excitement when they saw Bird returning. They all had assumed she was either dead or gone forever.

Clay was escorted to a teepee on the edge of the camp and told to stay here. Bird left him and disappeared into one of the other teepees. After about thirty minutes, she came out with an older man who accompanied her to where Clay waited. She introduced him as chief something or other, Clay never understood what she said, but Clay went through all the motions of being glad to meet him and thanked him for his hospitality. Bird translated for the chief who stood smiling and nodding his head. "You can stay in this lodge. It belonged to my mama and papa. It is mine now. You will stay with me."

Clay didn't know what to say. He didn't want to leave Bird with the idea that he was going to be living with her. He decided right away he should set this straight before it got any more out of hand. "Listen, Bird; I won't be staying here. I'll be leaving tomorrow or the next day."

"Clay, you can't do that. If you leave here, they will kill you." Bird said with tears in her eyes. "As long as you stay in the village or are with some of the men or me, you are safe, but if you leave, you are an enemy. I don't want that to happen. You are good man; I want you to stay with me."

"Bird, I only came along to help you get back to your people. I had no intention of staying. Can't you talk to them and explain that to them?"

"I can try, but I don't think it will do any good. That is the way things are."

"Ok, don't worry about it, I'll work something out. Who is the one I'll need to talk to?"

"Chief Black Hawk is the one who will make the decision. But once you leave the village, he will have no control over what happens."

Clay was thinking about that while looking about the village, and trying to plan how to get out of here. That's when he noticed his horses were gone. "Bird, where are my horses?"

"They are with the other horses," as she pointed toward the horse herd.

Well, that certainly complicates matters, Clay was thinking.

"When can you talk to Chief Black Hawk?"

"I'll talk to him now. He is in his lodge." With that, she walked away toward the largest lodge in the center of the village.

Clay walked around the village to see what the reaction would be. He walked toward the horse herd, which was about a half-mile away. His two horses were off to one side since they hadn't started mingling with the others yet. That may make it easier to get them and get out of here without being detected. Before he reached the herd, one of the teenage boys came over and spoke to him in Comanche. Clay had no idea what he said, but motioned to his horses and continued walking.

The young boy rode along beside him until he reached his horses and began talking and petting them. He was keeping an eye on the boy the whole time. He didn't want to get an arrow in his back. The boy sat on his horse and watched Clay. After a few minutes, Clay took Blue by the mane and started leading him back toward the village. The Boy didn't try to stop him, so Clay kept going. He was leading Blue, and Socks was following. He arrived back to his lodge and put halters on them and staked them nearby. He didn't know if this was going to work, but it's the only thing he could come up with at the moment. He sat on the ground and watched the horses graze.

Just as the sun was going behind the mountain, Bird came back. She didn't look happy. She sat on the ground beside Clay and didn't say anything. Finally, Clay asked, "Well, what did he say?"

"He said you can go anytime, but once you leave the village, he can't help you. You will be on your own."

They sat side by side without talking until the sun was gone, and the village was dark. Bird leaned against Clay and laid her head on his shoulder. He put his arm around her waist and pulled her closer. After a few minutes, Bird stood, took his hand, and led him into the lodge. A small fire burned in the middle of the floor, putting out just enough light to see where everything was. There was a bed of animal hides and blankets on one side, and stacks of other things around the walls. Clay couldn't tell what any of it was, but it didn't matter since he wasn't going to be here when the sun came up.

Bird led him to the bed and motioned for him to lie down. When he was on the bed, she removed his boots and placed them at the foot of the bed. She then proceeded to undress. When she was completely naked, she lay beside Clay and began removing his clothes.

Clay had such mixed feelings he was powerless to stop her. He had not been with a woman since the death of Ellen. Since her death, he had not thought of any other woman. He still saw her every night in his sleep. He could see her, feel her next to him, and smell her. When he awakens, and she isn't there, his heart breaks, and he can't stop the tears from flowing.

With that image of Ellen in his mind, he held up his hand and got off the bed. "Bird, I can't do this. Let me explain." He opened up his heart and told her everything. How Ellen had died, his son Carter, how his heart still belonged to Ellen, and he wasn't ready to be with another woman. "I'm sorry, Bird, I don't want to hurt you. I think the world of you, but I'm still in love with Ellen, even if she is gone, I can't get over her this soon. Do you understand?"

"Yes, I understand, but can you give me just this one night before you go?"

"Bird, I'm honored that you want to give yourself to me. But I'm not ready. It's too soon. Maybe if I come back this way in a year or so, things will be different."

"If you leave, and get away don't come back, they will kill you," she said, with tears running down her cheeks. "That's just the way things are. That is The Peoples way."

He took her in his arms and hugged her tight. Then he picked up his saddle and packs and carried them to his horses. He saddled Blue and put the pack-saddle on Socks. He knew Socks would follow Blue if they should get separated. He wasn't sure if Blue would follow Socks. When everything he owned was loaded, he turned to Bird and hugged her again. With nothing else to say, he mounted Blue and rode away.

CHAPTER

FOUR

H e rode to the stream, went in the water, and followed it downstream. Bird had told him this stream merged with a larger stream farther to the east.

He kept the horses at a slow walk, so they didn't make too much noise. He let them pick their way because they could see much better at night than he could.

Every few minutes, he stopped to listen if anyone was following him. He didn't hear anything other than the slight trickle of water as it passed over the rocks and debris, so he continued. After several hours he came to the larger creek that Bird told him about. It was running to the south-east. It was broader and deeper, up to his horses' chest, so he had to keep close to the bank. There were rocks, and brush along the edge that gave him some trouble, but the horses worked their way around them. When the sky in the east started getting lighter, he was looking for a place to hide. From here on, he would do his traveling at night. He is in Comanche territory, and they know the area much better than he does, so his best option is to try not to be seen. He didn't want to have to kill any of Birds people or be killed by them.

When it was light enough to see, he came upon a small stream feeding in from the right, and followed it for a half-mile or so until it played out. There was a rock shelf on one side that came down to the edge of the water. He turned Blue onto the rocks and followed it until it ended in a grove of pine and cottonwood trees. Pine straw and leaves covered the ground so he wouldn't leave much sign, but a good tracker wouldn't have any trouble following him if they managed to get this far.

He and his horses were exhausted. He found the thickest underbrush and trees in the area and settled down for the day intending to stay here and let his horses rest until nightfall then head out again.

He found a place where he could see down his back trail for two hundred feet and prepared to spend the day. He didn't think anyone would be coming along for several hours yet, so he leaned against a tree and was soon asleep. The sun was straight overhead when he awoke and looked around, trying to get his bearings. He had been asleep for at least four hours. He checked his horses and saw them grazing where he had left them. He stood up and stretched to get the kinks out of his back. He moved the horses to new grass and then walked back up the trail to where it left the creek. He didn't see or hear anything, so he returned to camp, and broke out the little food he had, which consisted of jerky, and more jerky.

He slept off and on throughout the day, and watched his back trail, but didn't see or hear anything to be concerned about. When the sun was behind the mountain, he saddled up and was ready to move out. Before he did, he walked back to where he left the creek to see if there was any activity. Again he didn't see or hear anything. He thought maybe he had gotten away with his hair after all.

He was a little leery of returning to the big creek that he had followed all the night before in case they had followed him that far. He knew the creek was running in a south-east direction, so he took a sighting on the stars, and tried to keep heading east, and south. He knew that would take him back to Texas eventually.

After five nights of traveling in the dark, he assumed he was safe from the Comanche. He rested up one whole day, and night, and left the next day at sunup. He was very careful that no one saw him. The Rabbit Ear Mountains were far behind him, and nothing but open prairie ahead. The grass was up past the knees of his horses, and he saw this as great grazing land for cattle.

A week of casual riding, camping by water holes at night, when he found one and letting the horses graze late evenings and early mornings. There was nothing out here but grass and a few buffalo from time to time until he came upon a well-worn trail pointed north and south. He thought, "What the heck, I wonder where this leads." He turned his horses north and followed the trail.

That night he was in his bedroll off the trail beside a small stream, he didn't know what time it was, he just knew he had been in bed for some time and was still awake when he heard voices coming from the trail not far away. He quickly went to his horses to keep them quiet. They were standing with their heads up, and their ears pointed toward the voices. He put his hand over their noses and whispered to them.

He didn't understand much of what he heard, but he heard enough to know that one man was in serious trouble and was about to get his neck stretched, and the people doing the stretching had no authority to do it.

Clay quickly saddled his horse and loaded all his gear on the packhorse. By the time he got on the trail, they were too far ahead for him to hear anything. After a few minutes of riding at a slow lope, he heard them and slowed to a walk. The noise they were making covered the noise he was making.

He slowed to a walk and continued to follow. He heard when they left the trail and went into a grove of trees not far down the hill. From what he had heard, he assumed this is where the evil deed was going to take place. He rode past where they had turned off until he found a place to leave his horses off the trail and out of sight. Taking his rifle, and checking his pistol, he hurriedly returned to where they left the trail and followed them into the trees. He hadn't gone far when he heard voices ahead. There was a lot of yelling and cussing going on, but Clay couldn't make out who was saying what. As he got closer, he moved off to one side and continued until he was only thirty feet away. The moon and stars were bright enough that he could see what was happening. A rope was hanging from a limb, and one end had a hangman's noose around the neck of the man doing all the yelling and cussing and the other end tied to the trunk of the tree. If he didn't do something quick, the man was going to be dead. From what Clay could see of him, he looked like a well-dressed, clean-cut young man. The man on the other side of the hanging giving all the orders, appeared to be a big man riding a big horse. He was wearing a wide-brimmed black hat so that Clay couldn't see much of his face, but it appeared he had a heavy dark mustache.

Clay couldn't afford to fire a shot and scare the victim's horse. That would get him hung for sure. He was off to the right rear of the action when he jacked a cartridge into the chamber of his rifle, and shouted, "That's enough, don't anyone move. Nobody is getting hung here tonight, but some of you may get shot if you don't do as I tell you. Now take that rope off that man, and untie his hands. NOW!".

No one moved until Clay said, "You in the black hat, you're about three seconds from getting a bullet between the eyes. I'm gonna count to three. If that rope is still on him, I start shooting."

"All right, all right, Shorty, take the rope off. There'll be another time, and we'll have two to hang then."

The man called Shorty removed the rope from the man's neck and untied his hands. The victim rode out of the circle of men coiling the rope and said, "I'll keep this rope. I know every one of you, and I will see that this rope gets plenty of use. Think about that when you lay down at night. I may be only a few feet away, and you," he said, pointing to the man in the black hat, "I have something special planned for you."

Clay told the men, "Now all of you drop your guns. Don't give me an excuse to shoot you, because I will."

The gun belts dropped to the ground. "Now, turn around, and ride out of here. Don't even think about coming back. So far, you've been lucky. Settle for that, and go."

The group turned their horses and rode away. Blackhat shouted back, "We'll get you next time, Wilcox."

When they were gone, Clay said to Wilcox, "Now, want to tell me what that was all about?"

"Sure, let's go somewhere we can have a fire, and make some coffee, and I'll tell you all about it."

Clay said, "No, this is as good a place as any."

"But I can't even see you."

"That's the way I want it. The fewer people see me, the better I like it. Who was the man in the black hat?"

"His name is Robert Blalock, but he likes to be called Bullet because he says if anyone crosses him or his, he'll get a bullet. He runs the biggest spread in these parts, and he wants everybody to know it."

"What's your name, and why was he trying to hang you?"

"I'm Clint Wilcox." He said as he dismounted and walked to Clay, holding out his hand. "I want to thank you for what you did. I thought I was a goner for sure." Clay shook his hand.

"He's accused me of stealing his cattle, but he can't show any proof of it, so he decided to take the law in his hands, and hang me anyway. Hell, if I wanted more cattle, all I have to do is round them up, they're running wild all over the place. The problem is Mr. Blalock thinks he owns all those too. So every time he sees a fresh brand on a critter, he accuses the owner of stealing his cattle. He's been running people out of the country or hanging them ever since he came into this country, and there ain't any law here to do anything about it."

"How long has he been here?" Clay asked.

"I would guess maybe six or seven years. His headquarters is a rawhide outfit about twelve to fifteen miles to the southwest of here."

"Fifteen miles and he claims all this empty land as his?"

"Yep, and he doesn't mess around about lettin' you know it. The problem I have with that is he doesn't appear to be running any kind of a cattle ranch that I ever heard of."

"What do you mean?"

"I never see any cattle with his brand on it."

"Who's the law in these parts, and why don't they do something about it?" Clay asked.

"There is no law here. Maybe the Texas Rangers, but I understand the new governor disbanded them. The closest town, if you want to call it that, is about ten miles that way," as he pointed northwest. "It's called Toyah, not much there except a saloon owned by Bullet's brother Clyde, and a general store owned by a Mr. Youngblood. Oh, there's a blacksmith shop, and livery stable, a cafe, and a few other small businesses. They don't even have a city marshall."

"Where do you live, Clint?"

"I have a place north from here about two miles alongside Toyah Creek."

"I think we need to get out of here in case those guys decide to come back. We may not be so lucky next time."

"You're probably right," Wilcox said as he mounted his horse.

Clay said, "My horse is back up the trail a piece. I'll see you around, maybe. I'm just passing through."

"Why don't you come over to my place and let me thank you properly?"

"You go ahead; I may drop by someday. Good luck to you."

Wilcox waved as he rode away. It had to be after midnight, so he saw no need to go back to his previous campsite. He got his horses and rode toward where Wilcox said Toyah Creek was. When he came to a small running stream, he assumed this must be it. He found a grassy spot and unloaded his camping gear and staked his horses on the grass. It was still several hours until sunup, so he crawled into his bedroll to get a couple of hours of sleep if he could.

As soon as he lay down, his mind started wandering. Ellen was there like she always was, but now she had a darker complexion and darker hair. She was smaller and younger by a few years. He was confused, and couldn't make sense of things until he awoke and realized he was combining Ellen and Bird.

When he finally got back to sleep, he didn't wake up until the sun had been up for an hour. The first thing he always did was look at his horses. They were grazing contentedly, so he knew there was nothing else around. He got a fire going, made a pot of coffee and heated a can of beans. That was his breakfast. Then he strolled down to check out the creek. The water was running clear and cool, so he dipped up a hand full and tasted it. It had a mineral taste to it, but he figured it wouldn't hurt him since all the animals drank it, and they seemed healthy enough.

He sat around his fire, drinking coffee, and contemplating the situation. It sounded like the situation he had just gotten out of down at Cuero, where one man was trying to run roughshod over everyone. Well, it wasn't his problem. He would be completely out of the area in another day.

He lounged around camp until after he ate lunch, giving his horses time to eat their fill of grass. Then he saddled and packed up and rode along Toyah Creek to see where it went, just out of curiosity more than anything else. He liked the area with the hills and valleys, with live creeks, lots of trees and underbrush. He flushed several longhorns and deer as he rode, but he just watched them run until they reached another hiding place. The creek bottom he followed was twenty to thirty feet below the surrounding plains in areas. After a mile or so, the hills dropped back from the creek and opened out on a broad flat valley. The stream still ran through it, but it was only a couple feet deep, and twenty to twenty-five feet wide. He stopped to gaze out over the valley before him when he saw a house and barn with corrals not far away. He assumed this must be Clint Wilcox's place since he hadn't mentioned anyone else living in the immediate area.

Clay was trying to decide if he should go down and call on Clint or not. He really didn't want to get mixed up in another range war, but he didn't like to see a young man taken advantage of either. Clint was only trying to make a living, much like Clay was. Clay had been fortunate that he had a herd of cattle and horses to sell to get his new start and move to Texas. He didn't know anything about Clint's finances, and it was none of his business.

After a few minutes of arguing with himself, he turned his horses toward Clint's place and rode on down. As he approached, he saw a man walk from the barn to the house and come back out with a rifle. When Clay was closer, he waved and kept his hands in sight. Clint was waiting for him on the porch when Clay rode up. Of course, Clint didn't know him because he never got a look at his face last night.

Clay removed his hat and wiped his forehead on his sleeve. "Mr. Wilcox, I believe, I'm Clay Wade, and we met last night."

"Yes, I recognize the voice now, get down and come in."

"Thanks." Clay stepped down and dropped the reins. He saw a nice looking young man in his mid-twenties, about six feet tall and one hundred ninety pounds with blond hair and blue eyes. He and Clay could have passed for brothers, being the same size and coloring. "Nice place you have here. I like the location and the views. Do you live here alone?"

"Yeah, just me and my animals."

"It must get awful lonesome," Clay said with a sad look.

"I don't mind it so much. I like the peace and quiet. That is until Blalock started causing trouble. Come on up here and have a seat."

Clay took a seat in one of the chairs on the porch and put his hat on the floor beside him.

"Speaking of Blalock, I saw you had to go to the house to get your rifle when you saw me coming. If it was me, and someone tried to hang me last night, I'd keep that rifle with me, and you aren't even wearing a handgun. It looks like you're inviting trouble. If I were after you, you would be dead and buried by now."

Wilcox looked surprised. He turned his head and looked all around like he was expecting someone to jump out at him.

Clay asked him, "Where're you from Clint?"

"I'm from Chicago, Illinois. My pa's a banker back there. He wanted me to work with him at the bank, but I didn't want to be a banker, so I came out here and started ranching, but I didn't expect this kind of trouble."

"Are you any good with that rifle?"

"I usually hit where I aim. Why?"

"I think you are in for a big surprise. Mr. Blalock is going to make your life miserable until he kills you or runs you out of the country. You need to get very good with that rifle, and you need a plan for defending this place. Blalock could ride in here and shoot you and burn this place to the ground, and you wouldn't be able to do a thing about it."

"Do you really think he would do that?" Clint asked.

"If he'll drag you off in the middle of the night and hang you, he'll do worse than that. Where were you when he grabbed you last night?"

"I was in bed asleep. The next thing I knew, I was dragged out of bed and thrown on a horse and told I was going to be hung by the neck until dead for stealing Blalock's cattle."

"So what's to keep him from doing it again tonight, or tomorrow night, or the next night?"

"I don't know. I hadn't thought about it."

"Did you think he was just going to let it drop and not finish what he started?" Clay asked.

"I guess I didn't think he was that serious."

Clay was utterly flabbergasted, "He had a rope around your neck, in the middle of the night, within seconds of hanging you, and you didn't think he was serious? Tell me, Mr. Wilcox, what would it take to make you think he was serious?"

Clint was looking embarrassed and said, "Things like that don't happen back home. I'm just not used to the life out here."

"Well, you better get used to it, or you won't live long enough for it to matter."

"What do you think I should do?"

"My first suggestion is to go back to Chicago." Clay said.

"I can't do that. Everybody would laugh at me. I made big plans about what I would do when I got out here. I can't go back a failure."

"So you are determined to stay here, and fight Blalock?"

"I'm going to stay here. I don't know about fighting Blalock."

47

"If you stay here, you're going to have to fight Blalock, or he will kill you and take everything you have." Clay informed him.

Wilcox was pacing up and down the porch and looking off across the valley while running his fingers through his hair. "What can I do?"

"How much ammunition do you have for your rifle?" Clay asked.

"I have most of a box, probably fifteen rounds or so."

Clay just shook his head. "You're going to need a lot more than that. Do you have a pistol?"

"Sure."

"Get it. Let me see it."

Clint went into the house and came back with an old forty-five that badly needed cleaning.

Clay went to his saddlebag and got his cleaning kit. While showing Clint every move, he took the pistol apart, cleaned and oiled, and reassembled it. Clay dry fired it several times and found it operated smoothly.

"How much ammunition do you have for this one?" Clay asked.

Clint said, "I have a full box, twenty cartridges."

Clay asked him, "Can you hit anything with it?"

Clint answered, "I don't know. I've never fired it."

Clay shook his head, "Oh boy, we have our work cut out for us."

Clint asked, "What do you mean?"

"Well, you say you are going to stay here, and you have a man determined to kill you. If we're going to prevent him from doing that, we have a lot of work to do. First, we have to get a lot more ammunition for these guns, and then you have to put in hours and hours of practice to get good with them. While that's happening, we have to come up with a way to defend this place and find another place to go to if we have to leave here. So, be thinking about it. If you have to leave here, and someone is trying to kill you, where would you go that he couldn't find you, and you have a good supply of food stashed away."

Clint was standing there with a shocked look on his face. "Do you think it'll come to that?"

"You're bettin' your life against it. But whether it does or not, you need to be prepared. Your life could very well depend on it." Clay said.

Clint still looked like he was in shock.

Clay asked him, "How long will it take to ride to Toyah and buy more ammunition?"

"If you're not in a hurry, it takes about two hours each way."

"Ok, we'll leave first thing tomorrow morning. In the meantime, we need to be deciding where you are going to be living until this thing gets settled."

"But I'm living right here."

"Not if you want to stay alive. Now, where are we going to stash a food supply?"

"I haven't thought about that either, but I did see what looked like it might be a small cave on the side of that hill over there."

"Good," Clay said, "Let's go take a look at it. We may as well take a bag of food with us since we are going there anyway."

"You're serious about this, aren't you?"

"I'm as serious as your death. You pack up everything you can get in a sack while I saddle your horse."

Clay went to the barn while Clint went into the house. Fifteen minutes later, they were riding away headed up the canyon. Clint stopped, and pointed, "The cave is over there, why are we going this way?"

"If someone is watching us, we don't want to lead him to our cash of food. Can you find this place in the dark?"

After a moment of hesitation, "Yeah, I think so."

"Is there a trail from this canyon over to where the cave is?" Clay asked.

"Yeah, about a mile farther along, we can cut over."

A mile farther up the canyon, they found the trail crossing over the hill. They climbed to the top of the mountain and stopped to check their back trail and to give the horses a breather. After a ten minute break, they continued down the other side. When they reached the bottom of the hill, they located a secluded spot and dismounted to wait until dark before approaching the cave. Clint pointed out the dark spot on the side of the mountain, which should be the cave. From where they were, it didn't look large enough for a dog to enter.

When the sun went down, they mounted up and continued toward the cave. It was completely dark before they got there, so they dismounted and waited for the moon to rise. They stood around in the dark, making plans. When the moon was high enough to light up the area, Clint led off again. He knew the general area of the cave, but it took almost an hour for them to find it. What Clay saw was a long crank in the wall of the mountain. It looked like maybe an earthquake had split the mountain open, and then brought the two parts back together again. The opening was just wide enough for a man to walk through if he turned sideways. Clay found a long stick and poked around in the bushes, and the cave entrance. When he didn't hear any rattles, he squeezed his way through the opening. When he was inside, and it was safe to have a light, he struck a match. What he saw left him in shock. "Holy cow, Clint, you gotta see this." Clint came through the hole and looked around in awe. "What in the world do we have here?"

The cave extended into the mountain and got broader and deeper the farther it went. In places, it was only three feet wide, and then it widened out to twenty feet or more. It was difficult to see how far it went with only the light from a match. When that match burned down, Clay struck another one on the wall. "We're going to need some flares so we can explore this baby." Clay said.

Clint said, "You can explore it. I'm not going any farther than this."

"Come on, Clint; I can see the headlines now. 'CLINT WILCOX DISCOVERS MASSIVE CAVE.'" Clay was laughing, and the echoes were rolling back and forth.

"Yeah, sure, I can see them too, 'CLINT WILCOX LOST IN MASSIVE CAVE NEVER SEEN AGAIN.'" Clint was not laughing.

"Let's bring the food in and stash it. Tomorrow we'll go to Toyah and stock up, make some flares so we can check this cave out, and find a suitable place to hide until it's safe to return home."

Clint went outside and passed the supplies through the hole to

Clay. And then they gathered every kind of tree and shrub they could find and piled it in front of the cave entrance. Clay said, "It won't keep anything out that wants to get in, but it'll at least warn us if something or someone has gone in there."

They mounted their horses and rode away. Clint said he knew a good camping spot deep in this canyon with plenty of grass and water. He led the way for what seemed a mile or more before they came to a wide place between the walls of the canyon. Trees grew right up against the walls on both sides, with a stream running along the wall on one side. "This is it. We should be safe here for a while."

By the time they were unsaddled and had the horses staked on grass within reach of the water, it was past midnight. The moon was still bright, so they could see well enough to set up camp.

Clay told Clint, "This looks like a good place, alright, but if someone rides up this canyon, they can't help but find us. Tomorrow after we get back from town with the supplies and get them stashed in the cave, I'll see if I can find a more secluded place. After all, we may be here a while. Do you know if Blalock is causing trouble for anyone else like he is you?"

"The only one I've heard about is an old Mexican who runs a herd of sheep all over these mountains. I came across him one time right after Blalock had killed a bunch of his sheep, and warned him to stay off his range."

"This Blalock sounds like a really likable guy." Clay remarked, "I think I'll ride over to his place and have a look around. I may even have a talk with him. Does he spend much time in town?"

"I don't know. I don't go there very often, and when I do, I don't stay long."

While they were talking, they were unrolling their bedrolls. They didn't bother with starting a fire, it was late, and they were tired and anxious to get to bed.

The sun was already peeking over the horizon when Clay roused up and checked his horses. They were standing undisturbed, so he forced himself out of his bed and got a fire going. About the time the coffee was starting to smell good, Clint came awake and said, "Is that coffee I smell?"

Clay answered, "That's what it's supposed to be. You tell me after you've sampled it."

Clay poured each of them a cup. Clint sat up in his bed and took a sip of the coffee. "Yep, that's coffee alright, a little stronger than I like, but its coffee," as he ran his fingers through his hair.

"You're in the west now, not Chicago, so this is about all you will get out here. Better get used to it."

They made a quick breakfast of jerky, and coffee, and saddled their horses and headed for town. Clay was riding Blue, and Socks was carrying the packs. Clay told Clint, "We need to cross back over this mountain and come at the home place from that direction. We don't want to leave a bunch of tracks showing everyone where we have our food stashed, and where we are camping. We'll only go to the cave at night in case someone is spying on us."

"You keep saying us, and we like you're going to be around for a while."

"Yeah, unless you don't want my help. I would sure feel bad if I rode off and left you to fight Blalock by yourself, and you got yourself killed. I've been through this kind of thing before, and I think I can help you if you want me to."

"I sure appreciate your help. I'm just not sure it's all that serious."

"You don't think hanging a man is serious? Mister, you sure are a slow learner. I hope you live long enough to learn it."

Clint rode off to find the trail over the mountain to Toyah Creek canyon. They came out of the canyon within sight of the house and stopped to look things over before riding into the open.

Everything looked peaceful enough, so they rode past the house and continued to Toyah. It took just under two hours to get there. They rode down the main street looking both ways but saw no sign of Blalock or his men. The general store had everything they needed, so they were packed, and leaving town in less than forty-five minutes.

Clay asked Clint, "Where is Blalock's place from here?"

"You follow that road out about ten miles. I've never been there, but from what I've heard, he or some of his men will meet you before you get there, and ask your business."

Both of them had their heads swiveling from side to side as they rode back to Clint's place. They had bought supplies for the house, and the cave, so they unloaded everything intended for the house and left the cave supplies in the panniers on the pack saddle to be delivered to the cave after dark tonight.

They prepared a quick lunch and talked about how to defend this place while they ate. They walked outside, and Clay looked the place over. He already had a pretty good idea of what he would do if the decision were his. He pointed a couple of things out to Clint and suggested, "If I were defending this place with only two men, I would have a man on each side of the house, out of sight. When Blalock rode in, I would warn him one time, and if he didn't leave immediately, I would shoot him dead. That would end all your problems unless someone else takes up the fight on his behalf."

Clint stood there with a shocked look. "You mean you would kill him?"

"In a Chicago minute. Like I said yesterday, you have a lot to learn, Clint."

After the sun went down, but before dark, they mounted up and headed toward the cave in the roundabout way. When they reached the top of the mountain crossing over from Toyah Creek canyon to the Cave canyon, as they had taken to calling it, Clay suggested they go out to the point of the mountain where it broke off overlooking his cabin. From there, they could see the valley for miles in all directions. Clay remarked, "This will be a good lookout point where we can keep an eye on your place without anyone seeing us, and we can see anyone coming in time to prepare for their visit."

Clint asked, "You mean I'm going to have to stay out here all the time, and can't even go down to my own house?"

"I'll tell you what, you go on down there, and do your thing just like normal, I'll stay up here and keep watch when I'm not busy searching out other things."

"What kind of other things?" Clint asked.

"I want to ride over to Blalock's place and see what kind of operation he has over there. So when I'm not here, you'll need to be on your toes and keep your rifle handy. Don't let anyone get close unless you know them."

All this defense planning reminded him of home, and Ellen, when they had to always be on the lookout for Thompson and his gang.

Clay took out his binoculars and scanned the valley before it got too dark to see. They ate a cold supper, then rode to the cave and deposited their supplies. From there, they rode straight back to the cabin, knowing no one could see them coming from the cave.

Clint slept in the house while Clay bunked in the barn. They didn't know if they would have trouble or not, so they prepared for it in case it came.

CHAPTER

FIVE

He was up before the sun taking a good look around the place. Clint prepared breakfast, and they ate and talked over today's plan. The house faced away from the canyons out toward the valley. It sat on high ground above Toyah Creek with another small hill off to the left. So with the creek on one side and the slight rise on the other, Clay pointed out to Clint, "One man could be down behind the bank of the creek on that side while the other one can be behind that rise over there. No one can see us until we rise from our hiding place and open fire. By then, it'll be too late for them to do anything about it."

Clint was bewildered by the whole thing. He was walking around, scratching his head, and kicking the ground.

Clay saddled Blue and rode out toward Blalock's place while Clint worked around his place, taking care of all the necessary chores.

Clay didn't know exactly where Blalock's place was. All he had was a general direction, so he rode that way watching for any other riders. He didn't ride in a straight line, though. He rode from one hilltop to another, doing his best not to skyline himself. If there were other riders out there, he wanted to see them first.

He had ridden what he guessed was about halfway when Blue's head came up, and his ears pointed forward. Clay immediately started looking for a place to hide. He saw a shallow draw off to his left about a hundred yards. When he galloped Blue into the draw, only his head and shoulders were sticking out above the rim, so he hunkered over, so his eyes were just above ground level and waited. He kept watching to see where Blue was looking. A couple of minutes went by before Clay heard horses coming in his direction. It sounded like they would pass to his right, so he turned Blue to the left and went deeper into the draw. Fortunately, the draw made a turn to the right, which allowed him to remain concealed when he went around the curve. He removed his hat and sat watching with just his eyes above the rim of the draw. Brush and bunchgrass covered the floor of the valley, and his blond hair blended in, so he wasn't too concerned about being seen unless they rode right up on him.

He watched as four men rode by about fifty yards to the west of him headed toward Clint's place. He was pretty sure one of them was Blalock. He couldn't be positive because he had only seen him in the dark with his hat on, but the big man in the lead was wearing a black hat and riding a black horse, and he had a thick black mustache.

Clay waited until they were past him, and then rode down the draw to where it got deeper, and he could straighten up without being seen. He didn't know where this was going to take him, but he had to find a way to get ahead of Blalock and warn Clint before they got there.

He rode what he guess was five hundred yards before the draw turned back to his left, and took him behind a hill from Blalock. He assumed Blalock would keep riding straight toward Clint's place, so Clay put the spurs to Blue, and raced down the opposite side of the hill. He knew he had about five miles to go to get there. Blalock didn't seem to be in any hurry, so Clay figured he had plenty of time. He took every opportunity to ride to the top of the hill to check on

Blalock's progress and saw he was already ahead of them. From there on, he concentrated on staying out of sight.

When he raced down the hill to Clint's place, Clint heard him coming and was standing at the barn door with a rifle in his hand. Blue was in a sweaty lather when Clay slid him to a stop in front of Clint and informed him they had company coming.

Each man knew what to do because they had rehearsed it in case something like this happened. Neither man wanted to get trapped in the house or barn, so they each had their battle stations outside, one on each side of the house about one hundred feet out. From there, they could cover the front, and back of the house, and the barn. If Blalock was planning to burn Clint out, he was going to be in for a big surprise.

Clay hurriedly put Blue in the barn out of sight, and both men took their positions. Each man had a rifle, a shotgun, and a pistol with plenty of ammunition.

They had been waiting for about twenty minutes when they saw Blalock and his three men approaching at a slow walk. Presumably, to look the place over as they rode closer.

Clint and Clay were lying flat on their bellies with their guns loaded and ready.

Blalock motioned for his men to spread out when they were still a hundred yards out. Clay already had his rifle aimed at Blalock. If it came to shooting, Blalock would be the first to die.

The riders were within fifty feet of the front of Clint's cabin when Blalock held up his hand to call a halt and sat looking the place over. There was no activity, and the place gave the appearance that no one was around. Finally, Blalock called out, "Hello, the house."

No one answered him, so he motioned his men to dismount and advance. They left their horses ground hitched, and with rifles in hand, they walked toward the house, still spread out with twenty feet or so between them. When they were twenty-five feet from the house, Clay called out, "Hold it right there and state your business."

Blalock and his men stopped, realized they were standing out there in the open and began looking around to locate where the voice came from. When they still didn't see anyone, Blalock said, "We came to talk to you, Wilcox, come out where we can see you."

Clay answered from his hiding place, "Anything you have to say, you can say it from right there. Now, what do you want?"

"You are not Wilcox, who are you?"

"The same man who could have blown your head off the other night when you tried to hang an innocent man, and the same one who can put a bullet between your eyes right now if you don't state your business or turn around and ride out of here. It's your choice. You have fifteen seconds to make up your mind."

Blalock was noticeably nervous as he stood looking around but still hasn't seen anyone. But he knew a rifle was pointed at his head, and a wrong move would get him killed.

"Time's up, Blalock," and Clay opened fire, putting bullets at their feet. They ran for their horses, but they were frightened by the gunfire, and Clay gave them something to be afraid of when he put several bullets at their feet also. The rock fragments and dirt flying up and hitting them did the job. They took off as fast as they could go with Blalock and his men running after them. There was no place for them to hide or take cover for several hundred yards. Before they got there, they were all out of breath and mad as a nest of hornets.

The horses were still running and probably would not stop until they got home, which was ten to fifteen miles away.

Clay brought Blue from the barn and mounted up, taking his binoculars, canteen, and rifle; he rode to the top of the hill overlooking the valley. From there, he could see Blalock and his men when they left their hiding place and started walking toward home. Clay kept watching until they went out of sight. He then rode down to tell Clint what was going on and that he was going to follow along and make sure they kept going.

"Want me to come with you?"

"That won't be necessary. I'm just going to watch them unless they turn back this way."

Clay rode out to where he could see Blalock and his men. They were walking in the right direction to be going home, so Clay followed along out of rifle range but close enough that they could see him watching. He kept them in sight until it got too dark to see and returned to Clint's place.

For the next three days, Clay and Clint did work around the place while keeping a sharp eye out for Blalock and his men. When they had about decided that Blalock had given up on running Clint off or killing him, they got a rude awakening in the middle of the night.

Clint, as usual, was sleeping in the house while Clay slept in the barn. Sometime after midnight, Clay was having a hard time getting to sleep, when he heard a large group of horses coming his way. He jumped out of bed, hurriedly put on his hat and boots, grabbed his rifle, and ran to the bedroom window where Clint was sleeping and banged on the window. "Clint, get up and get out of there; they are coming, hurry." Clay then ran to his post behind the hill to the south of the house while Clint grabbed his rifle and pistol and went to his position on the other side below the bank of the creek.

When the men were fifty feet or so from the house, Clay yelled for them to stop, and state your business. As soon as he yelled the order to stop, Blalock gave the order to charge the house. Gunfire broke out all around the place. Clay and Clint were both pouring lead at Blalock as fast as they could pull the trigger and ratchet a new round in the chamber. There was total confusion in Blalock's crowd. They didn't know where the lead was coming from. They were shooting at the house until some of them saw the gun flashes, and directed their fire at them. By then, several of Blalock's men were on the ground, and a couple more had ridden away barely hanging to their saddles. After about half a minute of this, someone yelled, "Let's get out of here!" and those that were able to put their horses in a stampede in the other direction.

When all the shooting stopped, and things quieted down, Clay and Clint slowly walked around to see the damage done. They found four of Blalock's men on the ground, either dead or wounded. Clint brought a lantern from the house so they could do a closer inspection. Three of the men were still alive and needed medical attention if they were going to live. Clay did what he could to bandage their wounds and try to stop the bleeding. They didn't expect Blalock to come back to see about his men, so Clint brought his wagon around, and the men were loaded aboard. The trip to Toyah and the doctor took two hours. It was still dark when they arrived at the doctor's home. After the third knock, the doctor opened the door in his nightshirt. "What in the devil is going on here? Don't you know it's the middle of the night?"

"Sorry to have to wake you this time of night, Doctor, but we have three wounded men here who need attention."

"Well, bring them on in and put 'em in that room wherever you can find a place to put 'em.

Clay and Clint brought the men in and placed them on the table, the bed, and a chair. Clay told the doctor when he came in, "These are Blalock's men. They attacked Clint's place last night. There are a couple more wounded out there somewhere. They'll probably be along later if they're able. You can bill Blalock for this. He put 'em up to it."

After leaving the doctor's office, Clay and Clint went to the café, had a good breakfast, picked up a few additional supplies, and returned home. When they came within sight of the place, they pulled up on a slight rise and looked the place over before riding in. Everything seemed to be in order, but they were still very cautious.

"Hey, Clint, this is a good time to check out that cave. Let's make several torches and go take a look."

"I'll go with you, but I'm not going any farther into that cave than the front door."

"Ah, come on, Clint, where's your adventurous spirit? That place may be full of gold just waiting for you to sack it up and haul it out."

"If you find any, you let me know. Until then, I'm staying where the sun shines."

They made their torches, took a can of coal oil, the additional supplies they bought and went to the cave. It was broad daylight, but since they had just taken a good look around, they thought it would be safe. They tied their horses near the cave entrance, pulled all the brush away that they had stacked there. Before entering, they soaked the torches with coal oil and stuck a match to one of them. Once inside, with the torch burning, they could see much more than the last time when they only had a match. They were both in awe at sight of what they saw before them. The cave widened and got much higher after a short distance. They could hear water dripping, and everything felt moist. The temperature was very comfortable.

Clay was holding the torch over his head and looking in fascination at the spectacle before him. At some places, the ceiling was so high the light didn't reach it, and in others, it was so low he had to duck to get through. After a hundred yards or so, he heard water falling. When he got closer, he saw a waterfall coming from somewhere above and falling into a pool somewhere below. There was a sharp drop off into the pool. He couldn't tell how far it was down to the water. He dropped a rock, and it took two seconds to hit the water. He still didn't know how far that was, just that it was a long way down. The smoke from his torch was drifting ahead of him farther into the cave, which told him there was another opening somewhere ahead, but again, there was no telling how far that might be.

"Well, I've seen about all I need to see how about you?" said Clay.

Clint said, "I saw all I needed to see in the first ten feet."

They headed back to the entrance while their torch was still burning. At the entrance, Clint gave a big sigh of relief. "I never want to do that again. I don't like tight, closed-in places. They make me feel trapped, and I want to scream and run out."

"Maybe we won't ever have to go any farther than this." Clay said hopefully.

From just inside the entrance, he looked out to make sure no one was waiting for them. When he saw nothing out of place, he told Clint, "Looks safe, come on."

When they were outside, and mounted, Clay told Clint, "I'm going to ride up this canyon where we camped the other night and see if I can find a more secluded place. If I'm not back by dark, don't worry, I'll camp out wherever I am at the time."

"Ok, you be careful. See you tomorrow."

"If I were you, I wouldn't sleep in the house. Blalock may come back, and you don't want him hanging you again."

"You got that right," Clint said as he rubbed his neck where the rope had been.

They each rode off in different directions. When Clint arrived back at the house, he fed all his animals, and when it was dark, he took his bedroll and moved off into the brush away from the house. The sky was clear, with no clouds, so he wasn't afraid of rain. He spread his bedroll, laid his rifle beside him, and lay down. But, since he wasn't used to sleeping outside, it took a while, but sleep finally came.

Clay rode up the canyon to where they camped the night before and started looking for whatever he could find. He wasn't looking for anything specific, just a place out of sight, and hopefully with some protection from the weather.

He followed the creek north as it wound its way around the foot of the mountain. He came upon a trail cutting off to the east and climbing toward the top. It didn't look promising, but he turned his horse onto it to see where it went. It switched back and forth as it worked its way toward the top. When he got there, he found a large flat surface with a small lake in the middle. Trees grew all around the edge and covered most of the top of the mesa. Clay stopped and took in the view, amazed at what he had found. After a few minutes, he touched his heels to Socks and rode around the lake. Fish were jumping every few minutes. He could see himself staying here for a long time.

On the far side of the lake was a rock formation that offered protection from the wind. Trees grew right up against the rock so thick that Clay almost missed it as he rode by, but when he saw what looked like an opening in the rock wall, he stopped and tied Socks to a bush and pushed his way through the brush, and was surprised at what he found.

Massive slabs of rock had fallen from above at some time in the far distant past and landed on other rocks forming a cave of sorts. It appeared to be about six feet wide at the opening and extended back toward the face of the mountain approximately thirty feet.

It would be the perfect place to stash food and use it as their hideout if the need ever arose.

He walked to the back of the cave to make sure no animals were living there. There was no wind blowing into the cave due to the trees growing so thick around it. With a fire in here, it should be comfortable enough, even on the coldest night, and there was plenty of room for their three horses. He would have to remember to bring plenty of feed for them. Grass grew all around the lake, but trees covered most of the top of the mesa preventing grass from growing very thick, and if it snowed, all of that would be covered.

He was pleased with what he had found. He continued to ride around the mesa and found his way back to the trail just as the sun was going out of sight behind the ridge.

He decided to spend the night here and go back to Clint's place first thing tomorrow morning. He went back to the cave in the rocks. There was plenty of deadfall limbs and brush about, so finding material for a fire was no problem. Before it was completely dark, he had enough wood gathered to keep his fire going all night. He got his coffee boiling and heated jerky in water until it was soft enough to eat without breaking his teeth. That and a couple of cold hard biscuits leftover from their lunch in Toyah was his supper. He could remember times when that would have been like a feast.

When he was finally able to get to sleep, his night was filled with dreams of Ellen and Carter. Very few nights went by where he was able to get a good night's sleep without being haunted by those dreams. He awoke several times with tears in his eyes. Then he had a terrible time getting back to sleep. When he finally decided sleep was a thing of the past for this night, he crawled out of his bedroll, put on his hat, and then his boots, brought Socks in close to the cave, and saddled him. He reheated the coffee leftover from last night and chewed on a piece of hard jerky for his breakfast. Then he mounted up to head back to Clint's place.

He let Socks have his head to find his way down the mountain and ended up at the creek and headed home.

He was still a mile or so from home nearing the end of the canyon, where it opened onto the valley where Clint's house stood when he thought he heard gunshots and stopped to listen. It only took a few seconds to determine that Clint was in trouble. He put his heels to Socks and took off as fast as the terrain would allow. When he reached the end of the canyon, and before he broke out into the open, he stopped to listen again and take in the situation. He was still too far away to see anything, but the gunshots told him Clint was still in the fight. He turned to his left to come up behind the hill that was close to the house on the south side. He reached the backside of the hill without drawing any fire. He tied Socks and took his rifle, canteen, and binoculars and crawled to the top of the hill where he could look over without being seen. He was about two hundred feet or so from the house. Between him and the house, he saw two men hunkered down behind some small rocks. On the other side of the house and in front and back, he spotted gun smoke. They had Clint surrounded. He was in the house and doing a good job of holding them off so far.

Clay took a few minutes to assess the situation and determine the best way for him to handle this. He knew he would have to take out the two right below him first. After that, he would have to select his targets as they presented themselves.

He took up his binoculars and looked at each man, hoping to find Blalock. He didn't spot him, but he counted eight men. So he took careful aim at one of the men below him and fired. He had aimed at the top of the man's shoulder. He didn't want to kill him if he didn't have to. He was just trying to take him out of the fight. As soon as he fired that first shot, he levered in another round and shot the second man before they realized someone was behind them. There was so much shooting that no one noticed there was another gun in the fight. Clay spotted his next target and took him out just as easily. That left five by his count. There was one behind the barn that Clay saw from time to time, and was ready for him the next time he stuck his head up. He was visible for only a moment, but Clay fired as soon as he saw him. The man ducked back out of sight, and the bullet only grazed him across the back. Now he knew someone was shooting at him from the hill behind him. The next time he showed it was only one eye peeking around the corner of the barn for only a second or two. Clay took aim where he saw the eye and waited. It was only a few seconds before the man peeked around the corner again. This time Clay was ready for him. When Clay fired splinters flew from the board next to the man's face, the man dropped his rifle, and staggered back, and was visible long enough for Clay to put another bullet in his thigh. That should take him out of the fight. Four left.

The four remaining must have caught on that they were losing the fight. Clay heard them calling back and forth, trying to get answers from the men Clay had shot. They were not answering, and that had the others worried.

Eventually, Clay saw a man sneaking away into the brush on the other side of the house. He aimed and put several bullets close enough to make him look for better cover. Those shots gave the shooters his position, and they started pouring lead in his direction. He was behind the hill, except for his head and shoulders, so he wasn't giving them much of a target. A couple of the shots came close but did no damage. He backed off from the top of the hill and ran twenty yards to his left and crawled to the top again. He saw one of the men sneaking toward the house and put a bullet so close to his face that the man yelled and tried to get the dirt out of his eyes. When Clay saw him last, he was crawling the other way as fast as could. Clay let him go.

The shooting slacked off and eventually stopped. Clay scanned the area with his binoculars and spotted four men riding away. Two of them looked like they were having trouble staying in the saddle. By the time he saw them, they were out of rifle range, so there was nothing he could do about it.

He called to Clint, "Hey Clint, are you ok in there? They've pulled out. It's all over."

A moment later, Clint stepped out the back door with no blood on him, and he didn't look like he was hurting. The two met near the barn and went to check on the men Clay had shot. Clay cautioned Clint about approaching them. "We don't know if they're still capable of shooting us or not, so until we know for sure, we assume we are." They approached each man carefully, took his guns away, and then checked to see how bad he was injured. It turned out all four of them were still alive but in no shape to cause any more trouble. Clay mounted his horse and rode around until he found their horses and brought them back and tied the wounded men on in a sitting position. There was a lot of moaning and complaining about the rough handling, but Clay and Clint finished the job. "My suggestion to you men is to go to Toyah and see the doctor. When he has you patched up, leave the territory. The climate here doesn't seem to be agreeing with you. All of you got off lucky this time. If y'all come around here again, we'll be shooting to kill. Do you understand what I'm telling you?"

They all nodded their heads that they did. "Ok, get out of here, and we better never see any of you again."

The man who was in the best shape of the four said he would see they got to the doctor.

When they were gone, Clay told Clint what he found on top of the mesa. They prepared another package of food to go to the cave in case they needed it in the future.

Clay was still determined to ride to Blalock's place to look it over, so he switched his saddle to Blue, and headed out.

Like he did the last time he was going there, he stopped to survey his surroundings before crossing over the top of each hill. This time he was able to get to Blalock's place without being seen. He took cover behind the trees and brush on top of a hill a half-mile or so from the headquarters. From there, he could see the layout clearly with his binoculars. Men were coming and going from the bunkhouse and barn. A few horses stood in a corral near the barn. In a fenced pasture farther back were more horses. He looked as far as he could see but didn't see one cow anywhere. Clay was scratching his head, and musing, "Hum, I thought this was supposed to be a cattle ranch."

The survivors who attacked Clint's place had arrived back here only a short time before Clay arrived. Horses were brought out and hitched to a wagon, and what looked like injured men got in the back. Clay counted five men getting in the wagon plus the driver. He concluded that must include the men who were injured the last time they attacked Clint. "We are racking up quite a score, Blalock. How do you like it?" Clay whispered to himself.

After the wagon left and was out of sight, one man rode off to the south and another to the west. Clay was prepared to sit here all day if need be to see what Blalock had planned if he could. Several more groups of riders came into the ranch headquarters from different directions. Clay started trying to get a headcount. From what he saw before the men began gathering, there were nine of them there. Then three groups of men came in with four and five to a group. That would put the headcount at around twenty-two if he saw all of them. He was wondering what Blalock had in mind when a scary thought hit him. "He's preparing to hit Clint with everything he has." When he had that thought, he eased back from the hilltop until he reached his horse. He jumped on Blue and headed back to warn Clint. It took him just about an hour to get there. Clint was at the woodpile splitting wood when Clay raced in. "Get our horses and all the grub you can pack. Blalock is coming with about twenty-five men. It looks like he plans to do away with you for good this time. We can't stay here and defend this place against that many. We have to get out of here. He'll probably burn the place unless he plans to use it for himself after he kills you. Grab everything you can carry. I'll bring the pack saddle, and we can load it down."

Within thirty minutes, they had the packs loaded and riding up Toyah canyon. When they reached the trail going over the mountain to Cave Canyon, they took it to the top of the mountain then rode out on the point overlooking Clint's place. With the binoculars, they could see everything that was happening down there.

They didn't have long to wait until they saw a large group of men riding toward the house. They spread out and came at the place in a skirmish line that stretched for a quarter-mile across the valley. When they were three hundred yards out, one of the men, they assumed it was Blalock, waved his arm, and the whole gang charged the house with guns blazing. They circled the house and barn as Indians are known to do. They shot at the buildings until there was not a window left in any of them. When they didn't receive return fire, they stopped shooting. Two men rushed the front door of the house while two more went to the bunkhouse. They came out in half a minute and said something to Blalock. He dismounted from his big black horse and stormed into the house. He came out in a couple of minutes and gave orders to his men. They all rushed the house and started throwing things out the doors and windows. The beds, chairs, tables, even the cookstove was dragged out and thrown on the pile. When the house was empty, and everything piled in the yard, coal oil was poured on it and set fire.

From where they were watching, there was nothing Clay and Clint could do without getting themselves killed, so they just watched. Both were so mad if they could have gotten their hand on Blalock, they would have cut his heart out.

Clay reached over and patted Clint on the shoulder, "Be patient Clint, he'll get his, only ten times worse. We know where he lives, and he has a lot more to lose than you do."

When Blalock and his men had done all the damage they intended to do, they rode away back toward home.

Clay and Clint stayed where they were until Blalock was out of sight then rode down to see what other damage they did.

Clint walked around in a daze surveying the destruction. "It took me years to accumulate all this, and Blalock destroyed it in a few minutes. I don't know what you plan to do, but I'm going to make Blalock pay. Before I'm through, he'll regret he ever started this."

"What do you want to do first?" Clay asked.

"I guess we better do like you said. Set up camp somewhere, then attack Blalock where it'll hurt him the most."

"And where is that?"

"At his home, just like he did mine."

"OK, that's what I would do. Come on; I have the perfect place to set up camp."

They rode to Cave Creek and followed it until they came to the trail leading to the top of the mesa and the rock cave. When they arrived, they unloaded the supplies and stashed them against the back wall. Clint walked around, looking the place over and shaking his head. Finally, he asked, "Is that trail we came up the only way up here?"

"I don't know. I haven't had time to look around yet, but we need to do that right away. We don't want anyone sneaking in on us through the back door."

They got busy gathering wood for their fire before it got too dark to see what they were doing. When the fire was going, and the coffee was ready, they sat back against the wall and sipped their coffee and ate from the supplies they had brought with them. While they were eating, they were kicking around ideas of how to get back at Blalock. Clint was in favor of going into his place at night and burning his house down around his ears. Clay couldn't argue against that too hard. He was leaning in that direction himself. Finally, Clay suggested, "How about we start with his barn. We can warn him what comes next if he don't leave you alone. If that don't stop him, then we burn his bunkhouse, if he still wants to kill you, we burn his house, and if he happens to be in it, too bad."

"Sounds like we are giving him too many breaks after what he did to my place and tried to do to me."

"You are probably right," Clay said, "but that's the difference in him and us. We aren't cold-blooded killers, and he is. But, there comes a time when you have to fight fire with fire. If that's the only thing he understands, then we can be just as cold-blooded as he can. We are just giving a warning before we do it. Kind of like a rattlesnake warning you before he strikes."

That brought back all the old memories of Ellen and how she died. He got up and walked out of the cave, leaving Clint wondering what had happened. He saw Clay was extremely upset and left him to his grieving. He didn't know what had brought it on, and he wasn't about to ask. If Clay wanted to tell him, he would do it in his own good time.

After Clint was in his bedroll fast asleep, Clay came in and poured himself another cup of coffee and sat staring into the flames. When Clint awoke later, seemed like several hours, Clay was still sitting staring into the fire.

CHAPTER

SIX

When Clint awoke at dawn the next morning, Clay was still sleeping. Clint knew he didn't get much sleep, so he went about his morning chores as quietly as possible, trying not to wake him. He took the horses to the lake to let them drink their fill and moved them to the grass along the banks of the lake. He saw the fish jumping, so he rigged a fishing hook and line and tried his luck. It didn't take any time at all until he had a nice string of perch for their breakfast and lunch. When Clay awoke, Clint had the fish in the skillet and the coffee perking. It took a moment for Clay to recognize where he was. "Is that fish I smell?"

"It sure is, but I'm going to eat your share if you sleep any longer."

Clint handed Clay a cup of coffee and a plate with two halves of fish. Clay dug in like he hadn't eaten in a week. "Now that is some of the best eating I've had in a long time."

Neither Clay nor Clint was noted for his cooking skills, so they got by on the skimpiest of meals. They made up for it when they were in a town, and in Clay's case, that wasn't very often lately.

Over the fish and coffee, they planned their day. First, they would ride back to Clint's place to see if Blalock had been back. Then they would ride to Blalock's place and stay hidden until everyone was asleep. Then they would go down and burn the barn. When the men came out to fight the fire, they would open fire with their rifles as long as they could see anything to shoot. Their main target would be Blalock if they could pick him out of the group of men he had working for him.

Clay asked Clint, "Blalock has at least twenty-five men working for him, but I didn't see a cow anywhere on his place, and I've never seen his brand on any cow anywhere on the range. Do you ever wonder what he has all those men doing?"

"No, I didn't know he had that many. That does bring up an interesting question, though." Clint said as he scratched his head in thought.

"What do you think about us trailing some of his men when they leave his place to see what they do? It can't be anything to do with his ranching activities."

Clint answered, "If we can do it without getting caught, I'm all in favor of it."

"I've had a little experience at that kind of stuff." Clay said, "I think we can pull it off."

"Are we still going to burn his barn tonight?" Clint wanted to know.

"Why not, he deserves it."

"Good, I'm with you."

They explored the mesa until mid-afternoon and then rode back to Clint's place to see if anyone had been around since the fire the day before. There was no sign that anyone had been there, so they headed for Blalock's place. From his earlier trip here, Clay knew the layout of the land and knew where they could wait without being seen until it was time to strike. From the top of the hill just north of the house, they saw Blalock's men coming and going. None of them seemed the least bit interested in guarding against an attack. Apparently, Blalock was so confident in his position, and strength that he wasn't worried about anyone attacking him in his own camp.

Clay pointed that out to Clint and said, "After tonight, he'll have a whole new perspective on that."

Clint was hoping Clay was right.

"We better get some rest before we start this war. It may be a long night." Clay said.

With that thought, they lay down and tried to get some shuteye while they could.

Sometime after midnight, Clay, and Clint were both awake about the same time. They couldn't afford to have a fire, so they drank water and chewed on jerky while they saddled their horses. When they were ready to ride and deliver Blalock's present, Clint asked, "How are we going to do this? This is all new to me."

Clay explained, "At the foot of this hill, there's a small gully or dry creek bed that runs pretty close to the back of the barn. We can leave the horses there, and walk to the back of the barn, and set the fire. By the time its burning good and the men become aware of it, we'll be back at our horses. When they come running out to fight the fire, we open fire. They should be easy to see in the firelight."

"Ok, I hope Blalock makes himself a target. I want a good shot at him. I'm going to try to put it right between his eyes."

Clay told him, "You'll stand a lot better chance of hitting him if you aim for the largest part of his body, like the chest or stomach."

"Yeah, I know you're right, I just want to see him suffer."

"If you shoot him in the head, he won't suffer at all. He'll just be dead."

"Ok, I'll aim for his gut. That should make him suffer."

Before they left Clint's place, they had soaked rags in coal oil. They now took those with them as they approached the backside of the barn. Clay and Clint went to opposite ends of the barn and stuffed rags in cracks in the barn walls. When the match was touched to the rags, it didn't take but a few seconds until the fire was climbing up the wall. Clay and Clint hurried back to their horses and waited to see what happened. Since the fire started on the backside of the barn, it took several minutes to become visible from the house and bunkhouse.

A shout came from the bunkhouse, "fire, fire, fire," The alarm was picked up by other men as they came running out. Most of them were in their long johns and no shoes. By that time, it was much too late to have a chance of putting it out, but some came running with buckets of water and started throwing it on the fire. Clay and Clint waited until several men were in the firelight before they started shooting. In the first volley, two men fell. Before they could get a second shot off, most of them had disappeared. They waited to see if Blalock showed himself, but after several minutes they thought they had better make some tracks away from here before Blalock could get his men organized.

When they left, they went in the opposite direction from Clint's place. They didn't want to make it too obvious who the culprit was, so they rode south until they came to a creek running from north to south. They took to the water and followed it north until it turned east. Then they cut across the country back toward Clint's place.

The sun was peaking over the hills in the east when they arrived. They didn't stop but continued to their rock cave. They were both tired to the bone when they arrived. They unsaddled their horses and staked them on the grass near the lake. There were still a few coals showing in the fire, so they coaxed them to life and heated the coffee. After two cups each, they were in their bedrolls sound asleep.

They slept until almost noon, ate a light lunch, and then returned to Clint's place and did some cleanup to get rid of the burn pile in the back yard. When they had done all they could, it was getting late in the day. Clay rode to the top of the hill to take a look around to see if anything was happening that they should know about. He scanned the valley with his binoculars but didn't see anything out of order, so he returned to the house. They prepared a light supper and prepared to get some sleep. Clint was getting used to sleeping on the ground, so he had no trouble getting to sleep. Clay, however, couldn't get to sleep until early in the morning. Ellen was everywhere he looked, in every thought, in every dream. He tossed and turned until he was utterly worn out, and finally fell asleep out of pure exhaustion.

They worked around the place the next three days with no sign of Blalock or any of his men. They were beginning to think he had gotten the message and was going to leave them alone.

They spent one day rounding up cattle and slapping Clint's brand on them. They spent the next day herding them back into the canyons behind Clint's place. They were hoping the animals would become accustomed to that area and stay close by. There was enough water and grass in the canyons to handle the number they drove in there.

The next day they made a trip to Toyah to get more supplies. Clint had been practicing with his rifle and pistol and had used up most of their ammunition. That was one of the main reasons they had come to town.

They tied the horses to the hitch rail in front of the general store and went in. Clint gave Mr. McCormick the list of things he needed. While he was filling the order, Clay and Clint walked across the street to the saloon and ordered a beer. They were standing with their backs to the bar when a big man got up from one of the tables and walked over to Wilcox. He stood for a full minute staring into Clint's face before he said anything. "You're that ten horn Wilcox ain't you?"

Wilcox looked him up and down before answering. "What's a ten horn? Don't believe I ever saw one of those critters. Let me buy you a drink, and you can describe one to me, and I'll see if I recognize him."

The rest of the patrons in the place burst out laughing. Clint didn't know if they were laughing at his remark or that he didn't know what a ten horn was.

"I'm Segundo for Mr. Blalock. We have orders to get rid of you any way we want to. He's through messing with you. You are just a thorn in his side that he wants out. I've been ordered to pull it."

Clint looked him over again. Thornton was several inches taller and twenty-five pounds heavier than Clint. Clay was waiting to see how Wilcox was going to handle this. It wasn't Clay's place to butt in, yet.

After another long pause, Clint asked, "Ok, when do you want to pull it?"

"Now's as good a time as any," Thornton said as he drew back his fist. Clint didn't wait to see what else Thornton was going to do.

He delivered a straight left to Thornton's nose with all the power he could muster. Thornton went flying backward until he hit a chair that tripped him, and he ended up flat on his back with blood pouring from his nose. Thornton was so surprised it took him a while to realize what had just happened. He let out a roar that reminded Clay of a bear. He lunged to his feet and came storming back with the force of a longhorn bull. Before he got to Clint, Clint sidestepped and hooked a right to Thornton's gut. When he bent over to get his breath, Clint shoved him into the bar headfirst. The bar was knocked back at least six inches, bottles, and glasses crashed to the floor.

Clay was almost as stunned as Thornton was. He never expected Clint to show this much fight.

Clint was standing back, waiting for Thornton to regain his breath. He was gasping, trying to get more air into his lungs when he turned around, and Clint landed another one in the gut. Thornton doubled over, and Clint came up with a right to the face knocking Thornton on his back again. He was slow getting up this time. When he was on his feet, he circled Clint with his fist in front of his face while he looked around to see if he was going to get any help. No one was offering, so he continued to circle. Clint kept turning with him until Thornton made another charge. This time Clint didn't dodge or sidestep, he delivered another straight left to the face which stood Thornton up straight. Blood covered his face and down his chest. Thornton still had not landed a punch to Clint. He swung several times, but Clint moved just enough to make them miss. Every time Thornton swung at Clint, Clint counter punched him in the face. Thornton circled some more. Finally, it looked like Clint had had enough of this game, and walked in with both fist landing as fast as he could deliver them. Thornton was backing up, trying to avoid the blows but having no luck at that.

When he reached the wall and had nowhere else to go, he put both hands in front of his face to ward off Clint's punches. Clint switched to Thornton's gut and kept pounding. When Thornton lowered his hands to protect his stomach, Clint went back to his face. Clint was delivering punches so fast there was nothing Thornton could do. Finally, Thornton collapsed to the floor. Clint stepped back, straightened his clothes, took one deep breath, and returned to the bar, picked up his beer, and took a sip. "Are you about ready to go?" he asked.

Clay answered, "Yeah, nothing happening here, might as well go."

Thornton's buddies were in shock and sat with their mouths open.

Clint and Clay walked across the street to pick up their supplies. Clay kept looking at Clint like he had never seen him before. Clint was acting like this happened twice a day every day.

The supplies were loaded, and they were riding out of town when Clay looked at Clint, and said, "Tell me I'm not dreaming. Did I really see what I just saw? Did you just beat the stuffing out of that guy, and he never laid a hand on you?"

"Oh, that. That was nothing; I used to do that several times a week back home."

"You got in fights like that several times a week? What were you, the chief trouble maker?"

"No, I was the boxing champ in college three years in a row." Clay was still looking at Clint like he didn't know him at all. Here's a man who doesn't know the first thing about guns or how to defend himself against someone who wants to hang him, but he beats the ears of a man much bigger than he is, and thinks it's nothing.

Clay was speechless the rest of the way home. They unpacked the supplies and put them away in the empty cabinets.

The fire didn't harm the cookstove that was dragged outside and thrown on the burn pile, so they brought it inside, and hooked the stove pipe to it, and ran it out through the wall. It wasn't long before the fire was going, and supper was ready in a few minutes. The pots and pans were brought back inside and cleaned up. All the furniture and bedding was gone. They would be sleeping on the ground, or the floor, for some time.

CHAPTER

SEVEN

lay and Clint continued to work around the place while keeping a close watch in case Blalock decided to cause more trouble. There was a lot of work to be done, but neither of them was any good at making furniture, so they settled for sleeping wherever they threw their bedrolls.

They spent at least three days a week, rounding up and branding mavericks. Clint guessed he had at least four hundred longhorns with his brand on them. An official round-up had never been done since Clint had been here, so he and Clay were thinking about trying to get all the ranchers together to round up everything in the area and put together a drive to a market somewhere. The main force behind this was that Clint needs money to replace the furniture lost to Blalock.

This was the wrong time of year to start a drive anywhere, but if they could get it organized, they could get it off to a good start in the spring.

Clay suggested that Clint go to the other ranchers in the area and get their thoughts on that idea while Clay stayed behind to guard the homestead. Clint was agreeable to that and left two days later to visit as many of the ranches as he could. He had no intention of visiting Blalock. He would probably hear about it from someone, but it wouldn't be from Clint.

Clint was gone for four days. Clay kept busy around the place doing odd jobs that had been put off for one reason or another while always keeping his eyes open for unwanted visitors. Luckily none showed up.

Clay and Clint were still sleeping out in the brush in a different place every night. Clint remarked one night as they were bedding down, "I'm getting used to this. It's not so bad, after all."

He changed his mind about midnight when the norther blew in and dropped the temperature from a comfortable sixty-something to an uncomfortable thirty-something with rain and sleet, with snow mixed in. They grabbed their bedding and ran to the barn just in time to keep from getting soaked.

There wasn't much chance anyone would be out causing trouble on a night like this, so they threw their bedroll down in the hayloft on a pile of hay and tried to get back to sleep. The hay was so much more comfortable than sleeping on the hard ground that both slept late the next morning.

While they were still snug and warm in the blankets, Clay suggested to Clint, "If you had a watchdog, we could sleep comfortably like this every night, and the dog would let us know if anything came around."

"Why didn't you bring that up when we were in town? We could have picked up a dog while we were there. I'm sure there are plenty of strays running around that the town folks would like to get rid of."

Clay says, "How about I ride in tomorrow, if the weather permits, and see what I can find? I kind of like sleeping in here."

"Suit yourself. I'm staying right here."

"You're going to get mighty hungry because I'm not bringing you your food."

"Aw Clay, what happened, I thought you loved me?"

"I wouldn't go that far. I kind of like you, especially after that display you put on with Thornton the other day. I don't want you mad at me."

"That was nothing; you should see me when I get warmed up."

"That would be something to see. I'll stick with picking up a dog."

The next few days kept them busy around the ranch, building and repairing the fence. But the thing that was the hardest and took the most time was cutting hay for feed and stacking it in the pastures. The winters in West Texas can be fierce at times, and if there isn't feed for the animals, they can drift for miles or freeze to death where they stand. One advantage of cutting hay is it builds muscle, on the cutter, not the eater. Clay and Clint were too tired and sore at the end of the day to fix anything to eat. They washed the dirt off and went to bed. In the morning, they were so stiff they could hardly move, but after the first half-hour back in the hay meadow, they were loosened up and going strong again.

They always kept their rifles and pistols close by and were constantly looking out for any unwanted company. Having a heavy pistol strapped around your waist while doing this kind of work was not comfortable at all, but when you consider the alternative, it wasn't so bad.

By the end of the week, they figured they had enough hay to last through the winter. The weather had warmed up enough that they went to the creek and jumped in. The water was so cold it made their baths very short. They climbed out, got dressed in clean clothes, and prepared a good meal for the first time in almost a week.

Both of them were a little confused about not hearing from Blalock since they burned his barn. They were getting more nervous every day. The suspense was the worst. They knew he was coming; they just didn't know when or how he was going to do it.

Several times a day, even when they were cutting hay, one of them rode to the top of the hill and took a look around. So far, they haven't seen anything, and that made them more anxious.

One day Clay said to Clint as they were working around the place, "Clint, I'm still curious as to what Blalock is doing over there at his place. He has no cows, only enough horses for his men to ride, and he has twenty-five or more men. What do they do?"

"I don't know, but I've been thinking along those same lines. You mentioned once before about following them when they leave his place to see where they go. Do you still want to give that a try? It could get dangerous."

"You're right about that." Clay said, "But if they discover us following them, I'll let you take care of them. I'll have nothing to worry about after what happened in town. When they see you coming, they'll probably run and hide."

"Very funny."

Clay suggested, "How about tomorrow morning I ride into Toyah and see if I can get a dog. We'll need one that's at least half-grown to be of any good right away. I can drop the dog off here on my way back, then ride over to Blalock's place, and see what's going on. That should put me at his place close to dark."

"That sounds good to me," Clint said. "What do you want me to be doing while you do that?"

"That's up to you. Just keep your eyes open and stay alert. Don't sleep in the house, and unless I get a dog, I don't recommend sleeping in the barn. It's too easy for someone to sneak up on you."

"Ok, you be careful too. You still have a lot of work to do around here." Clint joked with a smile.

Clay remarked about him being a slave driver and went to check on his horses.

The next morning Clay rode out on Blue leading Socks with the pack saddle and panniers. If he got a young dog, he would need a way to carry him. He didn't expect the dog would follow a total stranger so he would put him in the pannier, and let him ride.

It took the usual two hours to get to Toyah. The sun was high overhead, and putting out a little too much heat, but that was better than too much cold. He rode down the main street looking both ways, and between the buildings for stray dogs. Up ahead, he saw a small boy sitting on the porch of a building holding a small puppy.

The boy looked like he had been wearing the same clothes for weeks. His face was dirty, he had no shoes, and his pants were six inches too short for him, and frayed at the bottom. Clay rode over, and stopped a few feet away and asked the boy if he had any more puppies. "I need one for a guard dog. Do you think that one will make a good guard dog?"

The boy looked Clay over like he didn't know if he could trust him or not. "I don't know, Mister, he's just a puppy. He's too little for a guard dog."

"Is he your dog?"

"Naw, he's just a stray, don't belong to nobody." The boy said.

"What's your name?"

The boy stood up as tall as he could stretch, and said, "My name is Charlie Williford Perkins, Sir."

Clay was smiling when he said, "That's a good name. Are you named after your papa?"

"Naw, I don't think so. I don't know who my papa is; I ain't ever seen him."

That made Clay feel about two inches tall.

"Where's your mother?"

"She works over at the saloon. She don't get home 'till real late every night."

"So you're kinda the overseer of the town, right?"

"I don't know what a, whatever you said is, but I do see what goes on in town."

"Well, then you can tell me if there are any other dogs that I might get for a guard dog, right?"

"Oh, sure, come on, I'll show you where they stay most of the time."

Charlie led the way around behind the stores and saloons. Several dogs were there digging through the garbage. Most of them were nothing but walking skeletons. The people in this town didn't throw away much that they could eat.

Clay looked at the four or five dogs standing around. A couple of them looked like they would be big if they got enough to eat and filled out more. There was one, in particular, that was tall with long legs, just as skinny as the others, but looked like he would fill out good. He got off his horse and reached in his saddlebag, and took out a piece of jerky and walked toward the dog. He stood his ground, and bristled up, the hair on his back standing on end, and a low growl came from his throat. Clay squatted down a few feet away and offered the jerky. The dog slowly crept forward and quickly reached out and grabbed the jerky with his teeth. Clay waited until he had eaten that piece and offered him another one. This time the dog didn't hesitate. He stepped right up and took the meat from Clay's hand.

Clay left and went to the general store to buy the few supplies on his list and returned to where the dog was lying in the shade of the building. When he saw Clay coming, he got to his feet and walked slowly toward him. Clay squatted down and gave the dog another piece of jerky. This time Clay was able to rub the top of the dog's head for just a moment before he pulled away.

Clay was squatting down, talking to the dog, when Charlie Williford Perkins came back to join him. He walked right to the dog and put his arm across his shoulder and pulled him close. The dog showed no resistance. While Charlie was petting the dog, Clay moved closer and stroked him on the head and talked softly to him. The dog relaxed after a couple of minutes and allowed Clay to pet him.

Clay asked Charlie, "Do you think you could help me get him in that pannier on the horse? I want to take him home with me if that's ok with you."

Charlie stood up and called the dog, "Come on, Elmer, you're goin' to a new home." Clay helped Charlie pick the dog up and put him in the pannier. The dog didn't know how to react. He looked like he wanted out, but it was a long way to the ground. Clay gave him another piece of jerky and petted him on the head. "Why do you call him Elmer?"

Charlie laughed, "Because he reminds me of Mr. Elmer McCormick at the general store."

When they started moving, Elmer wanted out, but Clay rode beside him, petting him on the head and talking to him until he settled down. Long before they got back to Clint's place, the dog was sound asleep.

Clay looked at him and said, "Elmer, you're some kind of watchdog."

Clint came out to meet them when they rode in. Elmer stuck his head out of the pannier and looked around. Clay dismounted and lifted the dog to the ground and gave him another piece of jerky.

"I guess we better tie him up until he gets used to being here."

Clint found a long rope, and loped it around Elmer's neck and tied him to the corner of the barn where he could get in out of the weather, or he could lie in the sun. It was up to Elmer. They gave him a chunk of venison out of the smokehouse and a bowl of water. When he looked up at Clay, he almost looked like he was smiling.

Clay grabbed a bite to eat and headed toward Blalock's place. He expected to take at least three hours to get there. There would still be several hours of daylight left, which would allow him that much time to spy on Blalock.

He took his usual precautions as he rode but didn't encounter anyone. He made sure he came out in a grove of trees overlooking Blalock's place. He left his horse a hundred feet or so back in the thickest brush he could find, took his binoculars, and crouched down under a scrub oak with limbs hanging to the ground. The sun was to his back so it wouldn't reflect off the binoculars. He pulled out a strip of jerky and prepared for a long wait.

Nothing was happening down there, so when it was too dark to see anything, Clay moved back down the hill and rode a mile or so away and set up camp. He chewed on jerky and drank water until he got sleepy and went to his bedroll.

Before daylight, the next morning, Clay was back at his observation point with his canteen and package of jerky, so he figured he could stay here several days if necessary.

Fortunately, the weather stayed clear and cool. All the next day, Clay watched. A rider came and went several times during the day but nothing out of the ordinary. At dark, he returned to his previous camp. This time he decided to have a fire and make a pot of coffee. He was far enough from the ranch and hidden in a thicket of oak and cedar that he didn't think anyone would see his fire.

He had been in bed and asleep for several hours when he heard what sounded like a large group of horses moving somewhere nearby. It sounded like they were just over the hill from his camp. He was out of his blankets and standing by his horses with his hand over their noses to keep them quiet. The horses were going toward Blalock's headquarters. Clay quickly saddled Blue and followed them. He went straight to his previous lookout point and settled down to wait for daylight. In the meantime, he couldn't see anything down there. When the sun was lighting up the eastern sky, he had his binoculars out and looking down at Blalock's ranch headquarters. All he could see so far was a herd of horses in one corral next to where the barn used to be. Saddles lined the fence where the men hung them late last night.

Shortly after the sun was up and shining brightly, Clay saw Blalock come out the back door of the main house and walk to the bunkhouse. A few minutes later, he and another man came out and went back to the big house. Clay assumed the other man was the leader of the men who came in late last night. "I wonder what they are up to. That sure is not the usual cattle ranch. Something really strange is going on here."

Clay watched all that day. Mid-afternoon, the men began to stir, and eventually ended up in the kitchen off the side of the bunkhouse. After eating, they came back and sat around outside, smoking, laughing, and talking. The big man came out of the house, and everyone got quiet. He spoke to two of the men who got up and followed him into the bunkhouse. The rest of the men stayed where they were. A few minutes later, another man came from the outhouse and started to go in the bunkhouse when the men sitting outside stopped him. For some reason, that man wasn't allowed to go in there where the boss was having a conversation with the other two men. That perked Clay's curiosity, but there was nothing he could do at this point except wait and watch. Eventually, the three men came out and joined the others sitting around talking and smoking.

That's the way things went for the rest of the day. Clay watched until it got too dark to see, and returned to his camp.

The next morning as Clay watched from his observation point

on the hill, the same two men, who met with the boss yesterday in the bunkhouse, came out, saddled their horses, and rode toward Toyah. Clay watched until they were out of sight. Nothing else was happening down at the ranch, so he mounted up and followed the two men. He stayed out of sight and kept watch through his binoculars. They went straight to the saloon, tied their horses outside, and went in. Clay hung back long enough so it wouldn't look like he followed them, and then he rode in and tied his horse next to theirs, and went in. It was right at lunchtime, so he figured it was late enough for a beer. He bellied up to the bar, took his beer, and turned around to observe the other patrons. There weren't but six men in the place. Clay and the two he followed made up half of that total. After a few more minutes, a man in a suit and tie came in and ordered a beer. He stood at the bar, drinking and watching the goings-on, much like Clay was.

Nothing happened for thirty minutes or so when the two Blalock men got up and walked out onto the front porch of the saloon. Mr. Suit and Tie finished his beer and walked out. He stopped a few feet from the Blalock men and took his time lighting a cigar. They gave the appearance of totally ignoring each other, but Clay could tell they were talking. They never looked at each other, but a short time later, Mr. Suit and Tie walked away, crossed the street, and went into the bank. Blalock's men stood around another few minutes, mounted up, and rode out of town back toward their ranch.

Clay turned to the bartender and asked, "Who is the guy in the suit and tie who just left?"

"Oh, that's Mr. Winthrop, he owns the bank. He also owns the stage line."

"I see," said Clay, "He's a pretty big man in these parts, I guess."

"Oh yes, nothing much happens around here that he doesn't have his hand in."

"I'm just curious. I've only been in town a couple of times, but I've never seen any lawman around. Who enforces the law in these parts?"

"I've only seen one since I been here. That was a U.S. Marshall that passed through last summer.

"Is there a Marshall's office in this part of Texas?" Clay asked.

"None that I know of, Austin is their headquarters. I guess they all work out of there."

That would make sense, I guess, Clay thought. "How about another beer?" Clay finished his second beer and then walked out to the boardwalk in front, and stood looking up and down the street. Not much was going on in town this morning, so he went to the general store and asked for some paper, a pencil, and an envelope. He then went back to the saloon, ordered another beer, and took a seat at a corner table by the front window, and composed a letter. He dropped the letter in the outgoing mailbox in the general store, had lunch at the cafe and headed back to Clint's place.

On the way back, he got that feeling of being watched, and the hair on the back of his neck was standing on end. He felt like he was riding into something that he wouldn't like. He stopped at the next place he came to where he could see for quite a distance. He pulled up behind a large mesquite bush where he wouldn't be sky lined and took his time surveying his surroundings. After looking around with his naked eye, he took out his binoculars and went over the ground again. He still didn't see anything unusual, but the feeling wouldn't leave him. The feeling got so strong he dismounted, and hunkered down behind the bushes and waited. He was hidden pretty well, and unless someone saw him ride into this patch of brush, they wouldn't spot him from any great distance. He had a feeling the trouble was behind him instead of in front. He was watching both but concentrating more on his back trail. After thirty minutes or so, he saw movement on top of the hill behind him. He put his binoculars on it and saw a rider cross over, and start down the hill following his trail. At this distance, even with the binoculars, he couldn't recognize the rider, but the horse looked like one he had seen somewhere before. Now that he had the man spotted, he felt a lot better. It was going to take the man at least thirty minutes to get to where Clay was waiting at the speed he was traveling. It was obvious he was following Clay's trial, and Clay wanted to know why.

Clay left his horses tied to the bush and moved off to the side, staying low so the man wouldn't see him. When he was fifty yards to the side, he turned and went back toward the man who was following him. When he had gone two hundred yards, he settled down out of sight behind the bushes and waited. Eventually, the man rode by concentrating on Clay's trail. Clay recognized him as one of the men in town talking to the banker.

The man saw Clay's horse and stopped. He sat watching a few minutes, and then dismounted and slipped his rifle from its boot on the saddle and hunkered down and watched Clay's horses for several minutes. Then he started sneaking toward them, being very careful not to make any noise. He was so focused on the horses that he didn't hear Clay when he stepped out behind him and ordered him to "hold it right there fellow. One wrong move and you're a dead man. Now drop the rifle."

The man stiffened like he was stuck with a hot iron. He straightened up and began to turn around slowly.

Clay told him again, "Don't turn around. Drop the rifle." The man stood still for a moment then laid the rifle on the ground.

"Now, take the pistol from the holster and drop it."

The man started lifting the pistol from its holster when suddenly he spun around drawing the pistol, and Clay shot him. The move was so sudden it caught Clay by surprise, and he didn't have time to choose where he shot him. The man collapsed to the ground holding his stomach. Clay walked up and kicked the gun away and quickly frisked him for more weapons. When he didn't find any, he opened the man's shirt to examine the damage. One look told him he didn't have long to live, but he would be in extreme pain until he did.

"Who are you working for, and why were you following me?"

The man was holding his stomach, groaning, and rolling from side to side. Clay had to ask him again. Finally, the man said he worked for Blalock. Clay then asked him, "Why were you following me?"

"We were told to get rid of you and that Wilcox guy."

"Why?"

"Because you showed him up in front of his men." The man was getting weaker, and Clay could hardly hear him. "I could sure use a drink."

"Sorry, I'm not a drinking man. Don't have anything except water. Will that do?"

Clay checked for a pulse but didn't find any. Clay sat for a minute, thinking over what had just happened. Then he remembers the man's partner. Where was he? He looked all around but didn't see anything or anyone, but he was uneasy, not knowing where the man was. He crawled back into the bushes and waited a long time to see what was going to happen. He had his binoculars and was scanning the entire area, but still didn't find anything. Finally, he loaded the man on his horse, tied him down so he would stay there, slapped the horse on the hip, and sent him on his way. Clay watched until the horse was out of sight, going in the direction of Blalock's headquarters.

Clay got his horses and went to his lookout point above Blalock's place. He had only been there a few minutes when the horse came walking in with the body. Clay was watching when the men came out and caught the horse and removed the body. Blalock came out, took one look, stomped his feet, and called a couple of men to him and told them something and stomped back into the house. The two men stuck their heads in the bunkhouse and said something, six more men came out and saddled their horses and rode out. Clay waited until they were out of sight, mounted his horse, and followed them.

Clay did his best to not expose himself by staying below the ridgeline, and not sky lining himself. When he did have to cross over the top of a hill, he did it quickly while staying behind bushes and cedar trees. He followed the men long enough to see they were headed toward Clint's place. He wasn't sure that's where they were going, but they were going in that direction, and he couldn't take a chance of them getting there before him, and catching Clint by surprise.

This was looking like a replay of the last time Blalock sent men to attack Clint. Clay remembered the route he took before and put his horses in a fast gallop. It took him almost an hour to get to where he could see Clint moving around by the barn. When he topped the last hill, he was a hundred yards away. He pulled up and yelled at Clint and pointed. Clint got the message, grabbed his rifle, and ran to his hole by the creek bank. At the last second, he ran back and grabbed the dog and took him with him. When he was crouched down in his hole, he wrapped the leash around his leg to keep the dog from running away when the shooting started. Clay left his horses behind the hill, and took his position and waited. He decided he was not going to give them any more warnings. This could go on forever if they didn't put a stop to it here and now.

Clay's rifle held fifteen shots. He laid out another fifteen on the ground beside him.

Blalock's men stopped two hundred yards before they reached the house. They sat there looking the place over. Finally, one of the men gave a hand signal and said something. The rest of the men spread out at ten-yard intervals and slowly advanced toward the house. When they were within fifty yards, they charged, firing their guns and yelling. Clay and Clint waited until they were almost to the house before they opened fire. Blalock's men were falling like flies and couldn't find where the shots were coming from, but before they figured that out, there were only two still in the fight. They turned their horses and made a break to get away. Clay led one of them just a fraction and pulled the trigger. The man straightened up and toppled out of the saddle. By then, he had his sights on the second man and brought him down also. Their horses were milling around, still excited from the running and gunshots. Clay and Clint left their positions and approached each man with caution, took their weapons, and checked their condition. Only two were still alive and looked like they would survive if they got medical attention soon.

The bodies were loaded on their horses, tied down, and sent home. The two wounded men were able to ride and sent on their way to the doctor in Toyah.

Clay mounted his horse and herded the horses with the bodies back to Blalock's place. He stopped just out of rifle range and was watching when the horses arrived at the barn. Men came out and removed the bodies. Again Blalock came stomping out. Even from a distance, Clay could see he was not a happy camper. He waved his arms around, shouted instructions that got men running around saddling horses and packing gear. When they were all ready to ride, Clay counted twenty-two men. He and Clint would not be able to hold off that many men by themselves. He made fast time back to Clint's place. It was dark before he got here. He called out to Clint before he reached the barn so he wouldn't get shot. Clint met him as Clay was removing the saddle from Blue. "We have to get out of here. Blalock's coming with twenty-two men. We can't fight that many from here. Grab what you need and let's get out of here."

Clint didn't waste time asking questions. He ran to the house and grabbed a bag that he had prepared for just such an emergency, and came running back out. Clay had changed the saddle to his other horse and saddled Clint's horse. He hung the bag on the saddle horn, mounted, and they headed for the rock cave. They already had a good supply of food stashed there, so all they would need to do is gather enough wood for tonight. They could do anything else they needed to do tomorrow.

They were out of sight up Toyah Canyon before Blalock's men showed. They went to the point of the mountain overlooking the house and waited to see what was going to happen. They didn't have to wait long. They couldn't see them, but they heard the group of men as they charged across the valley and didn't slow down until they were almost to the house. Clay and Clint saw the gun flashes as they opened fire from a hundred yards out. They heard yelling, and more shots, and then everything got quiet. It was only a few minutes until they saw flames coming out the doors and windows. Clint was furious, and Clay had to hold him back to keep him from charging down there and getting himself killed. "Take it easy, Clint; they're gonna get theirs, just be patient. Come on. We don't need to watch this. Let's get to the cave and plan Mr. Blalock's party." Reluctantly Clint turned away, mounted his horse, and followed Clay.

They arrived at the rock cave well before daylight and tried to get some sleep. Neither of them slept very well for the rest of the night.

Both were tossing and turning for different reasons. When daylight came peaking in, they were awake but still so tired they didn't want to get out of their bedrolls.

After coffee and a light breakfast, they saddled their horses and rode back to the lookout point to check the damage done last night. The buildings were nothing but piles of ashes, the corral fences had been torn down and thrown in a pile and burned. There was nothing left of six years of hard work. Clint was having a hard time holding back the tears, and he was so mad he was shaking. "What do you suggest we do first to make Blalock pay for this?" Clint asked Clay.

"I've always been a believer in fighting fire with fire. I have a few ideas. Let's go back to the cave and get ready to stage a war."

"Now, you're talking."

"On second thought, we're going to need a lot more ammunition. Let's ride into Toyah and stock up on supplies, and see what else we might come up with."

Two hours later they rode into Toyah, went to the café and had a nice lunch. When they were finished eating, they went to the general merchandise store to get more ammunition and see what else they could find that would be useful in staging a war. Finally, he asked the merchant if he had any dynamite. "Yeah, I sure do, and it comes in these tubes, already prepared. All you do is stuff a fuse in the end, stick a match to it and run like hell. They tell me one stick will level a house."

"How much do you have?"

"I got a whole case. Twenty sticks of the stuff. Not much callin' for it. It's been here a while."

"Good, I'll take six of them."

When they left the store, they had the dynamite and enough ammunition to fight off an army. They arrived back at the rock cave at mid-afternoon, got everything sorted, and made their plans for the attack on Blalock.

They ate an early supper and got a couple of hours of sleep. Both were having trouble sleeping, so they gave up trying and saddled their horses. It took them until after midnight to get to Blalock's place.

The moon was shining bright, so they had no trouble picking out the buildings. They scouted the area and didn't see any sign of a guard. They left their horses on the backside of the hill that overlooked the place and went forward on foot.

Clay had his binoculars and scanned the place again when they got closer. But he still didn't see a guard.

"Clint, what do you think about using this dynamite on the bunkhouse and the main house? We can plant it at the kitchen end, so we don't kill anyone."

"I thought we came here to kill Blalock. What changed your mind?"

"I just have a problem killing a man when he's not looking at me. We can give him one more chance to leave the country before we kill him."

"I think you're too easy on him."

"I saw too many men killed during the war, and after I got home. I don't want to keep adding to the body count if I don't have to."

"Ok, let's do it," Clint said with enthusiasm.

"I checked the burn rate on this fuse. It will take just about one minute to burn one foot, so I cut the fuses one foot long. So when you light it, you have one minute to get out of the way of the blast. You want to take the bunkhouse, and I'll take the main house?"

"Sure, that suits me."

They each cautiously approached their targets and planted the dynamite where they wanted it. When the fuses were burning, they ran as hard as they could back toward their lookout point. Before they were halfway there, the bunkhouse exploded, and a few seconds later, the house went up. Clay had planted his charge under the house beside the fireplace. When it blew, the fireplace crumbled and flew into a million pieces. That end of the house went in all directions, the roof collapsed, and a fire started. Men came staggering from the bunkhouse running around in their underwear barefooted, wondering what happened. It took several more minutes for Blalock to show from the main house. He was cussing a blue streak, waving a gun around, looking for someone to shoot. When he didn't see anyone except his own men, he yelled at them to find out what happened.

Clint and Clay were watching from the hilltop and heard Blalock bellowing. Clint heard his name mentioned several times, and not in a nice way. Blalock definitely had plans for Clint. Clay didn't think Blalock knew his name, or he would've heard his plans for Clay also.

They sat on top of the hill for the next two hours, watching Blalock go through his act, while the men went out and gathered up the horses that scattered like leaves when the blast went off.

They watched a little longer, and then mounted up and went back to their rock cave, prepared a meal, and rolled up in their bedrolls planning to sleep most of the day.

It was near mid-afternoon when they started to show some life. They got up, ate breakfast, and rode to the top of the hill overlooking Clint's place. After watching for several minutes, and not seeing any activity down there, they headed on over toward Blalock's place, being very careful not to expose themselves, in case Blalock was watching or had guards out. The place looked deserted, so Clint said, "Maybe this is the time we can slip down there and leave that note telling him that if he doesn't leave the country in the next few days, we're gonna come back and finish the job he started."

The only paper they had to write on was the wrapper that was on the dynamite. Clay wrote a note telling Blalock to leave the country, or they would finish what he started. Clint rode to the door of the house and tacked the note on it while Clay was covering him from the bushes on the hillside. Then they rode back to the rock cave, which they were now calling home.

CHAPTER

EIGHT

They laid around in the cave for a few days between trips to spy on Blalock. They saw men come and go a few times, but they didn't come anywhere near Clint's place. On the third day, Clay and Clint rode into Toyah to pick up more supplies and see if they could get any more information about Blalock's activities. When they arrived in town, the first thing they did was go to the saloon and order a beer. They were standing with their backs to the bar with their elbows resting on it, sipping their beers, when Clay asked the bartender if Blalock's man had been in town lately. The bartender says, "Yeah, they were in here the other day, and they were all fit to be tied. They said something about the house and the bunkhouse blowing up. A bunch of the guys had scratches and bruises, and they were talking about how they were gonna get that Wilcox guy if it was the last thing they did."

Clay asked, "About how often does this Blalock and his men come to town?"

The bartender answered, "I don't know if there's any regular schedule, they come and go. They'll come in here and have a couple of beers, and sometimes cause some trouble, nothing real serious so far, why would you need to know, Clay?"

"Blalock's been causing Clint here a bunch of problems lately. Burned his place to the ground, tore all of his corrals down, and told him to get out of the country. So we went over to Blalock's place and returned the favor. I was just wondering if he had been in town and said anything.

"So, that explains why he was so mad."

They hung around town for another couple of hours, had dinner at the café, and picked up a few supplies at the general store, and rode back home without seeing any sign of Blalock or his men. The next day they are back at the top of the hill overlooking Blalock's place.

During the third day of spying on Blalock, they saw the whole gang of men come riding back and turn their horses loose in one of the corrals. They threw their gear on the ground and started a fire in the middle of the barnyard since they had no kitchen and prepared their meal.

Clay and Clint were watching from the top of the hill and thinking. "Things are about to get interesting around here. I sure would like to know what he has planned."

Shortly after they finished eating, Blalock and one other man saddled their horses and left heading toward Toyah. Clay said, "Maybe this is our chance to even things up with Mr. Blalock. Why don't we follow him, and if he goes into Toyah, maybe we can have a showdown and put an end to this foolishness."

Clint said, "I'm all in favor of that."

On the way to Toyah, they stayed far enough back not to be seen, but close enough to be sure where Blalock was going.

When they arrived in Toyah, they saw Blalock's big black horse standing in front of the saloon, so they tied up next to him and went in. Blalock and the banker were sitting at a back table with their heads close together like they didn't want anyone to hear what they had to say.

Clay came in the door in front of Clint, so when Blalock looked up and saw Clay, he didn't know him since he had never seen Clay before. They went on with their conversation. Clint and Clay ordered a beer, took it to a table by the front window and sat where they could keep an eye on Blalock, and see who came and went along the street.

They finished their first beer, and the bartender brought them another one. As he placed the beers on the table, he leaned in close and said to Clay and Clint, "I would sure appreciate it if y'all would finish your beers and leave. I don't want any trouble in here, especially with Blalock.

"OK, not a problem." They finished their beer and walked outside and sat on the bench on the porch. After a few minutes, Blalock and the banker came out. As they were parting only a few feet from where Clay and Clint were sitting, they heard Blalock tell the banker, "Don't you screw this one up."

The Banker said, "You do your part, and I'll do mine."

The banker continued toward his bank, and Blalock went to his horse and mounted. As he turns his horse away from the hitching rail, he saw Clint sitting on the bench. His face got deathly white, and he looked like he wanted to go for his gun. That's when Clay stood up and said, "Hello, Mr. Blalock," with emphasis on the Mr., "How are things going out at your place? I heard there was a little excitement out there the other night. I hope it didn't disturb your sleep."

Blalock was fit to be tied. He didn't know which way to turn or what to say.

"What's the matter, Blalock, cat got your tongue?"

Blalock was stammering and stuttering with spittle splattering from his mouth when he finally yelled, "I'm gonna kill you if it's the last thing I do."

"Ok, how about now? Get off that horse." Clay was walking toward him as he was talking. Blalock was backing his horse away. Clay reached out and caught the bridle, and then grabbed Blalock by the vest and yanked him off his horse into the street. Blalock landed on his back and was struggling to rise when Clint walked up and pulled Clay back, "Let me handle this Clay. I'm the one he's been trying to hang. Get up, Blalock; I want to have a conversation with you in the only language you understand."

Blalock got to his feet with a smile on his face and walked into Clint, "I've been waiting for this. I'm gonna beat you to a pulp, and then I'm gonna stomp you into the ground." Clint struck so fast Blalock didn't see it coming. Before he knew what happened, he was on his back in the middle of the street with Clint standing over him. Blalock jumped to his feet and charged Clint. As he was coming in, Clint hit him in the face and knocked him down again. Blalock got to his feet again and made a dive at Clint's legs, trying to get him on the ground where his added weight could be used to his advantage. Clint stepped aside and let him go past and landed a punch in Blalock's kidney that sent him crashing to the ground again.

A small crowd of people was gathering on the street to see the fight. Blalock got to his feet again. This time he circled Clint waiting for a chance to land a punch. Clint was slowly closing in on him while Blalock was backing away. Blalock considered himself a fighter and a brawler, but he couldn't land a punch on this young man much smaller than he was. Clint kept advancing, and Blalock was backpedaling. Clint dodged all Blalocks' attempts to hit him. Blalock kept backing up until he backed into the hitch rack and couldn't go any farther. He made his stand there and started throwing punches. Clint blocked most of them, but once in a while, one got through. They stood toe to toe trading punches. It looked like Clint may be getting the worst of it for a while. Clint was younger and in better shape, and it soon began to show. Blalock was gasping for breath when Clint stepped back, making Blalock's punch miss and landed one in Blalock's gut that folded him over. Clint came up with an uppercut to the chin that put Blalock on his back. He laid there a moment, trying to comprehend what happened. Clint was standing back, catching his breath, and waiting for Blalock to get on his feet. Both men could hardly stand. Their arms felt like they weighed a hundred pounds each. Both were struggling to get their breath.

Clay was keeping an eye on the crowd to keep anyone from interfering. As he scanned the crowd, he recognized the Blalock man who rode into town with him. He was standing against the wall of the bank being as inconspicuous as possible. Clay moved to where he could keep an eye on him and not expose his back. The banker was standing by his bank door, watching Blalock take a beating.

Blalock struggled to his feet. Clint walked in and landed a flurry of punches so fast Blalock didn't have a chance to cover up. He was back peddling while Clint continued to pound him in the face. When he raised his hands to protect his face, Clint landed two hard punches to his gut. Clint thought he had Blalock whipped and got careless. When he did, Blalock landed a lucky punch that put Clint on his back. Clint was stunned for a moment. When he opened his eyes, Blalock was in the air, trying to jump on Clint's stomach.

Clint rolled to the side just in time to make Blalock miss.

Clint spun around on the ground and kicked Blalock on the side of his knee. The knee buckled, and Blalock fell to the ground, but both men were up at the same time. Blalock was limping and couldn't put weight on his injured leg. Both were covered in blood and sweat, and their shirts were in shreds. Clint continued to crowd Blalock, and Blalock continued to back away. Blalock tried to make a fight of it, but every time he did, Clint hit him several times before he could move away. Blalock had blood running all down his face onto his tattered shirt and vest. Because of the injured leg, he was having trouble moving, and Clint was hitting him at will. After a couple more minutes of this, Clint moved in and finished the fight with a few fast and furious punches. Blalock ended up on his face in the middle of the street. Clay walked to the water trough and dipped his hat full and carried it to where Blalock was lying. With the toe of his boot, he rolled him over onto his back and poured the water in his face. He blew and sputtered, trying to get the water out of his eyes and nose. When he realized he was lying in the street, he tried to get to his feet but staggered and fell. Clint came over and offered his hand. When Blalock saw Clint standing over him, he cringed backward to get away and fell on his butt again. The crowd laughed while Blalock struggled to his feet and leaned against the hitch rack. "Stay away from me."

Clint walked to within two feet of him and told him, between gasping for breath so that everyone could hear. "Blalock, you tried to hang me in the middle of the night, you couldn't pull that off, and so you tried to kill me by attacking my home in the middle of the night. When you couldn't kill me there, you burned all my possessions. You came back a few nights later and burned my house. This is the only warning you are going to get, Blalock. Leave this country by tomorrow night. If you are still here after tomorrow, I'll kill you where I find you. Do you understand me, Blalock?" When Blalock didn't answer, Clint backhanded him across the face. "Do you understand me, Blalock?"

"Yeah, yeah."

Blalock stood there in shock. No one had ever talked to him this way, and no one had ever given him a whipping like he just got, and from a much smaller man. Without saying another word, he limped to his horse, and after several attempts, he got mounted and rode slowly out of town. Clay saw Blalock's man get his horse, and follow Blalock out of town.

Clint and Clay went back to the saloon, where the bartender handed Clint a wet rag to wipe the blood off and served them beers on the house. "I'm glad to see Blalock finally get what he had coming. He's been walking over people around here far too long."

Clint asked, "Doesn't his brother own this saloon?"

"Yeah, he does, but he doesn't come around much, and I don't like him any better than his brother. He has a place out of town about a mile west of here. He stays there most of the time. He comes around about twice a week to collect his money, and always gripes because there ain't more of it."

"What does he do for a living? Is this his only source of income?"

"I think he may be in cahoots with his brother Robert, and I don't know what Robert does. He don't seem to run any cattle on his spread. I've never heard of him making a roundup or driving any to market anywhere, so I don't know where he gets his money. But he has a lot of men hanging around his place. They come in here and raise a ruckus ever so often, and they always have money to spend."

Clay was scratching his head, "Yeah, I've been wondering about that too." Then he remembered the letter he had written several weeks back. "I'll be right back." He went to the post office, which was in the general store, and asked if he had any mail. The postmaster/owner of the store said, "Yeah, came in yesterday. What with the fight and all I forgot all about it." He handed Clay the latter. Clay took it outside and sat on the bench. It was addressed to Clay Wade, general delivery, Toyah, Texas. No return address. He took out his knife and slit the envelope open and pulled out one sheet of paper. A woman obviously did the writing since most men don't write that neat. The letter was in response to his letter to the Texas Rangers in Austin.

Mr. Clay Wade
General Delivery
Toyah, Texas,

Mr. Wade,

Your letter to the Texas Rangers was forwarded to me because the new governor disbanded the Rangers when he took office. The U.S. Marshalls office has taken over their duties. The man you described in your letter matches the description of Robert Sutton. He is wanted in Galveston, Texas, for bank robbery and beating the bank teller.

A deputy U.S. Marshall will be contacting you. He should be there by the 20th of the month.

Sincerely,
C. W. Baker
Chief U.S. Marshall
Austin, Texas

Clay read the letter, folded it, and put it in his pocket. He sat there, digesting what he had just read, and then returned to the saloon and told Clint about the letter. When the bartender came by, they asked for another beer, and since the place was not busy, Clay invited him to join them. The bartender went by the name of Harry. That had to have started as a joke because there was not a hair on his head except around his ears. He did sport a full red beard and mustache that he kept neatly trimmed. He was in his thirties, a little overweight, about five feet ten inches or so. He was always dressed neat and treated his customers well. He brought over three beers and sat down.

Clay asked him, "What day of the month is this, Harry?"

Harry turned around and looked at a calendar hanging on the wall behind the bar, "Looks like it's the seventeenth, why do you ask?"

"In the next two or three days, a man is going to be here looking for me. If you'll direct him out to Clint's place, I sure would appreciate it."

"Do you have a name or description for this man?"

"No, never saw him before."

"If you don't know him, I assume he don't know you either, so how is it he is going to ask for you when he don't know you?"

"Well," Clay responded with a smile, "He has my name. That's all I know."

"I see. Ok, I'll send him your way."

They sat drinking their beers and talking about the weather and anything else that came to mind until their beer was gone.

"Thanks, Harry, you about ready to head home, Clint?"

"I guess we better head that way, it's gonna be dark before we get there. Elmer's gonna be wondering what happened to us."

They took the long way home just in case Blalock had men waiting along the trail.

It was good dark when they reached Clint's place. There was nothing there except the remains of what used to be a house and barn. They rode past without saying anything. An hour later, they reached the rock cave. Elmer was waiting for them and was barking before they reached the top of the switchback trail and leveled out by the lake. Clay and Clint dismounted and played with Elmer and fed him some scraps they picked up in town. They couldn't tell if he was happier to see them or the food. They soon decided it was the food when he turned his back on them and ate all the food in a few seconds. While they were unsaddling their horses, they took the leash off Elmer and let him run and play a while. When they finished their meal and coffee, they laid back and enjoyed the cool of the evening. Elmer came and lay beside them and was soon asleep. They saw no need to tie him up for the night. Since he has been living with them, he has filled out and grown taller. He is almost full-grown now and follows them everywhere they go if he isn't tied to something.

The next morning they rode to Clint's homestead to start rebuilding. It took them two full days just to clear the burned debris away so they could start the rebuild.

Clint had drawn up the plans for the new house and barn with a few minor changes from the original. The materials were ordered when they were in town the last time and should be arriving in a few days.

They were still clearing debris and burning what had not already burned when Elmer jumped up and started barking. Clay and Clint picked up their rifles and stood ready until they could identify the rider coming. They didn't know him. He was riding a tall, long-legged buckskin that moved like he had somewhere to be in a hurry and wasn't wasting any time getting there.

When he got to within thirty feet or so of where Clint and Clay were standing with their rifles held loosely cradled across their arms, he spoke to the horse, and he stopped immediately. The rider sat looking at them a moment. They saw that the thong was removed from the pistol on his right hip, and his hand was hanging close to it in case he needed it quickly. After another half-minute, Clint asked, "Can I help you with something?"

"Yes, I'm looking for Clay Wade."

Clay took a couple of steps closer and said, "I'm Clay Wade."

"I'm Deputy U.S. Marshall Wes O'Riley. I'm told you may have information on a fugitive we are looking for."

"We might have, get down and come on in, Marshall, except there's no place to come into." A couple of large cottonwood trees provided good shade down by the creek, so the Marshall dismounted and followed them to the shade where they all made themselves as comfortable as possible, considering they had no chairs.

When they were all squatting or sitting, the Marshall asked Clay to tell him everything he could about this Robert Blalock. Clay and Clint filled him in on what had happened since Blalock started giving Clint trouble. When they finished telling their story, Marshall O'Riley took a small notebook from his pocket and flipped through several pages until he found what he was looking for. He made a few notes and then asked, "Where is this Blalock's place from here?"

Clint gave him directions on how to find the place but cautioned him about riding up there in the open. "You are likely to get shot before you get a chance to introduce yourself."

"He's a little touchy, is he?"

"I guess you could put it that way, or maybe he just don't want to make any new friends." They all got a chuckle out of that.

Then Clay told him, "You probably need to know about his connection with the banker in town also. There's something suspicious going on there, but we don't know what it is." Then Clay told him about the meeting in the saloon and overhearing their conversation when they left.

"That does sound like something we need to look into, alright."

Clint looked up at the sky and remarked, "It's getting late. Let's head on back to our camp and grab a bite to eat. We don't stay here at night since Blalock burned me out."

Clint and Clay saddled their horses and led the Marshall to the rock cave where they all settled in for the night.

The marshall walked around, checking the place out. "This is a nice setup you have here. A guy could just about live here permanently."

They dug into their stash of supplies and prepared a meal while they talked about their situation and what they needed to do.

The next morning early, Marshall O'Riley asked Clay to ride with him over to Blalock's place. When they arrived at Clay's usual lookout point, the Marshall stopped in the shade and sat looking the place over. "There doesn't appear to be any activity down there."

Clay told him, "There never is much of anything going on here. Even when there are a lot of men here, they don't do anything. You'll notice there are no cattle or horses around, but this looks like it's deserted. There's usually someone around, even if they aren't doing anything."

They watched for several more minutes, and then the marshall suggested, "Well, we may as well go on down and pay them a visit." Clay saw the marshall remove the thong from the hammer on his pistol, so Clay did also. They walked their horses down the hill to within about thirty feet of the front of what was left of the house and stopped.

"Hello, the house," O'Riley called out.

When there was no answer after a half minute, he called again. When he still didn't get an answer, he said, "Let's check out back." They rode around the house to the back and still didn't see or hear anyone.

O'Riley told Clay, "You wait here and cover me. I'm gonna check these buildings."

He dismounted and dropped his reins on the ground and checked to make sure his gun was loose in the holster and walked to the bunkhouse.

Clay backed his horse off to the side where he had everything in front of him, and stepped down from the saddle and pulled his rifle from the scabbard, and stood ready for whatever happened. He watched as Wes went from building to building, and found no one. He returned to where Clay was waiting, and they both walked to the house and pushed the door open. The place was in shambles with pieces of furniture and clothes strewn about. One end of the house was missing where the chimney used to stand. Wes stood looking around, and said, "Looks like there was an explosion of some kind. The bunkhouse looks the same way. I wonder what happened."

Clay responded, "Looks like they must have made somebody mad."

They went back outside and found tracks where a large group of horses had gone off to the west. "These tracks look like they're probably two to three days old, wouldn't you say?" asked O'Riley.

"That's what it looks like to me. That's about the same time that Clint gave Blalock a thrashing in Toyah and told him if he ever saw him again, he would shoot him on sight. Apparently, he took Clint at his word."

"Clint gave Blalock a thrashing? You gotta be kidding me."

"No, I'm not kidding you. I saw it, and I still find it hard to believe. Blalock only got in one good lick, and that's because Clint thought he had him whipped and got careless. No sir, that's one guy you don't want to get in a fight with."

"I'll have to remember that. Let's follow these tracks apiece and see if we can determine where they may have gone."

After following the tracks for over a mile, and they were still heading west, O'Riley said, "El Paso is the closest town of any size in that direction. If I had to make a guess, I would say that's where they're going. It'll take them the better part of a week to get there. Although there is any number of places they can go in that direction. Are you up to tagging along, and help me round them up? We've been trying to find this guy for a long time if it really is this Robert Sutton. Even if it ain't, I'd still like to know what he's up to. Something sure stinks about this guy."

"Sure, I'll help you, but I need to go back and get my other horse, and we're gonna need more supplies if we're gonna be on the trail that long."

"Well," O'Riley said, "We're already two or three days behind, so another one ain't gonna make much difference."

They turned around and rode back to Clint's place. It was too late in the day when they got there to start anything else, so they prepared to spend the night and get an early start tomorrow. Clint was disappointed when he heard that Clay would be moving on tomorrow. "I was sure hoping you were gonna be around to help me rebuild my place."

Clay responded, "I never thought I would be here this long. I only stopped because Blalock was intent on hanging you, and I wanted to see the show. I'm kinda disappointed that he couldn't pull that off."

Clint chuckled, "Yeah, I am too. That would have been some show, alright."

Clay proceeded to get all his gear together so he would be ready to ride at the break of dawn. He checked both horses over real good as well as his saddle and other equipment. They went to Toyah and stocked up on supplies, and then picked up Blalock's trail west of his place.

It didn't take long for Clay to realize that Wes was the better tracker unless he was saying stuff just to impress Clay. Clay kept his mouth shut and took it all in figuring time will tell.

Two days later, Blalock's trail turned off the main trail and went in a northwest direction. After following it for a half-mile, Wes said, "Well Clay, Looks like our boys are going into the Guadalupe Mountains. This is gonna get interesting. There's some rugged country up ahead. If they get in there, we may never find them. Have you ever been to this area before?"

"No, this is my first trip. I'm counting on you not to lead me into an ambush."

"Hey, that's what I'm counting on you for."

By nightfall, it was obvious that Blalock had a definite destination in mind. His trail was leading as straight as possible into the most rugged terrain in the Guadalupe's. The trail was mostly rock, which left almost no tracks. Occasionally they saw where a horseshoe had left a scrape on the rock or the droppings from a horse scattered along the trail. There weren't many places where they could turn off, so both men were busy watching for any place where someone could ambush them.

When it was getting almost too dark to see the trail, they started looking for a place to make camp. The terrain was not offering them much of a choice. It was mostly just following the low land between the hills. The trail, what they could see of it, still looked to be two to three days old as it switched back and forth across the stream that ran between the steep hills on both sides. With no place to stop, all they could do was keep riding and hope something showed up. Finally, they came to a wide spot in the canyon that offered a small flat place beside the stream. They couldn't see what else was around them, but they stopped and made camp. Wes told Clay, "I sure hope it don't rain up north. If a flash flood comes through here, we'll probably be in Mexico tomorrow morning."

"You sure know how to prepare a guy for a good night's sleep, don't you?"

They threw their bedrolls on the smoothest place they could find, which wasn't very smooth and prepared for a miserable night. They couldn't risk having a fire, so they chewed on jerky, and drank water, and rolled up in their blankets, and tried to sleep.

If anyone rode through this canyon tonight, they would make enough noise to wake the dead long before they got near, so they didn't think it was necessary to stand guard.

When morning finally came, they were almost too tired to crawl out of bed.

They didn't get much sleep because of the hard rocky ground, so they were up early and looked around to see where they were. The horses were standing quietly nearby, and the stream was trickling so peaceful it was hard to believe they were on the trail of a bloody killer and bank robber.

"Well," Clay said, "This don't look like Mexico, so I guess we didn't get any rain last night."

"Have you ever been to Mexico?" Wes asked.

"Now that you mention it, no, I ain't."

"Then how do you know this is not Mexico."

"Cause you're not speaking Spanish," Clay said with a chuckle.

There was enough dry wood washed up along the stream that they got a fire going and made coffee and heated a can of beans for their breakfast.

All that day, they followed the trail deeper into the mountain. Streams flowed into the canyon from both sides, but they didn't see any sign that Blalock had turned off at any of them. They started being more careful when they came to a turn or hill in the trail. One of them dismounted and walked to where they could see what was around the turn or over the hill before proceeding. If they got caught here, they wouldn't stand a chance of getting out alive. There was just no place to find cover.

The farther they rode, the more careful and nervous they became, knowing they could ride up on Blalock's whole gang at any time. During the day, they risked having a small fire. When they camped that night, they had no fire and made do with water and cold jerky. It was too risky to travel at night because the sound echoed off the canyon walls and carried too far. Blalock would know they were coming long before they got close.

The next morning as they were breaking camp, O'Riley asked Clay, "Have you ever been, or considered being, an officer of the law?"

Clay gave O'Riley a quick look and said, "Yes, I have. I've been a deputy sheriff a couple of times. Why do you ask?"

"I've been authorized to swear you in as a deputy marshall if you're interested. We need someone in this part of the country. We're spread way too thin to do the job we need to do. It could be a temporary or permanent job. From what I've seen, I think you would be good at it."

"I don't know, Wes. I'll have to give that some thought. I have some demons I have to get rid of before I can start thinking of anything permanent."

"Do you want to tell me about it?"

So for the second time, Clay told the whole story from the time he joined the union army to losing Ellen in a freak accident.

Wes listened without interrupting. When Clay stopped talking and walked away to be alone, Wes understood and continued getting everything loaded and ready to move out. After a few minutes, Clay returned and mounted his horse and led off up the trail. Wes never mentioned their conversation again. He figured if Clay wanted to talk about it, he would bring it up again.

That night as they were lying around their camp getting ready for another restless night, Wes pulled a marshall's badge from his pack and handed it to Clay. "Here Clay, take this, I don't know what we're gonna run into but to make it official consider yourself deputized. When we get to a telegraph, I'll notify my boss so he can put you on the payroll."

CHAPTER

NINE

That day was like the many before it as they followed the trail through the Guadalupe Mountains. They were trapped in the bottom of the canyon where no breeze reached them, but during the middle of the day, the sun beamed down on them so hot they could hardly breathe. Sweat poured off them and the horses so fast they had to stop often for everyone to get water. When the sun finally passed over and went behind the mountain, the temperature dropped until it was fairly comfortable. After the sun set, it got cold enough for a coat and a blanket.

Their camp was set up as far from the water and the trail as the terrain would allow. As one was setting up the camp, the other rode ahead a mile or so to make sure Blalock and his gang were not just around the bend.

Their supplies were getting low since there had been no place to replenish them for the last week. All they had left was a little coffee and some jerky. They took inventory and tried to calculate how far they could stretch it. They decided not near far enough. It looked like they would need to either shoot something to eat or leave the trail and try to find the closest store. Shooting was almost out of the question. The sound would travel up and down this canyon and alert anyone within miles that they were here. Wes took a well-worn map from his saddlebag and spread it on the ground by the fire. Both men hunkered down and looked at the map. Wes pointed with a stick, "Looks like we've been following this river here. Says it's the Delaware River. I wonder if it's named after the Delaware Indians. Don't hear anything about them around here, though." After a few minutes of scanning the map, along with some head-scratching and some grunts, he finally said, "Clay, I think we are likely to starve to death if we don't get out of here. There's nothing anywhere even remotely close where we can get supplies. There is this place that indicates it's a ranch. I don't know anything about it and never heard of it, but that looks like the closest place to get anything. That's right here," as he pointed to the map. "But where are we in relation to that? It looks like a trail or road going off to the south along here. We haven't seen anything that looks like a road or trail to a ranch, have we?"

"No, I'm sure we would have noticed if we had."

"Ok, we'll keep going the way we have been and see if we can locate that ranch. We should be able to get enough supplies to last a few more days until we can work our way out of here, or come up to Blalock and his gang, and get supplies from them, after we have them tied up and under arrest."

"You are a very optimistic man," Clay said with a chuckle.

"Don't pay to be any other way."

When they had eaten their meager meal, they rolled in their blankets and were soon asleep.

Sometime during the night, Clay was awakened by a sound that brought him straight up out of his blanket with cold chills running up and down his spine. It sounded like a woman, or a child, crying. He looked around, but it was too dark to see anything, but he still heard the noise off in the distance. He was convinced it was someone crying. He reached over and touched Wes's arm. He came awake instantly and looked at Clay, "What's up?" he whispered.

Clay whispered back, "Listen a minute."

In another minute or so, they heard the crying again. Wes sat up startled, and asked in a whisper, "What in the world is that?"

"Sounds like someone crying," Clay whispered back.

"That's what it sounds like to me, too, but where is it coming from?"

"I don't know," Clay whispered, "but it sure gives me the willies."

Wes whispered back, "The way sound carries up and down these canyons, it could be coming from anywhere."

Clay remarked, "I don't know what time it is, but I won't get any more sleep tonight. We may as well get ready to move out as soon as it's light enough to see what we're doing."

Since it was the middle of the night, they thought it would be safe to have a fire, so they put together the wood they gathered the night before, got the fire going, and used the last of their coffee to make a pot. They chewed on jerky and drank coffee until things started getting light enough to see. They had not heard the crying anymore, but it was still on their mind as they rode out of camp.

Clay said, "I sure hate to ride off and leave a woman in trouble, if that's what that was, but I don't know what else to do."

"Yeah, I guess all we can do is keep our eyes open and hope something gives us a clue as to what's going on."

Around the next bend, they saw a wagon road cutting off to the south. "This must be the road that shows on the map to that ranch," Wes said.

They followed the road as it wound around through the hills, staying close to the river on their left, but far enough back to avoid most of the small tributaries that flowed into it. After a mile or so, they rounded a bend and saw the ranch buildings sitting in a nice little valley. Waterfalls fed into it from several different places, which had everything nice and green. A house sat at the foot of the trail, with a corral and barn off to the side. There were a few horses and cattle spread across the valley. They sat watching the place for a few minutes when Wes remarked. "Something is wrong down there. Everything's too quiet."

They watched a few more minutes, and then both men pulled their rifles and gave their horses a nudge that started them slowly walking toward the house. The horses had their heads up with their ears pointed forward like they knew something was about to happen.

As they approached the house, without a word spoken, they separated to come at it from opposite sides. When they were fifty feet or so from the front of the house, and still hadn't seen any movement, they stopped, and Wes called, "Hello the house."

After a half minute with no answer, he called again and still got no response.

Wes dismounted, and with his rife held across his arm with his finger on the trigger, he approached the front door and knocked. When he got no answer, he lifted the latch, and standing to one side, pushed the door open with the barrel of his rifle. What he saw inside made his heart skip a beat. The place was in shambles. All the cabinets and drawers had been emptied, and the contents were strewn about the room. He slowly eased into the room as his eyes swiftly took in everything. There was a loft over the kitchen that had him worried. If someone was up there with a gun, he could be in trouble. "Hello, is anyone here?" The house was deathly quiet. He moved to the first room on the left and slowly pushed the door open. Everything in this room was scattered like the front room. As he turned to leave the room, he heard a noise that sent chills up his spine. He whirled about with his rifle ready to fire but saw nothing. He waited, but nothing happened. He slowly eased farther into the room, and as he neared the bed, he heard it again and thought he knew what it was.

"You can come out now. I'm not gonna hurt you. I'm Deputy United States Marshall Wes O'Riley. We're here to help you."

There was another louder whimper, and a small head poked out from behind the bed. The eyes were red and bloodshot from crying, and dirty streaks ran down her face. Her hair was matted and tangled, and when she stood, Wes saw her clothes were dirty, and she looked like she hadn't had anything to eat in a while.

Wes suddenly realized he was still pointing his rifle at her and slowly lowered it to his side.

"Hi, I'm Wes, what's your name?"

When Wes pushed the door open and went inside, Clay dismounted and moved to where he could cover the barn and the other building. When he heard Wes talking inside, he eased around to the back of the house and came in through the back door while keeping an eye on the rest of the place. He didn't know who Wes was talking to, but it didn't sound threatening, so he relaxed, and seeing Wes standing in one bedroom, he checked out the rest of the house. No one else was there, but it was evident someone had done a job of wrecking things. When he walked into the room behind Wes, the little girl screamed and hid behind the bed again. Wes walked to where she could see him and said, "It's ok, he's with me, he's a marshall too. We're gonna get you out of here."

She slowly peaked over the side of the bed and stared at Clay. He put his gun away and said, "Hi, I'm Clay. What's your name?"

She looked at Wes as if to say, "Can I trust him?"

Wes read her mind and said, "It's ok. No one's gonna hurt you." He eased over and sat on the bed next to her. "Where are your folks?"

She still didn't say anything. "Do you speak English?" Still no answer.

"Clay, do you speak Spanish?"

"Very Little." He came around to where he could see her and ask in Spanish, "Hablas inglés?"

She still just stared at them.

Clay said to Wes, "I'll see if I can find something to eat. She looks like she's starved."

"Ok, I'll stay here and see what I can find out."

Clay went to the kitchen and went through all the cabinets and cupboards. When he found nothing, he took his rifle and went outside. There were several buildings out there, one of which looked like it may be a bunkhouse. He was hoping to find a kitchen for the working hands, so he went to check it out. When he pushed the door open and carefully stepped inside, he saw the same mess that was in the house. The bunk beds were all turned upside down, and clothes scattered around the floor like someone was searching for something.

There was no kitchen or any place to stock food supplies. He went from there to the barn. There was evidence of a fight here; empty cartridge shell lying about and blood on the floor. Looking farther into the barn, he found an older man shot to ribbons, lying on the floor in a puddle of blood. He looked like he had been dead a couple of days. The blood under him was dry and hard. He assumed this was the little girl's father, or maybe a hired hand. Searching farther through the barn didn't reveal anything, but when he went back outside, he found a trail of blood leading into the brush behind the barn. He followed it with his gun at the ready, in case whoever left the blood trail was still alive. After a hundred feet or so, he came upon a young man, or more like a boy, dead, with several bullet holes in him. After making sure he had searched the place thoroughly, he returned to the house to let Wes know what he found. "There's nothing to eat here. Apparently, whoever did this took everything." He motioned for Wes to follow him outside, where he told him about the two bodies. "Has she said anything?"

"No, she appears to be in shock. All she does is cry and stare."

Clay said, "I'm gonna take my horse and see if I can find something for supper. I'll try to be back before dark." He mounted and rode out behind the buildings to see what he could find. There was a nice creek running through the valley, and he thought he might find a deer around there about sundown. He found a place where he could hide downwind from the creek and took up a position where he had a good view of anything that came along. It was still a couple of hours before sundown, so he was prepared to wait a while. Several cows and calves were grazing across the valley, slowly working their way toward the water. If a deer didn't show up before dark, he was determined to take one of the calves as a last resort.

He sat waiting, dozing, and enjoying the peace and quiet, but concerned about the little girl. What in the world were they gonna do with her? They couldn't leave her here, and they couldn't take her with them. They were on the trail of a bunch of outlaws, probably the same ones who made this mess.

Right as the sun was setting, he saw movement across the creek at the edge of the brush. He slowly raised his rifle and was ready when the four-point buck stepped into the open. Clay didn't waste any time in making the shot. The buck was field dressed, thrown across his saddle, and carried back to the barn where he hung it from a rafter and skinned it. Wes had a fire going in the stove when he walked in with a chunk of deer meat in his hands. They sliced it in thin strips and fried it until the aroma had their stomachs growling.

The little girl still had not said a word. Wes found three plates that were not broken and put them on the table and dished up the venison. The little girl ate everything they put in front of her. All they had to drink was water, but they made a meal of what they had.

Just as they were finishing off the last of the meat, the little girl started crying and said, "They killed my papa and brother."

Wes and Clay were taken by surprise and took a moment to think of something to say.

Wes asked, "Was anyone else here when they came, any more of your family?"

"No, just Papa and Bubba."

"Do you have any other relatives?"

"Papa has a sister, but I don't know where she lives. I've never seen her." She started crying again, "I don't have anybody to take of me."

"We're gonna take of you, don't you worry your pretty head about that," Wes said as he put his arm around her and pulled her close. She fell into his arms and hugged him like there was no tomorrow, and she probably felt like there wasn't.

They sat like that until Wes noticed she was asleep. He picked her up and carried her to the bedroom where they found her and tucked her in. When he was sure she was asleep, he went back to the table and asked Clay, "What in the world are we gonna do with her?"

"I don't know, but we sure can't leave her here. Maybe she can tell us where the closest town is, and we can find someone there to take her in."

"Yeah, that sounds like the best plan, if there's someone there who will do it."

Clay suggested, "Why don't we turn in. I think tomorrow's gonna be a long day."

They went out and put their horses in the barn, gave them a couple of forks of hay, and went back to the house.

Wes said, "I don't wanna leave her alone in case she wakes up and gets scared, so I'll sleep in the room with her."

The next morning Clay and Wes were sitting at the dining table, chewing on the leftover venison from the night before, when the little girl came in rubbing her eyes and looking around like she was trying to place where she was.

"Well good morning, Beautiful, did you sleep well?"

She took another moment or two to realize where she was and what had happened, and then started crying again. Wes went to her and put his arms around her and pulled her close, "Its ok. We're gonna take care of you."

After she calmed down enough to answer their questions, they asked her again, "You never did tell us your name, what is it?"

She sat up straight and said, "My name is Maria Victoria Isabella Cortez."

"Wow," Clay said, "that's quite a mouthful. How did you happen to get all those names?"

"Maria is my name; Victoria was my mama's mama's name, Isabella was my Papa's mama's name, and Cortez is my papa's last name."

Wes says, "So we'll just call you Maria, since that's your name, ok?"

"Sure, and I'll just call you Wes and you Clay."

"That'll work. Now, can you tell us where the closest town is?"

"I don't know if it's the closest, but we always do our shopping at Nichols Creek Station. It's almost a full day from here by wagon, so we don't go very often."

"After you eat," Wes told her, "we'll see if we can get you a change of clothes, wash your pretty face, and take a ride over there. Do you know anyone who lives there?"

"No, not really, I know Mr. Nichols, the man that runs the store, but that's all."

"Does he have a wife and children?"

"He has a wife, but I don't know about any children."

"I know this is not easy for you, Maria, but we have to find a place for you to live. You can't stay here alone."

"Why can't I stay with you and Clay?"

"We really like you, but we aren't gonna be staying in one place. We travel around looking for bad guys, and sometimes there's trouble, so you can't be around that. Do you understand?"

"Yeah, I guess so."

Clay was looking out the window while that conversation was taking place. He turned back to Wes and said, "Do you hear that wind picking up out there? It sounds like we may have a storm coming. If we get trapped here with no food, we're gonna get awfully hungry."

Maria spoke up, "We won't get hungry; there's lots of food in the root cellar."

Wes and Clay looked at each other, and in unison, asked, "Where's the root cellar?"

She pointed at the floor.

They looked down but didn't see anything and looked at her with a question on their faces.

She snickered and said, "It's under the table."

They looked under the table but still didn't see anything.

She got up from her chair and told them, "Pull the table over here."

They took hold of the table and lifted to the side. Maria reached down, and stuck her finger in a knothole in the floor, and pulled a trap door up, exposing a ladder leading to a large hole in the ground.

"Down there." She said and climbed down the ladder with Clay, and Wes following her. When she reached the bottom, she took a lamp and matches from a shelf. With the lamp lighting the room, and they could see, their mouth dropped open, and both said, "Holy cow. This is not just a root cellar. This is a cave. How far does this go?"

Maria laughed, and said, "A long way, me and my brother used to play down here sometime, but Mama didn't like it, she said it was too dangerous. There are big holes back there, and big rock post-like things that go way up, and more that come down from the ceiling with water dripping off them. It's really spooky."

"How far back in there have you gone?"

"I don't know how to tell distance, but we went a long way. We had a torch, and it started going out, and we had to run real fast to get out before it got dark."

Clay said, "I'll bet that was scary."

"Yeah, it really was. I didn't go back there again, and my brother wouldn't go by himself."

"Ok, where's that food? Let's see what we got here."

She showed them where the food was stored, and they were surprised to see so much. There were boxes of potatoes, onions, carrots, and jars of all kinds of fruit, and a large can of coffee.

Clay remarked, "You were right Maria, we won't go hungry with all this food, and there is plenty of deer around, so we should have enough meat to hold us for a while."

They each grabbed a hand full of potatoes, an onion, a couple of jars of fruit, and went back up the ladder to the kitchen. They moved the table back to its usual place and looked outside. The wind was whipping around and rattling the windows, and the rain came pouring down. They stood looking out for a few minutes, but it was raining so hard they couldn't even see as far as the barn.

Wes shook his head, "Man, I'm sure glad we aren't out in that. You would surely get your face washed, Maria. Come on; let's see if we can find some clean clothes to put on you."

Wes and Maria went to the room that Maria said was hers while Clay was getting a fire going in the stove.

When they came back to the kitchen, Clay had a pretty good meal just about ready. He took another look out the window and told them, "That rain has turned to ice. The ground is completely covered with it. I don't think we will be going anywhere anytime soon."

There was enough wood in the wood box by the stove to keep a fire going for a day or two, so they made another pot of coffee and sat in front of the fire listening to the storm blowing outside. Maria told them about her family, how her grandfather had started this ranch when he was a young man and then left it to his son, and he was planning to leave it to his son. But now he and his son were both dead, and she started crying. Wes held her until she stopped crying and went to her room and curled up in bed, and went to sleep.

Just before dark, as Clay was looking out the window, a group of horsemen came rushing up to the barn. They all dismounted, and Clay heard one of them tell another one, "Put the horses in the barn and give them a bit of oats and hay, they've earned it. Then come on inside."

As they were dismounting, Clay suddenly recognized the man giving the orders as none other than Mister Blalock, the very man they were looking for. He called to Wes as he drew his gun, "Hey Wes, that's Blalock coming in, get ready."

Wes jumped to his feet and ran into the kitchen. When Blalock and his men came through the door, Wes was behind them, and Clay was across the room with his gun pointed at them. Apparently, they didn't notice the smoke coming from the chimney as they rode up because seeing someone in the house was a shock, and they froze in their tracks.

Clay said, "Welcome, MISTER Blalock, or should I call you, Mr. Sutton?"

Blalock/Sutton did a double-take and said, "How did you know…..?"

"We know a lot more than you give us credit for, Sutton. By the way, you are under arrest for bank robbery and assault in Galveston. Drop your gun and get your hands in the air. The rest of you do the same."

Then Clay recognized one of the other men as the banker from Toyah, and the third man looked enough like Blalock/Sutton to be his brother.

"Well, well. What do we have here?"

"What are you doing here, Wade? You have no authority to arrest anyone, besides that, you can't take all of us, and there's more outside coming in."

"I may not get all of you, but I'll sure get you, and what I don't get the man behind you will."

"Don't try pulling that childish stunt on me, Wade."

The man who looked like Blalock spoke up, "He's not fooling, there's another one behind us with a gun."

Wes spoke up, "I'm Wes O'Riley, U.S. Deputy Marshall, and as Wade said, you are all under arrest. Now drop those guns or use them, makes no difference to me, you'll be a lot less trouble for us if you're dead, so don't tempt me."

They all slowly unbuckled their gun belts and let them fall to the floor.

Wes searched each of them for weapons and told them, "Now get over in that corner, sit down, and keep your mouths shut, or I'll shut it for you."

They went to the corner and sat on the floor where Clay could keep them covered, and also watch the door. Just as they were sitting down, the door burst open, and three more men rush in, "Hey Boss, there are three horses in the...."

Clay said, "Welcome to the party, Gentlemen. Keep your hands away from those guns if you want to live."

They looked around the room taking in the situation, and trying to decide what to do next when Wes stepped up behind them and lifted their guns from the holsters before they could make up their minds. He searched them for more weapons, put them in a pile with the other guns, and told them, "Get over there and sit down. Keep 'em covered Clay while I find something to tie 'em up."

Clay pulled a chair away from the table and flipped it around backward and straddled it facing them.

All of them seemed to still be in shock at the turn of events. Several times Sutton looked like he wanted to say something but couldn't get his thoughts together enough to say it. After a few more minutes, he went into a cussing fit, threatening all kinds of bad things to Wes and Clay when he got his hands on them. "I should have killed you back in Toyah. You've been nothing but trouble for me ever since you showed up."

"Well, ain't that a shame. I'm really sorry to inconvenience you, Mr. Sutton, but your troubles have just begun."

Wes had snow and ice hanging off him when he came in with a

rope, which he cut into three-foot lengths and tied all the men's hands and feet and left them sitting on the floor. He knew there was a strong possibility that they would work their way around and untie each other, so he made them sit in a line, one behind the other, all facing the same direction, with their hands tied behind their backs. That way, they wouldn't be able to untie the man next to them.

When Wes returned from the barn with the rope, he also had all the saddlebags belonging to Sutton and his men. After the prisoners were tied, the saddlebags were dumped onto the kitchen table. One of them was stuffed much fuller than the others, so Wes opened it first. "Wow, Clay, look what we have here."

Clay came over from watching the prisoners and saw what Wes was referring to. The table was covered with money of all denominations. Some were in bundles marked with the Toyah Bank label.

"I guess this explains what Mr. Sutton had going with the banker," Clay remarked.

"Yep, it looks like we caught two jailbirds with one trap."

Clay chuckled, "I couldn't have said it better myself."

Wes was the better cook of the two, so while Clay watched the prisoners, Wes put together a meal. The men were untied, two at a time, and allowed to eat while Wes and Clay sat watching. When they finished and were securely tied again, two more were released and allowed to eat.

Just as the last of the men were finishing eating, Maria came into the room. When she saw all the men sitting along the wall, she screamed and pointed, "That's the men that killed Papa and Bubba."

Wes took her in his arms and said, "It's ok, Honey, they can't hurt you, they are all tied up, and we'll be taking them to jail where a judge will make them pay for what they did."

Maria finally calmed down and agreed to come to the table and eat. After eating, she returned to her room, but as she walked by Blalock/Sutton, she stopped momentarily and spat in his face, and stuck her tongue out at him.

Wes and Clay couldn't keep from laughing, and that infuriated Sutton even more.

The snow and sleet continued to fall for three more days before there was any let-up. By then, there were two to three feet of snow banked against the buildings. Clay and Wes, with the help of Maria, were kept busy taking care of the horses and feeding the prisoners. Maria said there were hundreds of cattle spread across the valley and in the canyons surrounding it. They would have to fend for themselves. There was no way to carry hay to them.

Late on the third day, the sky cleared and the sun came out, just before going back out of sight behind the mountain. The next morning was cold but clear, and the snow was slowly melting where the sun was hitting it. They figured they would be able to travel the next day, so they got everything packed and ready to load that night.

Wes and Clay had taken turns guarding the prisoners during the nights and days. Both were showing signs of lack of sleep by the time they were ready to ride the next morning. Knowing it was going to take all day, and maybe longer, to reach Nichols Creek Station, they made every effort to get an early start, but Sutton and his men did everything they could to delay their departure. Finally, they reached their limit, and Wes and Clay grabbed Sutton, and threw him across his saddle, belly down, and tied him in place. "Does anyone else want to ride this way? You have thirty seconds to get on your horse, or we'll put you on it. Now move."

When they were all mounted, their hands were tied to the horn of the saddle, and their feet tied together under the horse, and Wes led off at a brisk trot, where the trail conditions allowed it.

Sutton was complaining from the start but was totally ignored until they made a brief stop to eat a bite of lunch. When he was allowed to sit upright in the saddle, he complained about the treatment he was getting until they threatened to tie him across his saddle again if he didn't shut up.

It was right at dark when they rode into the station. Mr. Nichols heard them coming and met them at the door, "What is the meaning of all this? Who are these men, and who are you?"

Wes and Clay showed their marshalls badges, and introduced themselves, and then turned to Maria and said, "I think you know this young lady. This is Maria Cortez; these men raided their place and killed her pa and brother. We've been trailing them since they left Toyah several days back and came upon Maria all alone at her place. She doesn't know of any other relatives, so we are hoping we can leave her here with you and your wife until some arrangement can be made."

Nichols stuck his head inside the door and called for his wife, "Ethel, came you come out here a minute?"

Mrs. Nichols came out and asked, "What is it, Herb?" and then she saw all the men, some with their hands tied, and little Maria sitting her horse off to the side. Mr. Nichols explained the situation in as few words as possible. When he was finished, Mrs. Nichols went over to Maria and lifted her down from the saddle and gave her a big hug that almost squeezed the breath out of her. "I've wanted a little girl just like you all my life, but now I know God was saving me for you. He's had this planned for a long, long time, you and me. You didn't know that, did you?" There were tears in Mrs. Nichols' eyes when she led Maria into the store and closed the door.

Clay took the package holding Maria's things from the packhorse and handed them to Mr. Nichols. "You wouldn't happen to have a place where we can lock these men up for the night, would you?"

"There's a root cellar back there. We can padlock the door, and there ain't no way they can dig their way out of there. It's solid rock, walls, and floor. It took me one whole summer of digging and blasting to get it that big."

The root cellar was like Mr. Nichols said. The prisoners were hustled in, and the door locked. Their hands remained tied, and their feet were tied together once they were inside and seated.

When they went in to eat with the Nichols, Maria looked like she was making herself right at home. She brought the plates and utensils to the table and helped Mrs. Nichols with the food like she had been doing it all her life, and maybe she had at home.

The next morning was bright and clear and much warmer than

the day before. The prisoners were fed and brought up one at a time and tied to their horse. When all were ready to leave, Wes and Clay said goodbye to Maria, "I know you will be happy here, Maria. You take care of Mrs. Nichols, ok?"

"Ok, y'all will come to see me sometime?"

"We sure will, every chance we get, you can count on it."

CHAPTER

TEN

Wes said to Clay as they were leaving the Nichols place, "I was studying this map last night, and as near as I can tell, it's right at a hundred miles from here to Pecos. It's gonna take us at least three days to get there, barring any trouble."

"The mood I'm in if they cause us any trouble, I'm ready to shoot 'em and shove 'em in a ravine, and let the wolves and bears have a meal if they can stand to eat this garbage."

Wes said, "I'm with you on that. Do you hear that men? You better be on your best behavior, or you'll never see the judge."

Late on the third day, the group of tired, cold and hungry men, made quite a show as Wes led the group of prisoners down the street of Pecos, with Clay bringing up the rear. The prisoners were turned over to the local authorities, who locked them in the county jail to await trial. The authorities in Galveston were notified that Sutton was in custody in Pecos, Texas. Due to the distance and time involved, they told the authorities in Pecos to try them on the murder charge there, and let them know how that turned out. If Sutton escaped the hangman there, they would come and get him and try him in Galveston on the bank robbery charge.

Wes and Clay waited around for the trial that was scheduled for the next week when the circuit judge was due to come through. They spent their time eating, and drinking coffee at the local diner, and flirting with the cute little waitress who worked there. Since this was Wes's home station, they knew each other pretty well. Clay soon picked up on the fact that there was more to this relationship than waitress and customer. Clay saw them holding hands as Wes walked her home at night when the diner closed, but he said nothing about it. It brought back memories of his and Ellen's time together. He couldn't decide if they were pleasant or sad memories, but they brought tears to his eyes. That's when he wanted to be alone with his thoughts and memories to try and sort things out. He was no closer to that a week later when Sutton's trial took place. He was found guilty of murdering Mr. Cortez, and his son, and sentenced to hang the next day. All of the other men, including the banker and Sutton's brother, were sentenced to forty years in the state prison at Huntsville, Texas. Several days later, a couple of deputy marshalls arrived with a prison wagon to transport the prisoners to Huntsville. Wes and Clay were free to take a few days off to rest up before their next assignment.

On the second day, Clay went to Wes and offered the badge back, saying he had to move on, "This sitting around is getting to me. I have to be doing something. He handed the badge to Wes, but he refused to accept it.

"Thanks, Wes, but I gotta go. Maybe I'll see you around sometime."

He walked away and mounted his horse. As he rode out of town leading his packhorse, he waved to Wes and the cute little waitress and disappeared in the distance.

For the next several years, he lost count of how many, he roamed. He lost track of days, months, seasons, and the years flew by. He served a summer in Montana as a sheriff's deputy, another summer and winter, as a scout for the army as they tried to get the Indians to report to their assigned reservation. He was wounded twice in skirmishes and spent a month in the post-hospital recovering. When he was released, he had had enough of scouting, so he took his leave, his horses, and rode away, intending to find a warmer climate. Instead, he met up with a pair of beaver trappers and spent the winter trapping beaver. When he left them the next spring, he was more determined than ever to find a warmer climate.

As he was riding south, he remembered the winter he spent in Cheyenne, Wyoming, and the friends he made there. With nothing else to do, he turned his horses in that direction. He crossed into Yellowstone and spent two weeks taking in the sites. Three weeks later, he rode into Cheyenne. The first place he stopped was the marshall's office.

Marshall Brown was sitting at his desk when Clay walked in, removed his hat, and said, "Still just sitting there getting fat. Don't you ever do any work?"

It took a moment or two for Marshall Brown to recognize him, but when he did, he jumped to his feet and came around the desk with a big smile on his face and grabbed Clay in a bear hug. Clay thought he was going to kiss him before he let him go. "What in the world happened to bring you back to this God-forsaken country, did Texas get too hot for you?"

"Well, it does get hot, but we kind of get used to it, and it's sure a lot better than freezing to death up here."

The marshall looked at the clock on the wall, "Look at that," he said, "it's time for a beer. Let's go get Doc and Everett, and drink a toast, or two, or maybe three. What do you say?"

"Oh, ok, if you insist." They laughed as they walked out, and led Clay's horses to the livery where Mr. Everett greeted him as warmly as the marshall did. When the horses were stabled and fed, they all walked to the doctor's office and caught Dr. Wolf just walking out to get a beer. "Well, look who's here just in time to buy a broken-down old doctor a beer."

Clay told him, "That's where we're headed. Come on."

They stormed into the saloon and took a table by the front

window. The bartender came over and shook Clay's hand, and asked, "What's the occasion that brings a Texan all the way to Wyoming to have a beer? You're not still chasing horse thieves, are you?"

Clay answered, "Just passing through. I'll only be here a day or two at the most."

"What's the hurry, don't you like us anymore?"

"Oh, I like you as much as I ever did."

"That's not saying a whole lot, is it?"

They laughed, and the bartender, Red, returned to his place behind the bar and continued polishing bar glasses.

When things settled down and got serious, Marshall Brown asked Clay, "What's troubling you, Clay; you're not your usual self, what's happened?"

Clay took a moment to clear the lump in his throat, and then he told them the whole story. When he finished, they could only shake their heads. Everyone was silent for a while, just sipping their beers and thinking about what Clay had just told them.

Finally, the doctor asked, "So you have just been wandering around trying to find yourself, right?"

"I guess that's the best way to put it."

Dr. Wolf continued, "But Clay, I think if you stop looking at what you have lost, what you don't have, and look at what you still have, you'll be much happier. You have a son that's growing up without his pa. Think about what's going through his mind. He's lost his ma and now his pa too. But he doesn't have to lose his pa, all you have to do is go home, and that little boy will be much happier. Have you given that any thought?"

After a minute or so, Clay said, "No, Doc., I guess I've only been thinking of myself."

"Well, give it some thought Son. Get on that horse and go home."

"Thanks, Doc, I'll do that."

"Do What?"

"Give some thought to that."

"Good, now Bartender, bring us another round."

The conversation at the table cheered up some, and they sat

enjoying the company, and the beers, when shots rang out, and someone yelled, "The banks being robbed!"

They all jumped to their feet and headed for the door. Marshall Brown and Clay drew their revolvers as they stepped out the door. A group of four horsemen was racing down the street directly at them, firing at everything in sight. When they saw the men in front of the saloon with guns drawn, they opened fire as they raced by. The Marshall got off two shots before he grunted and folded over, and fell to the ground. Doctor Wolf was standing right there and started examining him to see how bad he was hurt, while Clay was still firing at the bank robbers. He was pretty sure he hit at least one of them, and maybe two, but they were all still mounted when they went out of sight.

Clay holstered his revolver and dropped to his knees beside Marshall Brown and Doctor Wolf, "How is he Doc?"

"Not good, help me get him to my office; a couple of you men give us a hand here." Four men stepped up and lifted the marshall, and carried him to the doctor's office, and laid him on the examining table.

"Now y'all get out so I can do my job; Mrs. White, get in here, please." She came rushing in, expecting the worse. She had heard the shots and was expecting a patient at any moment, but was surprised to see it was the marshall.

Clay was standing by the table a few moments later when the marshall opened his eyes and looked around the room. When he saw Clay, he reached out with a trembling hand and took him by the arm and pulled him close. With the other hand, he removed his badge and handed it to Clay and whispered, "Here Clay, go get 'em, make 'em pay for killing me."

Clay told him, "You just rest easy, Marshall, they ain't killed you yet, but I'll get 'em if it's the last thing I do. You be here when I get back, you hear me."

"Can't promise…. I'll be here, but ….I'll try. Good luck to you, and be careful." He whispered.

Clay held his hand a moment longer until he saw the marshall was either asleep or unconscious, and then released the hand, and went to get his horses from the livery stable. When he arrived, Mr. Everett had his horses saddled and ready to go. "How did you know I was going to need 'em?" Clay asked.

"Nobody else would take on a job like this. It had to be you. Good luck. I put a sack of feed in the pack for the horses."

"Thanks, Mr. Everett, I'll be seeing you."

Clay mounted up and took the trail left by the bank robbers. They started out headed north, but after a few miles, they turned east toward Nebraska. Clay didn't know a thing about that area, so all he could do was try to follow the tracks.

It was already late in the day when the bank robbery took place. Clay assumed it was planned that way, so any pursuit would have to wait until morning while the robbers got a good lead. When it was too dark to see the trail, Clay stopped and made camp. He chewed on jerky and drank water until his hunger and thirst were satisfied, and then rolled up in his blanket and went to sleep.

His only experience with this country was from a few years back, which involved temperatures in the teens and snow up to his hip pockets. He knew he wouldn't have that problem this time of the year since it was springtime, and the temps were very pleasant, except at night when it could get downright cold.

When he rolled out of his blankets the next morning, he was shivering until he got his boots and coat on. He didn't take the time to start a fire and make coffee, so he was back on the trail within a few minutes. He picked up the trail, still heading east. From the looks of the tracks and the fact that he had not seen where they stopped for anything since leaving town, he had to assume they rode all night. That would put them a good eight to nine hours ahead of him. But knowing they were going to have to stop sometime, he was confident he would make up the time somewhere along the trail.

He took to the trail when it was light enough to see, kept his horses at a trot until about noon when he stopped for a brief snack and shifted his saddle to his other horse. Two hours later, he came to what looked like a recent camp beside a running creek. There were ashes from a campfire, and miscellaneous items of trash thrown about. He dug into the ashes and found some hot spots indicating this was someone's camp last night. He saw a trail along the bank of the stream and followed it to a corral with four worn out, sweat-stained horses standing with their heads down. At first, Clay thought the men may still be around, but when he didn't find any saddles or other gear, he knew they had fresh horses waiting here. Now they were riding fresh horses, and Clay's were getting tired. He immediately gave up the idea of catching them while they were still running. All he could do was follow the trail until they stopped somewhere. They must have a destination in mind, or they wouldn't have had fresh horses waiting for them. He made a note of the brands on the horses for future reference. There was plenty of water here for them, but they would run out of food in another day or so if they were kept penned up, so he opened the gate and let them out. He had a pretty good idea they would eventually find their way back home, where ever that was.

The trail leading away from the camp was in a northern direction. After a few hours of following the trail, he was getting into a more rugged country. It was cut up with canyons and ravines, most of them with running water. The farther he went, the deeper the canyons and the higher the mountains. He found himself riding between two walls so close his feet were almost touching on both sides. This went on for what seemed like a half-mile or more until he rode out onto a ledge that overlooked a large valley with cabins and corrals. He quickly drew back out of sight and tied his horses to a bush. With his binoculars, he crawled up to where he was concealed behind brush and rocks but had a good view of the valley below.

This looked like a permanent setup, not a temporary hideout for a gang passing through. He was wondering if this was a working ranch, and honest people lived down there, and these outlaws had barged in on them, or were the outlaws' part of the family?

He couldn't go storming down there and get shot or shoot the wrong people. Besides that, four to one odds were not a good bet in any game, and this was not a game. If the outlaws were part of the ranch, then the odds were even greater against him. Everyone down there would be shooting at him, and he had been shot too many times and didn't like the feeling he got from it. "I think I'll just sit here and watch until dark. If I don't know anymore by then, I'll try sneaking down there and learn what I can."

He moved his horses farther off the trail, in case someone else came along, he didn't want them to discover him watching the place until he was ready. When they were hidden as safe as he could get them, he took his canteen and a bag of jerky, and went back to his lookout point, and settled down to wait until dark. Several times he caught himself dozing and got up to walk around to get woke up again. He wasn't worried about being seen because the ledge was covered in brush and trees. As long as he stayed away from the edge, he was safe.

Every few minutes, he raised his binoculars and scanned the scene below. So far, there had been no activity at all. He could see the horses in the corral by the barn and more roaming free across the valley with cows with calves, but no humans. Just as the sun went behind the mountain across the valley, two men came out of the house and went to the barn. A few minutes later, they came out and saddled two horses and rode out the other side of the valley. That must be how the supplies were brought in because they sure couldn't get through the way he came in unless it was by packhorse.

He watched the two men until they were out of sight. By then, it was too dark to see anything farther than a few yards. He checked on his horses, and gave each a hat full of water, and moved them to a new patch of grass. Leaving his rifle on the saddle, he proceeded down the trail until he reached level ground a hundred yards or so from the front of the house. During the time he was watching, he had not seen any dogs, but he was still leery that one or more might be laying up somewhere. He circled the building but didn't see anything out of place, so he moved in closer until he could see through the windows.

He was looking through the window into what looked like a living/dining room when he heard a mean, gruff voice say, "Get in there and fix me something to eat and be quick about it."

A feminine voice came back at him, "If you want to eat, you fix it yourself."

Clay heard a slap and a whimper, "You want some more of that? Sass me again, and you'll get plenty more of it. Now get in there and start cooking."

A moment later, a young woman crossed in front of the window, going toward the kitchen. She had tears running down her cheeks, and she was wiping the blood off her lip and holding her cheek. Clay moved around so he could see more of the room. An older man and woman that appeared to be in their fifties were tied up sitting on the floor leaning against the wall. Another man walked in from another room, rubbing his eyes and running his fingers through his hair that was standing straight up and asked, "When do we eat around here?" One arm was bandaged and in a sling.

Clay thought, *Good, I got some lead in one of them.*

The first man answered, "As soon as that lazy woman gets it ready."

"When's that gonna be?"

"Go in there and ask her, don't pester me with your problems."

The second man walked into the kitchen, "What's takin' you so long, Honey?" He put his good arm around her and pulled her close. She turned around so quick he didn't have a chance to avoid the heavy iron skillet as she brought it around with frying bacon and hot grease. The skillet hit him square in the face; the hot grease covered his face and ran down his neck into his shirt. He screamed and staggered across the room, holding his face. The young woman stood with a frightened look on her face trembling from head to foot.

The first man came storming into the room, "What happened?"

"She tried to kill me. I think I'm blind, I can't see a thing, and my face is on fire."

The girl ran from the room, crying. Clay ran to the back door and opened it far enough to see the two men still in the kitchen, and then ran to the man tied up on the floor and cut the rawhide string on his hands and feet. The girl was standing staring at him with her hand over her mouth. Clay whispered, "You two cut your mother loose and get out of here. Are there any more of them besides those two?"

"No, the others left earlier." The man answered in a whisper.

Clay turned toward the kitchen, drew his revolver, and quietly walked to the door. The wounded man was lying on the floor, moaning, and cursing; the other man was standing over him when Clay walked up behind him and took his gun from the holster and pushed it into the man's back. "Don't move, I'm Deputy Marshall Clay Wade, you're both under arrest. Lay on the floor beside your partner with your hands behind your back." Clay gave the man a shove to help him get on the floor and then removed the revolver from the injured man's holster and stuck it behind his belt. When both were on the floor and disarmed, he was looking for something to tie them with when the girl's father came in with a shotgun in his hands.

"Stand back, Marshall; I'll take care of them from here on," as he pulled both hammers back to full cock.

"Hold on, Mister. I can't let you do that; you'll mess up your wife's kitchen."

"I'm sure she won't mind, get out of the way."

"No, hold on a minute," as he stepped in front of the shotgun, and pushed it to the side. "I have to take these men back to Cheyenne to stand trial for robbing the bank and shootin' the marshall. I don't know if he's still living or not, but I'm pretty sure they'll hang either way, so let the law handle it, ok?"

Clay took the shotgun from his hands and leaned it against the wall. "Do you have something we can tie them up with?"

"Yeah, I got a roll of barb wire that will work just fine."

"I think some rope or stout string will work?"

"I'll find something."

He was back in a few minutes with a ball of rawhide.

When both were tied up like a pig going to market, Clay asked, "Now, do you have a place we can stash them until I can get them back to Cheyenne?"

"Yeah, throw em in the root cellar, and let 'em rot."

Clay asked, "What about the other two that left earlier today? When are they expected back?"

"They rode over to the trading post to get some supplies and liquor. They won't be back until sometime late tomorrow."

"Ok, help me get them locked up, and we can relax some, I hope."

"By the way, I'm Horace Adams, my wife is Effie, and the daughter is Marilyn. We sure are glad you came along when you did. They had some bad stuff planned for Marilyn."

"You're probably right. I'm glad I got here in time to help."

Mr. Adams called the two ladies back into the house and introduced Clay. "Now, would y'all mind putting something on to eat? I'm starved, and I bet Mr. Wade is too?"

"Call me Clay, that Mister stuff makes me feel old."

"Then you call me Horace. I don't cotton to that formal stuff either. Come on in here, and sit while they get supper on the table."

"I need to go get my horses from up on the bluff by the trail."

"I'll ride up with you, its pitch black out there; I wouldn't want you getting' lost."

They saddled two horses and brought Clays down and put them in the corral with oats and hay.

Clay remarked, "I'll have to get them out of sight before those other two come back. I wouldn't want them warned that anything has changed here while they've been gone."

The stove was already hot, and the coffee had boiled until it was strong enough to walk to the table by its self when Marilyn brought the pot and poured each of them a cup.

Horace asked Clay, "How did you happen to be so close on their trail if they shot the marshall?"

"I was standing right beside him when he was shot. He handed me his badge and told me to go get 'em, so here I am."

"I like a man that follows orders. Were you in the war, Clay?"

"Yeah, all four years of it."

"Yeah, I was too, spent the last two years in a rebel prison camp. They just about killed me. I come out of there weighing eighty-five pounds, nothing but skin and bones. My Effie didn't even recognize me when I finally got home. She and the girl were livin' with her folks up in Cody then. When I finally got most of my strength back, we came down here and built this place. Just now getting' it kind of the way we want it. I thought it was all gonna end yesterday when them guys showed up flashin' their guns around. I sure wasn't lookin' forward to bein' tied up there and watching what they were planning for Marilyn. They made it really clear what they were gonna do, and there wasn't a dang thing I could do to stop 'em."

Clay took a sip of his coffee, "Well, it's all over now. We'll be ready when those two get back, and then I'll haul 'em off to jail."

"Are you gonna be able to handle four of them all by yourself?"

"I think so; I've had a little experience with this kind of thing. They won't give me any trouble."

Clay and Mr. Adams took a lantern and checked on the prisoners in the cellar. When they were sure they would still be there tomorrow morning, Mr. Adams showed Clay to the bedroom where he would sleep. He wasted no time turning in and didn't move until he heard a noise coming from the kitchen. The aroma of coffee and bacon brought him out of bed. He quickly dressed, ran his fingers through his hair, and went to the kitchen. Marilyn was the only one there, and she had the coffee perking, and the smell of bacon was making his stomach growl. "Is the coffee ready?"

"Sure, sit at the table; I'll bring you a cup."

"Where's the cup? I can pour it."

"Right there on the shelf; help yourself," she said.

"Thanks."

He poured his coffee and stood by the stove leaning against the wall, watching her finish putting the breakfast together. She was tall for a woman, maybe five feet nine or so, and every inch stacked in the right place and proportion. The summer dress she was wearing fit her to a T and showed every curve, and Clay couldn't take his eyes off her.

She kept glancing at him and got embarrassed with him watching her.

"You're embarrassing me. I'm not used to anyone looking at me like that."

"I'm sorry, I don't mean to. I guess it's because I haven't been around a pretty woman in a long time."

"Now, you're really embarrassing me."

"I'm sorry; I'll go sit at the table."

"No, that's ok," she said, putting her hand on his arm, "stay here if you want to."

After a few moments of silence, she asked him, "Why is it that you haven't been around women in a long time."

"It's a long story; I don't want to bore you with it."

"For some reason, I don't think I'll be bored."

"Maybe some other time."

"Ok. So, where will you be going when you get these men back to Cheyenne?"

"I don't know. I haven't given it any thought. I just go from one day to the next. Where ever it leads me."

"How long have you been living like that?" she asked.

He thought about it a moment before answering. "It must be going on five years, I guess. I seem to have lost track. It's been a difficult time."

"Why don't you tell me about it? It'll probably do you good to get it off your chest, as they say."

She poured herself a cup of coffee and said, "Let's sit at the table, and you tell me about it."

A half-hour later, they were still sitting at the table, holding their still full cups of cold coffee.

"Where is your son now?" She asked.

"I guess he's still with Ed and Lisa. That's where he was when I left. I know he's well cared for."

"I'm sure he is, but every boy needs his father," she told him.

He sat with his head down for a long time, with neither of them talking. He took a sip of coffee and made an ugly face, "I've been talking so long my coffee has gotten cold."

He took their cups to the kitchen and refilled them, and returned to the table.

They sat drinking coffee, each of them lost in their own thoughts.

Her parents came in and said, "Good morning, folks, how's the coffee this morning?"

"Strong, black and hot, just like I like it," Clay said with a smile.

Marilyn got everyone another cup of coffee and served breakfast. While they were eating, they were discussing the possible problems of Clay handling four prisoners alone. Mr. Adams said he would be glad to ride along and help keep an eye on them if Clay didn't mind since he needed to pick up some things in Cheyenne anyway.

"I don't mind at all. Your help will be most welcome." Clay said.

Shortly after lunch, Clay moved his horses from the barn to a grove of trees out of sight of the house and staked them on a patch of grass. He was waiting in the barn when the two bank robbers returned. While they were busily unsaddling their horses, Clay slipped up behind them and took their guns. They were too surprised to react until it was too late. Clay tied their hands behind them and put them in the root cellar with the other two. They were all still there the next morning when Clay came to check on them.

Clay and Marilyn were sitting at the breakfast table when Mr. and Mrs. Adams came in.

Breakfast was very quiet that morning as if everyone had something else on their mind.

Mr. Adams asked Clay, "When do you want to leave?"

Clay answered, "The sooner, the better. The earlier we leave, the earlier, we'll get there."

"Effie, why don't you fix up a food bag for us? Better fix enough for all six of us."

Marilyn spoke up, "Better make that seven, I'm going too."

Everyone looked at Marilyn in surprise. Her mother asked, "What are you going for?"

"I'm tired of being stuck here with no one my age to talk to and no one even close enough to visit. I'm going to pack my clothes and stay in town for a while. I'll try to find a job doing something, anything to break the monotony. A person could die of loneliness away out here so far from everything."

Mrs. Adams looked like she was going to cry, "Why Honey, I had no idea you felt that way, you never said anything."

"What good would it have done? There's nothing you could do."

"Well, your pa, and I will surely miss you. You've never been away from us a day in your life."

"I'm well aware of that, Mom. That's why I have to go."

She went to her room and packed everything she could get in a carpetbag and came back to the breakfast table dressed in riding clothes. "I'm ready to go."

Her dad said, "Wow, that was quick."

"I don't have that much to pack."

Clay rose from the table, "I guess I better go saddle some horses."

"I'll help you," Marilyn said as she picked up her bag and headed for the door.

Mr. Adams came out and helped get all the horses ready. The prisoners were brought out one at a time and tied to their saddles. There was a lot of complaining and griping coming from them, but no one was paying much attention. Finally, Clay told them to shut up, or he would slap a gag in their mouth, and they would ride that way all day. Things got quiet after that.

The ride to Cheyenne took them a day and a half. The one night on the trail passed without incident. The prisoners were guarded constantly and never got a chance to cause trouble. Marilyn took the first watch while Clay and Horace tried to get a couple of hours of sleep. Horace took the second watch, and Clay took over when Horace woke him at around two in the morning. Marilyn was up before six o'clock and told Clay to get some sleep while she prepared breakfast. She called them to come and eat just as the sun was peaking over the horizon. They ate a quick meal and were on the trail within an hour. It was the middle of the afternoon when they rode down the main street of Cheyenne. It looked like the entire town turned out to watch them ride up to the marshall's office and unload the prisoners into the jail. The first person to come in the door was Dr. Wolf. Clay asked him, "How is the marshall, Doctor?"

"He's gonna be fine. Give him a few more days in bed, and he'll be up and around. The bullet didn't hit any vital organs. He lost a lot of blood, but he's gonna be fine."

Clay said, "You may want to take a look at two of the prisoners.

One has a busted wing, and the other has some pretty bad burns. He's complaining about a lot of pain, but he may be just making that up for attention."

"I'll check it out. Bring them in here away from the others."

The doctor cleaned and disinfectant the wounds and burns, applied clean bandages and told them to stop their complaining; it's only a scratch.

Clay arranged for rooms for Horace and Marilyn at the new hotel that opened since he was here last, and then he treated them to supper at the diner across from the jail.

Clay was asked to stay in town until Marshall Brown was on his feet and able to resume his marshaling duties. He gladly agreed. He was looking forward to spending more time with Marilyn. After all, it has been over five years since he lost Ellen, and he has spent no time at all with a woman, and Marilyn was easy to spend time with.

CHAPTER

ELEVEN

Horace Adams bought the supplies he came for, and they were all loaded on his packhorse early the next morning when he met Marilyn and Clay at the diner for breakfast.

"Marilyn, It's gonna be awful lonesome around the place without you there to fight with. But I understand where you're coming from. All your ma and I ask is let us know where you end up, and if you get a chance, you come to see us. You know how we get our mail so write to us. I guess we'll get it sooner or later."

"Ok, Pa, I will. I'm gonna miss y'all too, but if I stay there any longer, I'll end up an old maid like Miss Watson, and I sure don't wanna do that."

"I don't blame you a bit. I'm gonna go now before I make a fool of myself."

He got up from the table and hurried out the door wiping his eyes.

Marilyn had tears in her eyes also, watching him leave. Clay took her hand, and she squeezed his and held it tight.

Finally, she got up and told Clay, "Let's go for a walk."

They left the diner and strolled down the street and found themselves walking out into the country. It was a pleasant sunny day with a light breeze blowing, and they continued walking, holding hands, and not saying much. They weren't paying attention to where they were going and ended up on the bank of a stream in a grove of cottonwood trees. They sat on the bank and watched the fish swimming in the water. After a while Marilyn laid her head on Clay's shoulder, he put his arm around her waist, and they sat like that for a long time until she turned her head and kissed him on the cheek. He immediately turned his head, and their lips met in a long, sweet, passionate kiss. Clay's heart was beating so fast he thought he would pass out. He had never felt like this, even with Ellen, or that other girl in Tennessee, whatever her name was, he couldn't remember right now. This was Marilyn's first serious experience with a man, and she was as excited and nervous as Clay. The longer they stayed there, the more heated things got, and before either of them realized it, the clothes were coming off, and neither wanted to stop.

Sometime later, as they lay catching their breath, they looked at each other and smiled. Clay asked, "Now what do we do?"

"What do you mean?"

"I'm not letting you get away. If I have to hogtie you and throw you across a horse, you're going with me when I leave here."

She smiled and asked, "And where do you plan to haul me off to?"

"Someplace where nobody will ever find us. I want you all to myself."

She giggled and said, "That sounds like fun for a while, but I'm afraid we'll get tired of just each other after a while."

"By then, we'll probably have a house full of kids to keep us busy."

"Wow, you seem to have given this some thought."

"I have, I've been dwelling on it for the last hour."

She laughed out loud, and he joined her. They hugged and kissed some more, and before they realized it, the sun was setting, and they were getting cold. They hurriedly got dressed and walked back to town. When they realized they had missed lunch, they had to laugh again. They went to the diner and ate and went to the marshall's office to see if anything needed to be done there. There had been no emergency while they were gone, so they sat and talked some more. Clay walked her to the hotel and kissed her at the door and went back to his office. He would be sleeping in a jail cell as long as he was here, which he was hoping wouldn't be very long. He was making plans for himself and Marilyn, which didn't involve Cheyenne, Wyoming.

They met for breakfast the next morning. Marilyn looked as fresh as a daisy and was smiling when she saw Clay waiting at the table. He had been to the barbershop and had a bath, shave, and haircut as soon as the shop was open. He wanted to look his best when he met her because he had an important question to ask.

After they finished eating, they left the diner and went to his office where they could talk in private. When they were alone, he asked her, "What would you say if I asked you to marry me and go to Texas?"

She was silent for a few moments and then said, "I don't know, I haven't given going to Texas much thought. But why don't you go ahead and ask me, I might surprise both of us."

Clay swallowed and took a deep breath, "Marilyn, will you marry me, and go to Texas with me and help me raise my son, and all the dozen or so others that we'll have?"

"Woo, that's an awful lot to ask a girl that you just met a few days ago, but the answer is yes, I'll marry you and go to Texas with you and help you raise your son. As far as the other dozen....Let's put that on hold for the time being and enjoy the first part, is that ok?"

"That is perfect. I love you."

"I love you too."

They spent the rest of the day in the office alone, making plans for leaving as soon as the marshall was able to resume his duties.

The next day they looked up the pastor of the local church and made arrangements to get married the following day. The pastor's wife witnessed the marriage, and they were Mr. and Mrs. Clay Wade before noon. Clay moved his few possessions into her room at the hotel, and they lived happily for the next three weeks when the marshall returned.

Marilyn wrote a letter to her parents and left it at the general store, which also served as the post office, telling them about the wedding and that they would be living on Clay's ranch in Texas. They were anxious to get on with their lives, so they left the next day riding south. They were in no hurry to get where they were going, but since he made up his mind to go home, he was anxious to do it. He was thinking about Carter and what he must look like. He would be almost eight years old now and probably didn't remember Clay. The more he thought about him, the more anxious he became and worried at the same time. How would Carter accept him? Would Carter accept him at all? The only parent he has known since he was two years old is Ed and Lisa, at least as far as Clay knew.

They took their time traveling through Colorado on the edge of the Rocky Mountains, camping when they came to a pretty place and living off the land as needed. The weather stayed pretty most of the time, cool at night, which made for good snuggling, but it could get hot during the day. It took them a month to get through Colorado and cross over Raton Pass into New Mexico. After they got away from the pass, the land was mostly open with rolling hills with streams running cool and clear. They camped near water almost every night and kept the fires low and hidden as best they could. There were signs of Indians at some of the water holes, but they were fortunate not to run into any so far.

One night as they were lying in bed almost asleep, they heard what sounded like many horses approaching the water. Clay grabbed his rifle, handed Marilyn his pistol and told her to stay put, and if anyone sticks his head in the tent except him, she should shoot, and keep shooting as long they are moving, and he snuck out of the tent. The fire was down to coals and ashes so it couldn't be seen from any distance, but it could probably be smelled if the wind was blowing in the right direction. He listened and thought he detected something different about these horses. It didn't sound like horses that were ridden. They stopped some distance back from the water and milled around for a half-hour and never came near the water. Clay figured it out after a few minutes. That is a herd of wild horses, and they have caught the scent of Clay, Marilyn, and their horses and are afraid to come near the water. After he had that figured out, he returned to the tent and called to Marilyn in a whisper so she wouldn't shoot him.

She had been so nervous she was almost crying, thinking they were going to be attacked by Indians. When she heard "wild horses," she had to laugh, "Wow, I was about ready to kill myself to keep from being kidnapped by Indians."

They lay awake, talking in whispers and listening to the horses in the distance and finally drifted off the sleep.

After their coffee and breakfast the next morning, they packed their camping gear and moved away from the water to allow the wild horses to drink. They stopped just over the hill and tied their horses to some bushes, and eased to the top of the hill with the binoculars. Lying flat on their stomachs, they took turns watching the horses as they came down to drink. The band was led by an old bay mare that was skittish as a deer. She checked the area out thoroughly before she let any of the horses get near the water. The lead stallion was off to the side on a rise of ground where he could see everything around. He was very nervous. From the way he was acting, Clay thought he might have had some dealings with humans before and remembered the experience. He was a golden palomino with almost white mane and tail that flowed in the wind. As Clay zoomed in on him with the binoculars, he could tell right away he was not a young horse. He had scars all over his body from fighting to protect and keep his herd of ladies, but he was a magnificent specimen of a horse.

When Marilyn saw him for the first time, she said, "Oh Clay," she whispered, "Look at him. He is beautiful. Just look at the muscles ripple every time he moves. What a horse."

When she finally gave the glass back to Clay, he looked the rest of the herd over and commented, "There are several young ones that look just as good as he does." He handed her the glass and whispered, "Look at those standing off to the side away from the main heard. That's the bachelors, the young stallions that have been driven out by the big palomino to keep them away from his mares. Man, I would love to be able to catch a couple of those and take 'em back to Texas. The boys back there would have a fit over them."

Marilyn looked at him at asked, "Well, why don't we?"

"Why don't we what?" he asked with a confused look.

"Catch 'em, and take them with us."

He laughed out loud, "You got to be kidding."

"No, I'm not. We can do it. It'll be fun."

"You're not serious. Do you know anything about catching wild horses? And then you have to tame 'em enough to be able to handle them, and they can be dangerous, and it's a lot of work."

"What else do we have to do?"

Clay laughed and buried his face in his arms.

"What have I gotten myself into?"

They spent the rest of the day staying out of sight and watching the horses from the top of the hill. Toward evening the herd came back to the water hole and drank. They lingered for over an hour, returning to drink occasionally, and then they all drifted away toward the south. Clay explained to Marilyn, "Wild horses like this have an area that they cover on a pretty regular schedule. It may take them a week or more to make the circle, but they keep coming back to the same water holes. If we can locate those water holes, we may be able to set a trap for them the next time they come around. Let's hang back, stay out of sight, and follow them to see where they go and if there's a pattern to any of it."

After sundown, they mounted their horses and followed the herd for a couple of miles to see if they were going to return to the water or keep going. When it was too dark to see them, the herd was still moving south at their own pace, grazing as they went. Clay and Marilyn returned to the water hole and set up their camp in the same place as the night before.

They were up early, packed, and ready to go before the sun came up. Marilyn was as excited as a child with a new toy. Clay had to laugh at her and tease her about it.

"This is all new to me." She said, "My life was so boring before I met you. I can't control myself."

"When this is all over, and we settle down, are you gonna get bored and wanna go chasing wild horses again?"

"Probably, and if you don't go with me, I'll find someone else." She said, laughing and kissed him.

Clay shook his head, smiling and asked, "What have I gotten myself into?"

"You keep asking that. If you don't know by now, I must be doing something wrong."

"Oh no," he said quickly, "You're doing everything perfectly; you just keep it up."

"Ok, then stop complaining." She said with a chuckle.

"I'm not complaining. I'm just trying to figure you out."

"You'll never do that, so you can stop trying."

All-day, they followed the trail left by the herd of wild horses. Just before sundown, they spotted them a mile or so ahead, still moving at a slow gazing walk. Clay and Marilyn backed off and made camp behind the last hill they passed. They stayed very quiet all night and moved forward early the next morning. The horses were nowhere to be seen, so they found their trail and followed it until they saw the horses standing around a water hole. They were still too far away to recognize any of them but assumed it was the same herd since the tracks led right to it. Again they backed off and made camp and stayed out of sight and made no noise that might frighten the horses. They were very careful to stay downwind so the wild herd wouldn't get their sent and flee. Several times during the next three days, they had to move to different sides of the herd as the wind changed directions so they would be downwind.

On the fourth day of following the herd, the trail led them into a narrow canyon with high walls on each side. "This might turn out to be a place where we can trap them. It all depends if there's another way out of here." They continued to follow the trail. After a half-mile, the canyon widened to two hundred feet and continued for another half mile before they came to a small pond of water fed by a small waterfall flowing down the wall of the canyon. The tracks were there where the horses had come for water the day before. "I didn't see any fresh tracks leaving here by the way we came in, so there's either another way out, or they're still in here somewhere," Clay told Marilyn.

"Let's hope they're still in here, and there's not another way out. That would make our job a lot easier."

"Yeah, it would, but that would be asking for too much. We're not likely to get that lucky."

"I don't know. We've been pretty lucky so far," she said with a mischievous smile.

"How is that?" he asked.

"Well, I found you, and you found me. I don't know about you, but I feel pretty lucky."

"You do have a nice way of looking at things, and yes, I feel lucky too."

They stopped by the pond and fixed a bite to eat for lunch, and then followed the trail left by the horses when they left the water hole. It led them through another tight canyon with high walls, and after a half-mile or so, it opened onto a valley with trees and a stream along one wall of the rim that enclosed the valley. Clay took out his binoculars and surveyed the area. "Well, well, look what we have here."

He gave the glass to Marilyn and said, "Look at the walls all the way around this valley. From here, I can't tell if a horse can climb out of here or not, but it sure looks we may have hit the jackpot. The horses are over there in the shade of those trees, and from the looks of the tracks in this canyon, they go both ways. So maybe they come to that pond for water, and then come into this valley to graze before they move on to the next water hole."

Marilyn said, "I'm looking at the walls all the way around, and I don't see anything that looks like a trail, or any kind of path that they could use to get out. I even see what looks like several deer and a few buffalo over there."

"If you're right, maybe we did get that lucky again."

They rode a little farther out onto the valley floor to get a better feel of the place before making any more plans. They rode almost to where the horses were resting in the shade, but when they saw Clay and Marilyn coming, they broke and ran to the other side of the valley as far as the walls would let them go. The big palomino stallion came charging toward them but stopped a hundred yards before he got to them and reared up on his hind legs, pawed the air, and then turned and ran back toward the mares and foals. The old bay mare led the herd as far away as she could against the back wall. They were standing in a tight bunch looking at Clay and Marilyn while the stallion was running back and forth between them and the herd.

Clay turned his horse and said, "Let's get back to the entrance and block it so they can't get out."

They hurried and reached the narrow entrance to the valley and stopped. "Let's set up camp right here. We'll have them blocked in, I hope. If there's another way out, they'll be gone tomorrow morning. If they're still here, we'll know we have them trapped."

They unloaded the packhorses and staked them on a patch of good grass. The camp was set up in the middle of the canyon that was only fifty feet wide at that point. They got a fire going, and the coffee was perking in a few minutes. Clay was looking the place over and making plans. Finally, he told Marilyn, "There's enough brush around here to build a fence right across here, and unless they make a mad charge and crash into it, they can't get past us."

They set up their tent and prepared to stay here for a while. The next three days were spent building the fence. It was hot, dirty work, but they worked well together, taking frequent breaks and resting in the shade when they felt like it. At night they kept the fire going and sat listening to the night sounds. They heard the big stallion come close and stomp the ground and snort, and then trot away. That happened several times during the night. Clay and Marilyn lay in the tent and listened to see what he would do. During the day when they took a break from building the fence, one of them saddled their horse and rode out to check on the horses. They rode as close as they could without spooking them and sat their horse and watched for a while, then ride around, getting closer each time. Every time they did that, they were able to ride closer before they started looking like they were going to run. The rider then backed off a little way and waited a few minutes and did it again. By the fourth day, they could ride within a hundred feet without spooking them. The big stallion didn't like any of it, the scent he was getting from the man and woman spelled danger to him, and he was getting more aggressive the closer they got. He charged at them and reared up and squealed, trying to frighten them away.

That night as they sat around the fire discussing what they needed to do, Clay said, "We need to get that stallion out of here. I have an idea that might work. We can give it a try tomorrow."

The fence was completed, and they had left a small section that was closed off with only poles across it that could be removed quickly, and allow them to come and go. The next morning they dropped the poles to open the gate and left it open while both of them rode toward the horse herd. When they were about halfway to them, Clay told Marilyn, "You wait here while I ride up there and try to cut that stallion out with a few of the mares, and get them running along that wall. I'll try to limit the number if I can, but I think it'll work better if a few of the mares go with the stallion; otherwise, he probably won't go. If you see that I can't stop the rest of the herd, you beat 'em back to the gate and block it. Fire your pistol if you have to, but turn 'em back. If it's the stallion and a few mares, let 'em go. All we want are the young stallions and, if possible, some of the young fillies. I don't think we can handle more than six."

"Ok," she said, "I hope this works."

"Me too, good luck. Be careful; don't let 'em run over you. If you have to, get out of the way and let 'em all go, I don't want you getting hurt."

Clay took the lariat from his saddle and slowly rode toward the herd but off to one side, leaving room for them to go between him and the wall. They started moving away from him with the stallion leading the way. When they saw the wide opening ahead of them, they made a break for it at full speed, racing toward the opening. Marilyn saw them coming and put the heels to her horse and kept pace with them. All of the bachelors were bringing up the rear. Clay closed in on the side, forcing a separation between them and the mares and foals ahead. When the bachelors saw Clay cut in front of them, they cut back and tried to come around behind him, but Marilyn saw what was happening and cut in front of them and raced them to the gate. Clay was right behind her when she arrived, and they successfully turned them back and quickly put the bars up, closing the exit.

When they had time to see what they had done, they saw ten young horses running back and forth, trying to get to the exit to follow the rest of the herd. After a few minutes, they settled down and stood watching Clay and Marilyn. Both parties stood staring a few minutes before Marilyn turned to Clay with a big smile and said, "We did it! I told you we could."

They gave each other a big hug and laughed out loud.

"I wonder if there's any of that coffee left."

"If not I'll make some more, I can use it too."

While they sat enjoying the coffee and thinking about what they had just done, Clay told her, "Now the hard part starts. We have to catch them, get halters on them, and get them used to being around us before we can do anything else with them. That's gonna take a while."

"How long do you think?"

"Wow, that's hard to tell. We have no place to pen them up so I can work with them. I'll have to rope them out in the open and hobble them, or in some way fix it so they can't run away. I'll have to give that some thought."

From a long length of rope he had in his pack, he began building halters. When he had three ready by lunch the next day, he saddled Socks and rode out to the bachelor herd. As he approached, they dashed to the far side of the valley and only stopped when they reached the wall. Clay continued riding and didn't crowd them, but just rode as near as they let him without running. He kept that up all the rest of that day and the next day. By the evening of the second day, he was able to ride within fifty feet as they stood watching him. He sat his horse and let them get accustomed to him being near. The next day he eased around them and drove them back near their camp and let them stand and graze while he remained nearby. He kept that up for the next two days, getting closer and closer all the time. The next day as they were trotting along in front of him, he was close enough to toss a loop over the head of one of them. That's when the fight began. When the young horse hit the end of the rope, and it tightened around his neck, he went crazy. Clay had all he could do to hang on. With the rope tied to the horn of his saddle, he followed along as the young horse fought trying to get away. That went on for over an hour. Both horses were covered with sweat and breathing hard.

Marilyn was holding her breath as she watched the fight from a distance.

Clay led the horse around the area in a circle, getting closer all the time as he took up the slack on the rope. Soon he was only three feet away. He kept talking in a quiet voice and didn't try to do anything to aggravate him more.

That went on for a couple hours until Clay was able to reach out and touch him on the neck. At first, he shied away, but when he realized it wasn't hurting, and actually felt good, he relaxed. After a few more minutes, Clay was rubbing him between his ears as he sat on Socks beside him. He actually seemed to be enjoying it.

Clay led him around some more, and then gently stepped down from the saddle on the opposite side of Socks from the colt. When he walked around in front of him, he shied away, but when the rope tightened on his neck, he stopped and watched Clay with big eyes and looked like he would bolt at any second. Clay slowly approached and rubbed him on the forehead while talking quietly. He soon relaxed and let Clay rub him along his neck and back, but when he approached his hindquarters, he got nervous again, so Clay moved back to his head and continued talking and petting.

When he was ready to release him, Clay reached in his pocket and took out a lump of sugar he carried for his horses and held it in front of the colt's face. He sniffed it, and after a minute or so, he took it from Clay's hand. Clay slowly and gently took a halter from his saddle and slipped it on the colt's head and attached the rope to it. Then he led both horses to a big log that Clay had cut for that purpose. He removed the rope from the saddle horn and tied it to the log with about twenty feet of slack between the horse and the log. He then slowly led Socks back to their camp and left the colt standing tied to the log. He could drag it if he pulled hard enough, but he couldn't run away with it.

Clay went to the campfire and poured himself a cup of coffee, and he and Marilyn stood watching the colt. He learned real quick he couldn't win fighting the rope, so he settled down and pawed the ground and whinnied for the other horses that were standing off in the distance watching the show. He was left tied to the log until the next morning when Clay spent a few minutes talking and petting before mounting Socks and leading him around for an hour. Clay tied him to the log and went after another horse.

This routine was continued every day. A new horse was roped and worked until he settled down and then tied to a log to learn not to fight the rope. It took ten days to go through the entire heard of young horses. At the end of the ten days, all of them had been worked enough to be handled without fear of someone getting hurt.

Clay and Marilyn were exhausted but exhilarated to the point of being giddy at times. They were enjoying every minute of it. They fell into bed every night so tired all they wanted to do was sleep.

The next ten days were spent breaking them to the saddle. When they all accepted the saddle without bucking, it was time for Clay to ride them. That went rather smooth because of the way he had taken them through the process. Only a couple of them gave him any trouble, but he handled it ok.

After a month, Clay was riding all the horses, and none of them were giving him any trouble. Then he tied three of them on a lead line and taught them to lead in a group so they wouldn't be a problem when they took to the trail.

They were sitting around the campfire one night when Clay said, "I think we are ready to move on down the trail, how about you?"

 CHAPTER

TWELVE

The next morning they were packed and ready to go before the sun came up. The horses were all tied in two lines, with Clay and Marilyn each leading five. They made quite a show as they left the canyon where they had lived for the last two months. Their food supply ran out over a week ago, and they had lived on venison, buffalo meat, and coffee.

They had no idea when or where they would come to a place to replenish their supplies, so they had smoked as much meat as they had time for and packed it to go with them.

After the first hour on the trail, the horses settled into their new role and were easy to handle.

When they emerged from the canyon, they turned east and came to Lite Creek and followed it going southeast. The creek was crooked and wound around the hills and through the valleys, so they rode within sight of it but far enough away to avoid all the crooks and turns.

Late that day, they came to a trading post on the banks of the creek that existed by trading with the Indians and ranchers in the area. They replenished their supplies and camped up the creek from the store. For the first time in over two weeks, they had something to eat except coffee and meat. They were up early the next morning and got underway before sunrise.

When this trip started, they were enthusiastic and looking forward to the experience, but that seemed like a long time ago. Now they were tired and wanted to put an end to it.

Along about mid-afternoon, Marilyn asked Clay, "Why do you keep looking back, are you afraid Pa's coming after you with a shotgun?"

"I hope that's all it is," he said, "but I don't think so. Someone's back there, and they're getting closer. I first saw them this morning, but they're still too far back to tell anything about 'em. I didn't want to alarm you, it may be nothing, but we need to keep an eye on 'em. Twelve horses and a beautiful woman would be a big strike for some men."

They kept riding, and Clay kept checking behind them. "When we come to a good place to do it, we'll change directions and see if they follow us. If they do, then we'll have to make plans accordingly."

Just before sundown, when they would normally be stopping for the night, they came to the end of a low hill on their left, "Let's turn here and stay behind this hill out of sight. If they make the turn, we'll know they're following us. They probably won't get here in time tonight to see where we left the trail, so we should be safe tonight. Tomorrow we'll be watching to see what they do."

They cut in behind the hill and rode until they came to another hill on their right. When they got around it, dark had taken over, so they stopped and made a cold camp. No fire tonight, the sky was clear, so no tent either. They threw their bedrolls on the ground in the smoothest place they could find in the dark. Not long after they turned in, all the rocks began to make an appearance, in their back, on their hips and shoulders; it was not a comfortable night. They were constantly changing positions, trying to avoid the rocks.

Morning came way too early. They were more tired than when

they laid down. When he could see, Clay took his binoculars and climbed the hill to check out their back trail. An hour after he stretched out on top of the hill, he saw three riders coming back down the trail. They apparently rode past it last night in the dark, hoping to come upon Clay and Marilyn after they made camp. When they couldn't find the trail this morning, they came back looking for it. Clay was watching when they reached the place where he and Marilyn turned off late yesterday. They stopped and talked for a couple of minutes and then followed their tracks. Clay watched a few more minutes, and when they continued following, he returned to camp. Marilyn had the coffee ready and breakfast served, so they hurriedly ate while he explained their situation. "We need to be looking for a place that we can defend. It looks like they could catch up to us by late today if they continue pushing like they are, so let's get saddled and make some tracks."

Fifteen minutes later, they were at a slow lope, still heading east and following the easiest route through the hills. At every rise in the ground, they stopped and checked their back trail, and each time the men back there were closer. "We're gonna have to find a place pretty quick and make a stand until we know what their intentions are." They picked up the pace some more and continued to watch for the best place to defend. When the men were less than a mile back late in the afternoon, they came upon a small canyon branching off to the side. They rode past it a hundred yards and then doubled back, riding off to the side of their original trail, and went into the canyon. It didn't look like much at first, but the deeper they went, the steeper the sides got. After half a mile, they saw a game trail going up the side of the canyon. Clay told Marilyn, "Take all the horses and keep riding. I'm gonna climb that wall and stop 'em right here." He dismounted and gave his reins to Marilyn, and with his rifle, canteen, and a small bag of jerky, he climbed the wall and took up a position behind a bolder at the top of the trail. Marilyn was soon out of sight around a curve. He had a view for a hundred yards up the trail and was waiting for them when they came around the bend a few minutes later. He waited until they were a hundred feet away and fired a shot into the ground in front of them. The horses reared and tried to run, but the men got them settled down. Clay called out to them, "Y'all hold it right there and tell me why you're following me."

They looked around to see where the shot and voice were coming from. When they couldn't spot him, one of the men, apparently the leader, spoke up, "We're not following anybody. We're just minding our own business. Why are you shooting at us?"

"I've been watching y'all since early yesterday," said Clay, "so when you say you're not following us, you're lying. Now you have two choices. You can try to get past me, in which case I'll shoot all of you before you go fifty feet, or you can turn around and go back where you came from, the choice is yours. But make up your mind quick. I'm not a patient man."

"I told you we're not following you."

Clay sat back and didn't answer. He was watching them but never said another word. The man kept talking, trying to get Clay to answer him. He had a comfortable place out of sight, so he let them stew. After fifteen minutes without a response from Clay, they rode forward again. Clay put another shot closer to the leader's horse this time. When the dirt and rock fragments hit the horse, he went into a pitching fit. After about four bucking jumps, the rider sailed into the air and landed on his head. The other two sat watching, not knowing what to do. A minute or two went by, and the man on the ground had not moved. One of the other men called to Clay, "Hey fellow. We need to check on our friend. He looks like he's hurt bad."

"Go ahead," Clay told him, "get him on a horse and get out of here."

One man jumped off his horse and ran to the man on the ground, while the second man rounded up his horse and brought it back to load the injured man.

Clay watched as they struggled to get the man on his horse, and they weren't getting any help from the injured man himself. To Clay, it looked like the man was dead.

They finally got him loaded and tied in place. When the other two were mounted, one of them yelled to Clay, "You ain't seen the last of us, Mister."

Clay yelled back, "Keep this in mind, Mister, the next time I see you on my trail. I'm gonna shoot you, and I'm not giving you any warning."

Clay watched them slowly ride away. He watched until they were out of sight, and then he came down from his hill and started walking. He had no idea how far Marilyn and gone before she stopped, so he was surprised when she stepped from behind a boulder with her rifle and stood waiting for him to come up to her. When she saw he was unhurt, she ran and hugged him. "Are you ok?"

"Sure, I'm fine, how about you?"

"I'm worried sick."

"It's over now, so you can stop worrying."

She had left the horses in the shade of a tree farther up the trail. They mounted up and rode until they exited the canyon and came out on level ground. The sun had gone down, but the moon and stars were already lighting up the plains, so they kept riding, wanting to put more distance between them and those men. They didn't want to set up their camp and have them come back and catch them sleeping. Clay suggested they change directions to throw them off track if they should try to follow them tonight. The horses had already had a long day, so they took their time while watching for a good place to stop for the night.

An hour or so later, they saw a grove of trees on the side of a hill and headed for it. They worked their way deep into the trees and brush and found an open spot and set up camp. They were so tired all they did was picket the horses, and throw their bedrolls on the ground, and hit the sack.

Clay was awakened the next morning by the sun shining in his eyes. He jumped up and looked around, surprised that he had slept so late. Marilyn was still sleeping, so he checked on the horses and saw that they were ok, and moved them to new grass. There wasn't much under the trees, but maybe they would find something to munch on. He got a fire going and filled the coffee pot from his canteen and put it on the fire. When it came to a boil, he dropped in a handful of coffee grounds, and sat back and waited until the coffee smell told him it was ready. He poured two cups and carried one to Marilyn and shook her. When she opened her eyes and rolled over, he kissed her on the lips and asked her, "Hey, sleepyhead, are you gonna sleep all day?"

She said, "Yes," and rolled back over and covered her head.

He laughed and said, "Your coffee is getting cold, and I'm leaving in twenty minutes."

She threw the blanket off and sat up, "You wouldn't dare go off without me, would you?"

"Never in my wildest nightmare."

They sat close, drinking their coffee and talking. Clay warmed some jerky to go with the coffee, and that was their breakfast. Later in the day, Clay checked their back trail, as he had frequently been doing, and told Marilyn, "There's a cloud of dust back there. I wonder if it's those same two men. If it is, they aren't getting any warning this time."

They kept riding while keeping an eye on the dust cloud that was getting closer. Just before sundown, they rode over a small hill and stopped. "Take the horses down in that wash over there and stay out of sight. I'm gonna wait right here, and when they come over that hill, if it's the same men, I'm gonna stop 'em for good."

Marilyn led the horses down the hill, and into the dry wash. The banks were just high enough to hide them. She dismounted, and knowing Blue and Socks would stand without being tied, she took her rifle and eased up the bank until she could see over the edge. She saw Clay squatting behind a small bush with his rifle ready, waiting. A half-hour later, just before it was too dark to see, the two men came galloping over the hill. Clay recognized them as the same two from earlier, raised his rifle, and shot both of them before they knew what was happening. They were lying on the ground, moaning and writhing in pain when Clay walked up to them and kicked their guns out of reach. One of them groaned, "Why did you shoot us?"

"I told you yesterday, if I saw you on my trail again, I was gonna shoot you. Didn't you believe me?"

"Can I have a drink?"

"All I have is water."

"Never mind, just let me die."

Clay checked on the other man and found him already dead. He returned to the dying man and sat beside him, "Is there anyone you would like me to notify?"

The man was breathing very shallow. Clay thought he had died until he whispered, "No, I don't want Ma to know how I died."

A few minutes later, he took his last breath and let it out slowly.

By then, it was completely dark, and he went to where Marilyn was waiting with the horses. She had watched the shooting, and when Clay told her the men were dead, she asked: "What are you going to do with them?"

"There's not much I can do. All I have is that small shovel, and the ground out there is almost solid rock. There's no way I can bury them, and there are not enough loose rocks around here to cover them, so all we can do is leave them. The varmints need to eat too. I hope it doesn't kill 'em."

"That is so sad," she said, "All they had to do was ride the other way and leave us alone."

"I guess some people are just not that smart. They must think nothing is gonna happen to them. It's always the other guy who gets shot and dies."

They collected the two horses left by the dead men and added them to their string. "We are collecting quite a herd here. Maybe we can sell some of them if we come to a town big enough."

They continued riding toward the southeast for the next few days. On the third day after the shooting, they came to a trading post sitting on the bank of a small creek. The water was moving slowly, but clear and cool. The horses drank their fill, and they filled their canteens and spent an hour resting and giving the horses a breather. Clay was watching the store while they sat in the shade of the cottonwood trees. There were several horses in a corral behind the store, but other than that, there was no activity that he could see. They waited until almost dark, and then they mounted up and leading all the extra horses, walked them down to the store, and tied them to the hitch rack in front. For some reason, Clay had an uneasy feeling about this place. He couldn't explain it, so he didn't say anything to Marilyn, but he removed the leather tie-down from his pistol and moved it to a more comfortable position. Marilyn didn't notice that, but when he pulled the rifle from its boot on his saddle and jacked a cartridge into the chamber, she gave him a wide-eyed look. He told her very quietly, "Stay behind me. I have a bad feeling about this place."

The building was made of adobe and only had one door and a window on the front wall. He pushed the door open with the end of his rifle barrel and stepped into the poorly lit interior. He couldn't see beyond ten feet, so he stopped in the doorway until his eyes adjusted to the poor lighting. Anyone inside would only see a silhouette of a man with a gun on his hip holding a rifle in his left hand. As his eyes adjusted, he saw a makeshift bar along the right wall, the window that he saw from the outside was at the end of the bar. The only other window was in the back wall. The interior was hot and dark, and the air was stale. When he could see enough to walk without stumbling over something, he walked to the bar and turned to take in the rest of the room. Four men were sitting at one table. They were all staring at Marilyn, who had come in behind him. From the way they were looking at her, he didn't think they even knew he was there. Finally, one of them got up and went behind the bar, "What can I do for you, folks?"

Clay half turned so he could keep his eyes on the men at the table, and told the man behind the bar, "We need some trail supplies," and gave him a list that he and Marilyn had prepared. "Do you have beer?"

"Sure do, made it myself, the best in the country."

He took a glass from under the bar, opened a quart jar, and poured the beer.

"How about you lady, what would you like?"

"Do you have anything other than beer?"

"Just water Ma'am."

"Ok, then give me a beer."

That got her a double-take look from the bartender, and one of the men at the table said under his breath, but loud enough that Clay heard him, "Well, what do you think about that, a woman drinking beer in a bar with the men."

Clay was still watching them out of the corner of his eye when the man rose from the table and walked unsteadily toward them. Clay turned full around facing him. The man was big, unshaven, and dirty. He looked like he must be over six feet four, and weigh over two hundred and fifty pounds. He only had eyes for Marilyn as he walked across the room. Marilyn had her back to him, waiting for her beer when he reached for her. Clay stepped between them and shoved the man's hand and arm away. "Before you make a fool of yourself, this is my wife, so leave her alone."

"Get out of my way, I ain't seen a woman like that in years, and I'm gonna have me so fun."

Without warning, Clay hit him with a right uppercut to the chin. The man's head snapped back, but he stood like nothing had happened and gave Clay a look with a wicked smile, and then his eyes crossed, and he wilted to the floor and stretched out flat on his back. Clay quickly turned to the other two and asked, "Anyone else want to play?"

Clay and Marilyn stood at the bar drinking their beers while their order was filled. Clay asked the man to put it in a sack so he could tie it to his saddle. When they were finished with their beer and had their supplies, they headed for the door with Clay keeping his eye on everyone in the room. The sun had already gone down, and it was almost dark when they came out the door. He asked Marilyn to take the sack of supplies and put them in one of the packs on the packhorse, while he stood watching the door and window. When the supplies were packed, Marilyn mounted her horse and said, "Ok, I'm ready," and pulled her rifle from the scabbard and sat with it pointed at the door. Clay mounted, and they rode back the way they came in. When they were out of sight of the store, they changed directions and rode for several hours before stopping to make camp.

They were hardly out of sight from the store when the big dirty man started coming around. He shook his head and, after several attempts, managed to sit up. He felt of his chin and looked around the room, trying to figure out what happened and why he was sitting on the floor. When it all came to him, he roared and came charging to his feet, "Where's that mangy coward? I'm gonna break him in two. Where is he?" he yelled.

The other men slowly backed away and put more distance between them. The bartender moved to put the bar between himself and Rufus, and told him, "They left a long time ago. You've been out for a while."

"What did he hit me with?"

The bartender told him, "He hit you with his fist."

"You're lying. No man ever knocked me down with his fist. I'm gonna kill 'em?"

One of the other men spoke up. "No, he's not lying, he hit you one lick, and you went down, and never moved."

"I don't believe it. You're all lying. When I get my hands on him, I'll take him apart, limb from limb, and feed him to the coyotes."

"You better take my advice for a change and leave that man alone, Rufus. He didn't look like he just left his mama's bosom. He's an old he-coon from high up the creek."

"I don't care where he's from," he shouted. "No man does that to me and walks away."

He stormed around the room, and ended up at the bar, slammed his fist down, and yelled, "Give me another beer and be quick about it."

His beer was delivered, and the bartender disappeared into the back somewhere. The beer was gone in a minute, and he yelled for another one. The bartender came running and served another one, and disappeared again. The other two patrons sat drinking their beer and staying quiet. After two more beers, Rufus returned to his chair at the table with his two friends. A few minutes later, he was sound asleep with his chin resting on his chest, and a half-finished beer sitting in front of him. The other three men quietly left the room and took seats on the front porch. The night was cool and pleasant. They sat talking quietly so as not to awaken the man inside. They knew him well and didn't want to antagonize him. He could be a brutal man when he was drunk. Being drunk and mad made the situation doubly dangerous. A little while later, only the bartender was left. The other two had snuck off to find a place to sleep.

The sun had been up a couple of hours before the drunk was awake enough to remember what happened the night before. He was lying on the floor by the table where he had been all night. He was slowly waking up until he remembered, and then he stumbled to his feet and started searching for his partners. They were nowhere to be found. They had seen him in this condition before and wanted no part of it. It always ended up with all of them in trouble. He found no one in the store and stormed outside. When he saw no one there, he went back into the store, yelling for the owner, "Abe, Abe, get out here!"

Abe stumbled into the room half asleep, rubbing his eyes looking around to see what the trouble was, and spotted Rufus standing at the bar, he stopped short, and asked, "What's all the commotion about?"

"Where did those two sorry excuses for men get off to?"

"I don't know Rufus, they probably went to bed somewhere, why don't you go look for 'em?"

"Don't tell me what to do, or I'll come around there and beat you senseless!"

Abe reached under the bar and came up with a 45 caliber revolver and told Rufus, "If you cross that bar, I'm gonna shoot you."

"You don't have the guts to shoot anybody."

"Do you want to bet your life on it? Come on over here."

To save face, Rufus said, "I don't have time to fool with you; I've got business with that coward that hit me when I wasn't lookin'."

Abe pushed his luck and said, "Oh, you were lookin' alright, he just knocked you out cold, and there wasn't any doubt about it either."

Rufus bristled up and charged the bar, "Why you sorry…" He was halfway over the bar when the bullet caught him in the face and knocked him back into the room. He landed on his back with blood leaking onto the floor.

Abe watched him a moment, and then said, "Good riddance, I've wanted to do that ever since the first time you walked in here."

A few minutes later, Rufus's two friends came in and looked at Rufus, and then Abe, and asked, "What happened?"

"He was comin' across the bar after me, and I shot him. Get him out of here, and bury him somewhere or dump him where the coyotes can get him, I don't care which."

They looked at the body as they walked around it to the bar, "That's gonna cost you a couple of beers."

"That's a cheap price to pay to get rid of him."

They drank their beer, and looked at the body again, and said, "Give us another beer, that's gonna be a dirty job."

Halfway through their second beer, one of them said, "I guess we get to keep his horse and tack, don't we?"

They finished their beer and walked over to the body, and went through his pockets. All they found were a few matches and cigarette papers, a pouch of tobacco, and two dollars in change. They dragged the body out the back door, and threw him across a horse and rode away. They were back in thirty minutes and demanded another beer. Abe was not too happy about giving away free beer but considered it worth it not to have to put up with Rufus any more.

With the two dollars they got from Rufus's pockets, they had a few more beers. They were both more than half drunk when Mike asked Lonnie, "Wonder where they got off to. That sure was a pretty bunch of horses they had. I'm thinkin' we ought to follow 'em, and take 'em off their hands. We could take 'em down to the fort, and sell 'em for some good money. Whatcha think?"

With a little slur in his speech, Lonnie said, "I don't know, Mike, that old boy looked like he could take care of himself pretty good. He sure didn't mess around when it came to takin' care of Rufus."

"Ah, he can't be all that tough, besides there are two of us and only one of him."

"Don't forget that woman. A man like him ain't gonna have no lily-livered woman taggin' along. You gotta consider her in this too."

"Yeah, but just think, when we get rid of him, we'll have her all to ourselves, and way out here ain't nobody gonna know what happened to 'em."

"She sure is a pretty thing. I ain't ever seen a woman like that."

The more beer they drank, and the more they talked about her, the more their courage built. Finally, Lonnie said to Mike, "Do you think we can follow their tracks?"

Mike was bleary-eyed, and his speech slurred when he said, "With that woman as the prize, I can follow their trail 'til it falls off the end of the world."

"Well, ok, let's go."

They stumbled out the door and went to saddle their horses. Abe watched them go, and shook his head, "There's two more I won't have to put up with anymore."

Lonnie and Mike found Clay and Marilyn's trail and followed it until the alcohol was wearing off, and the headaches set in. They came to a creek with clear running water and stopped to rest and fell asleep. When they awoke, it was dark. They realized they had no supplies, and they were hungry, and their heads were pounding. They forgot why they were out here in the first place, so they turned around and rode back to Abe's store.

CHAPTER

THIRTEEN

lay and Marilyn were miles away by the time Rufus finally fell asleep that night, so they had no way of knowing what happened after they left. They awoke late the next morning and took their time breaking camp. It was almost noon before they were saddled and riding out. Clay had taken to switching his saddle to the young horses and was riding several of them every day. All of them were turning out to be good horses and were quick learners. A couple of them had a nice easy gait that made for a comfortable ride. After he had ridden them a few times and saw they were no trouble, he encouraged Marilyn to ride the chocolate palomino filly with the easy gait. After riding for a few minutes, she remarked, "Wow, I never knew a horse could be this smooth. I'm claiming this one for myself; you keep your hands off her."

Clay laughed, "Yeah, I thought you would like that."

They continued riding south and east across the wide-open planes of West Texas for several days without seeing another soul. Their supplies were getting low again, and they were looking for any sign of a settlement when they came upon a well-worn trail and followed it, knowing sooner or later it would lead them to something. The Next day, around mid-morning, they saw smoke in the distance. When they came over the hill, there was a small town sitting on the bank of a creek. They looked the place over as they slowly rode down the one street. It wasn't much of a town with only one saloon, a livery stable, a mercantile that advertised "anything you want we have it," a barbershop, a diner, and a few other small businesses, all of them on the one street. There wasn't any sign of a hotel, so they would be sleeping on the ground again. They were getting awfully tired of that, but they were used to it by now.

They tied their string of horses at the hitching rail in front of the store and went in the diner and had a good meal prepared by someone else. They lingered after their meal, and when the waitress came over and asked if they would like some apple pie to follow that meal, they both smiled and said yes.

They finished their apple pie and went to the store to purchase the supplies they needed. They were in the store for about forty-five minutes and came out with their supplies to find several men standing around admiring their horses. Fifteen horses made quite a sight, and most of them, being beautiful young stallions, caught the eye of anyone who happened to look their way.

The supplies were being stashed in the packs when a man asked, "Hey feller, where did you get these horses?"

Clay was standing between his horses, where the man couldn't see what he did when he slipped the thong off his revolver and lifted it slightly to make sure it was loose in the holster. He checked to see where Marilyn was before he stepped from behind his horse, and answered, "Well, some of them I raised from babies, some we captured from a wild herd, and some we took from men who tried to steal them from us. Why, do you want to buy some of 'em?"

"No, I think you stole 'em. Those horses come from my ranch. You drove 'em off a couple of nights back."

Clay started walking toward the man as he said, "Mister, I don't know who you think you are, but you just called me a horse thief."

"I'm Major Ledbetter; I own the biggest ranch in these parts."

Clay interrupted him, "I don't care who you are or what you say you own, now you either retract that, and say it out loud so everyone can hear you, or go for that gun." By that time, Clay was only three feet from the man and looking him straight in the eye. The man was well dressed, wearing boots that looked like they were just polished, and looked like a prosperous rancher, and must be used to getting his way around here. But when Clay stopped right in front of him and challenged him to back up his talk, he hesitated and looked around at all the men watching. He realized he had just made a fool of himself. If he backed down, he would be the laughing stock of the county, and if he didn't back down, he had a strong feeling he was going to be dead. This man facing him didn't look like he was the least bit afraid of him. He cleared his throat and said, "Let me have a better look at 'em. I could be mistaken."

"You go ahead and take your time looking at 'em," Clay told him, "but what I said still stands."

Ledbetter walked around the horses pretending to examine them while Clay stayed right with him only a few feet away. The man kept looking back to see if Clay was still there. Sweat broke out on his face, and he didn't know how to get out of this situation. He kept glancing at the other men like he was expecting help, but they were not moving. Then he saw Marilyn standing with her back to the wall of the store with her rifle leveled at them. One glance, and there was no doubt that she would use it if they made any move toward her man.

The big rancher took his time looking at the horses, hoping someone would step in and distract Clay, and give him a chance to go for his gun. When no one stepped up to help, he finally cleared his throat again, and turned toward Clay, and said in a low voice where no one else could hear him, "Ok Cowboy, you win this round, but you're still in my territory, and I swing a wide loop. You ain't got away with nothing yet."

Clay stepped closer to where their noses were almost touching and told him, "You must have forgotten what I told you. Apologize, and retract what you said, and do it so everyone can hear you, or go for your gun."

"I've never apologized for anything in my life, and I'm not starting with you."

The last word was barely out of his mouth when Clay hit him square in the face. Clay didn't know if he fell from the shock, or if he had knocked him down, but Major Ledbetter was laying on his back in the middle of the street with Clay standing over him. Ledbetter shook his head and attempted to get to his feet. He staggered and fell once before he could stand. When he was steady on his feet, Clay walked into him again. This time he hit him in the stomach as hard as he could. A big gust of air came out, and Ledbetter's face turned white, and he was gasping, trying to get air back in his lungs when Clay landed another blow to the side of his jaw. Major Ledbetter found himself lying in the street again with Clay standing over him. When Clay thought Ledbetter could understand him, he told him again, "Apologize, and retract what you said, or get up, and fight, or are you the kind of coward that has other men do your fighting for you?" He said it loud enough that everyone on the street heard him.

Ledbetter got to his feet and backed away from Clay and told him, "I don't stoop so low as to fight scum like you."

One quick step and Clay was in his face again and slapped him with his open hand, and then backhanded him coming back. Ledbetter staggered back and grabbed his face in shock. But by now, he was getting furious and embarrassed that anyone would and could manhandle him this way. He came charging at Clay, roaring like a bear with his fist up ready to fight. He swung a wicked right that Clay easily pushed aside, and landed three blows to the face before he could get out of Clay's reach. He staggered back and raised his hands to protect his face, and Clay sunk his fist up to the wrist in Ledbetter's stomach. Ledbetter had had enough, but he didn't know how to stop it. He dropped his hand to cover his stomach and got another blow to the face. The blows were coming so fast there was no way he could avoid them. Blood was dripping from his nose, his eyes were beginning to swell, his head was spinning, and his sight was blurred, but the blows kept coming. He was so busy trying to keep from getting hit he had no time to fight back.

To the spectators, it was obvious that Clay was just taking his time, and landing punches that were tearing Ledbetter's face to ribbons. Clay wasn't trying to knock him out. He wanted to punish this loudmouth who thought he was better than anyone and teach him a lesson. Clay kept landing punches to the face, and gut, while Ledbetter was backing up, and trying to cover up. Clay was finding the openings, and landing punches faster than Ledbetter could block them. Ledbetter finally backed into the hitch rack across the street from where they started and could go no farther. Clay walked in and really started pounding him good. Ledbetter slowly sank to the ground out cold. Clay grabbed him by the front of his shirt and dragged him to the watering trough, and threw him in. Clay thought for a few seconds he wasn't going to come up, but he finally shot to the surface gasping for air, spitting water, and trying to wipe it from his eyes. When he realized where he was, he quickly tried to rise from the trough, but he couldn't make it. He finally settled back and covered his face with both hands.

Clay grabbed him by his shirt collar, and dragged him from the trough, and told him, "Stand up, you sniveling coward."

"Don't hit me anymore, I've had enough, I apologize for what I said."

"Louder, we can't hear you."

In a slightly louder voice, he said, "I'm sorry for calling you a horse thief."

Clay told him, "Loud enough for everyone to hear you, did I steal those horses from you?"

"No, I was mistaken. I never saw them before."

Clay turned to the crowd of fifteen or so men, and a few women, who saw the whole thing and told them, "You heard him, now my wife and I are gonna ride out of here, and if anybody follows us, I'm not gonna like it. Is there anyone here who doesn't understand what I just said?"

No one spoke up, so Clay went to his horse, mounted, pulled his revolver, and waited for Marilyn to get mounted. They turned their horses and rode slowly out of town with Clay turned so he could watch the people still standing in the street.

When they were out of sight over the hill, he holstered his gun and turned to Marilyn and said, "I'm sorry you had to see that. But some men are just arrogant enough to think they can take whatever they want, whenever they want."

"I thought it was a good show. I was a little worried there at first, but then I saw you had it under control. That guy was just a big bully."

They hadn't ridden far when they heard a horse coming up behind them at a fast gallop.

Clay quickly pulled his rifle from the scabbard, and stepped down from the saddle, and turned facing the rider. The man had both empty hands in the air and was slowing to a trot, then to a walk, as he got closer. There was something familiar about this rider, but Clay couldn't put his finger on it right away. As he got closer, he became more familiar, but when the man stopped his horse and said, "Howdy, Captain Wade, I never expected to see you in these parts. I thought you were goin' back to Tennessee."

"Well, I'll be a...Sergeant Wallace, of all people to run into. What in the world or you doing way out here?"

Sergeant Wallace stepped down from his saddle, and the two men grabbed each other and shook hands like long lost friends.

Clay finally remembered Marilyn, and turned to her, and said: "Marilyn, this is Sergeant Wallace, we served together for four years during the war, Sergeant, this is my wife, Marilyn."

Sergeant Wallace stepped forward and extended his hand and shook Marilyn's and said, "I'm really pleased to meet you, Mrs. Wade." Turning back to Clay, he said, "I saw the show you put on back in town. It was all I could do to keep from cheering. That so-called Major has needed that for a long time. He goes around strutting like a peacock daring anybody to speak to him or get in his way. When I saw who he was talking to, I said to myself right then; this is gonna be interesting."

Clay asked him, "Where are you staying, anywhere around here?"

"I was ridin' for the Major, but I just quit. Now I'm ridin' for you. Where are we goin'?"

"Marilyn and I are headed down to south Texas, close to Cuero. Do you know where that is?"

"No, never heard of it, but it don't matter. Unless you shoot me or tell me you don't want me around, I'm goin' where you go."

"Well, I'm not gonna do either. So I guess we're stuck with each other."

"Ok, Captain, you give the orders, and I'll see that they are carried out."

"Ok, the first order is, forget that captain stuff, the war has been over a long time, just call me Clay, and I'll call you...what is your first name anyway?"

"Luther, I'm named after my ma's brother. I never liked him, and I never liked that name, so I prefer just to be called Sarg. I've been called that so long I kind of like it."

"Ok, Sarg it is. Is there a good place anywhere around here to set up camp?"

"Yeah, just up ahead, there's a place with good water and shade. If any of the Majors men come around, they'll probably try to start trouble. He thinks he owns everything from here to yonder, but if they do, it'll be just like old-times, you and me takin' on the whole confederate army. So I guess we can handle a few cowhands if they show up."

"Let's hope they don't. I've seen enough fighting to last me a lifetime."

"Yeah, I know what you mean."

As they were riding to the camp sight, Clay and Sarg caught up on what they had been doing since they saw each other last. That was the night that Clay was shot and thought he was going to die on the battlefield. *Long Trail To Texas, Clay Wade, Book One.*

The horses were staked out on a good patch of grass along a creek, and the camp was made upstream under a big cottonwood tree. With the fire going, and coffee brewing, they sat back and told Marilyn stories of their time during the war. Of course, there were many things they couldn't even mention in front of her, but they told what they could, and laughed at the funny stuff, and clouded up, and got quiet when they remembered men they had gotten close to that didn't make it out alive.

Sarg told Clay, "When I saw you back there in town, I thought I saw a ghost. The last time I saw you was that day in Virginia when you were shot. I saw your horse go down, and then you were shot, and I thought you were dead. The lead was flying around us so fast I didn't have a chance to get to you to check on you. What happened after that?"

Clay was quiet for a few moments, but then he told Sarg what happened. Once he got started he couldn't stop and ended up talking for over a half-hour telling his life story, about his folks being notified that he had been killed in action, and arriving back home to find his girlfriend, thinking he was dead, married to another man, his parents dead, the homestead bought up by a carpetbagger, the running battle to recover the livestock that the carpetbagger tried to steal, and then marrying Ellen, and Carter being born, then the baby girl dying her first winter. The final straw was when he found Ellen dead.

"Since then, I've just been a lost man. I haven't cared whether I lived or died, or about anything else until I met Marilyn. I guess you could say she saved my life, for what it's worth."

Marilyn had heard the story before, but she sat quietly, listening, with tears in her eyes, feeling sorry for Clay.

After a moment of silence, Sarg said, "Yeah, sounds like you've really had a rough time."

The men sat by the fire and talked over old times long after Marilyn had turned in and was asleep.

Breakfast was finished the next morning, and the horses were saddled ready to ride out when, with no warning, Sarg walked behind Clay, pulled his revolver, and hit Clay behind the ear. Clay crumpled to the ground, unconscious. Marilyn screamed and rushed to Clay's side and took his head in her lap. Blood was seeping from a cut and dripping onto her riding skirt. "Why, why did you do that?" She screamed. "He's your friend, why did you do that?"

Sarg just looked at her and chuckled as he lifted Clay's pistol from its holster. "That's what he thought. I thought I killed him that night in Virginia. It was quite a shock today to see him still walking around."

"But why? I thought y'all were friends."

"I've hated his guts for years." He got his canteen, and poured water in Clay's face, and waited for him to come around. The water soaked Marilyn's clothes, but Sarg didn't care. When Clay started regaining his senses, Sarg stepped back, holding his revolver pointed at Clay. A few minutes later, Clay reached up and touched his head, groaned, and looked at the blood on his hand. "What happened?" He whispered

Marilyn explained, "That man you thought was your friend hit you with his pistol and knocked you out. You have a bad cut on your head."

Clay looked around until he saw Sarg standing a few feet away, smiling, with his pistol pointed at him. "Why, what is the meaning of this?" He asked, holding his bleeding head.

"You really don't know, do you?"

"No, what are you talking about?"

"You always got everything, and I got nothing. We enlisted at the same time, but you got all the promotions, and I got passed over every time. We were privates at the same time, and then you made corporal, and I was still a private. They put you in charge of all the details, and I was the man that did all the grunt work. Then you made Sargent, and I'm still a private doing all the work. Every time an opening came up, you got the promotion. I hated your guts. Then finally, I got a promotion to corporal. Two measly stripes, while you had stripes all the way down your arm. Then the straw that broke the camel's back was when you got that battlefield commission. Now Mr. Bigshot, you're an officer with bars on your collar, and I had to salute you. You were no better than me, but you were shoutin' the orders, and I had to jump through hoops to do what you said." The longer

Sarg talked, the louder he got. "Every time you gave me an order, I wanted to shoot you between the eyes. Who do you think sent that letter to your folks telling them you were dead?" Sarg laughed out loud, remembering how he pulled that off. "Remember that little snotty-nosed private that was the orderly for the general? Well, I threatened to make sure he got shot in the next firefight we got into if he didn't write that letter." He laughed again, "Then I saw my chance. You thought the rebels shot you, didn't you? I never enjoyed anything as much as puttin' that bullet in you, and watchin' you fall. If I had known you weren't dead, I'd have come over there and finished the job." He laughed again, "What do you think about that, CAPTAIN?" He shouted at Clay and laughed again. "Now I got you right where I want you. I got your woman, your horses, and all your gear. Now you're gonna suffer like I suffered all those years."

Clay was still lying with his head in Marilyn's lap, trying to understand what was happening. Everything was confused, and his head was spinning and felt like it was going to burst, but he refused to let Sarg see any sign of pain. His mind was going ninety to nothing, trying to think of what he could do. His vision was slightly blurred, but he could hear. He didn't know if he could move or not. From somewhere, he got the idea to remain still and pretend he was hurt worse than he really was.

Marilyn was crying and holding him so tight it almost hurt.

Sarg came over and grabbed Marilyn by the arm, "Come on, we're leaving. He can lay there and think about what I'm doing with his wife." He laughed again and jerked her to her feet. Clay's head fell to the ground, and he didn't move. He listened as Sarg dragged her to the horses, picked her up, and threw her on her horse. She fought him all the way, but he knew if he tried to interfere at this point, Sarg would shoot him. If that happened, Marilyn would be left to fend for herself. He remained perfectly still hoping not to get shot. A few minutes later, he heard the horses leaving, and Marilyn screaming and crying his name. When they were far enough away that he couldn't hear them, he rolled to his side and sat up. His head was spinning, and his vision was still slightly blurred, but he considered himself lucky to be alive at this point. He was finally able to get to his feet by holding to a tree until his head stopped spinning. He looked around their camp for anything he could use as a weapon, but there was nothing there. He then remembered they already had everything loaded before he was knocked unconscious. He didn't even have a canteen, and his mouth was already so dry it felt like he hadn't had a drink in days. There was a stream nearby, so he staggered down there and drank his fill, and tried to wash the blood from his head, and face. He felt some better, but his head was still throbbing. There was nothing he could do about that, so he took out on their trail. Fifteen horses leave a trail that anyone could follow, so he started putting one foot in front of the other and stayed with it. He knew the chance of catching up with them was slim, but he had no other choice. That was the only thing he could do, so he set his mind to it, and kept plodding along.

After only fifteen minutes, he had to stop to rest. He felt weak like he was going to pass out and staggered to the nearest shade and fell down. When he awoke sometime later, he could tell by the length of the shadows that he must have been out for an hour or more. He forced himself to get to his feet. He stood holding to a tree until the dizziness slacked off some, and then started walking. The tracks of his horses were still there, so like a dog on a leash, he followed them.

By early afternoon the sun was so hot it felt like it was burning a hole in his head through his hat, and his feet felt like they were on fire. He knew they had blisters, but he had nothing to doctor them with, and if he removed his boots, his feet would swell, and he would never be able to get them on again. He put a pebble in his mouth to try to get some saliva flowing if there was any left.

Hours later, he was still hobbling along their trail and found where they stopped for their noon break. They had a fire, and must have made coffee, and maybe cooked something. He only spent a few minutes examining the area and took advantage of their stop to try to shorten the distance between them. He was moving at a pace he hoped he could maintain all day. The blisters on his feet had burst and become raw and bleeding in his boots, and the pain was almost unbearable. Nothing is worse than walking in riding boots, but again, there was nothing he could do about it, so he did his best to put it out of his mind, and kept walking.

Several times he roused up and found he was lying face down in the trail. He had no idea how long he had been lying there. The shadows were getting long, and he was worried about Marilyn knowing what Sarg would probably do when they stopped for the night.

The trail was leading to the north, and Clay had no idea what lay in that direction, but apparently, Sarg had some destination in mind. Clay hoped he could catch up before they reached where ever that was.

Things probably would get very unpleasant for Marilyn when they got there, and it could start even sooner. With that thought, and knowing night was coming on, he tried to pick up the pace. But his feet were in such bad shape he couldn't do it. It was all he could do to keep walking, and that was getting more difficult and painful with every step. With a little luck, maybe he could overtake them before morning if he could keep moving through the night. Even that was looking doubtful. He tried to put those thoughts out of his mind and concentrate on putting one foot in front of the other. He came to a stream and fell on his stomach and buried his face in the water, and drank until he was full. He rolled over on his back to rest just a minute or two. When he awoke, it was completely dark. He struggled to his feet and cursed himself for falling asleep when Marilyn's life depended on him.

The blood was sloshing in his boots, but he tried not to think about it. After a few minutes of walking, the pain was so intense he had to stop to give his feet a break. It didn't help much. They still hurt to the point of being almost unbearable. If Marilyn's life didn't depend on him, he would have quit long go.

He lost all track of time. It was just one foot in front of the other all through the night. When he just couldn't go anymore, he sat and rested a few minutes, and then struggled to his feet and walked some more.

Marilyn fought with all her might when Sarg was loading her on her horse, but he was so much stronger, she didn't have a chance.

When they rode away, leaving Clay on the ground bloody and helpless, she was screaming and crying, but Sarg just laughed, "I want him to suffer until his last breath. I've waited over ten years for this."

Marilyn kept looking back, hoping to see Clay, but they were too far away now. She knew he didn't have a horse or any supplies, and there was nothing she could do about it. She never felt so helpless in her life.

They rode all day, except for the brief stop for a snack around midday. The traveling was slow with leading so many horses, but Sarg was in no hurry. The horses were walking at their own pace, which wasn't very fast. That gave Marilyn a little hope of Clay catching up to them. Night came, and they stopped by a small stream and set up their camp. "Get us some chow cooked woman. I'm starved."

She was just opening her mouth to tell him to get his own when she remembered what happened the last time she did that. The coffee pot was always the first thing to get going. While the water was getting hot, she prepared the rest of the meal, and it all came together about the same time. Sarg took his plate and sat next to a tree and ate, but Marilyn couldn't force herself to eat anything. She knew she should eat something to keep her strength up for what was to come.

Sarg never took his eyes off Marilyn the whole time he was eating. When he finished, he threw his plate toward her and said, "Clean that up, and put it away, then come over here."

The sun had gone down and would be dark in a few minutes when she took the plates and walked the short distance to the creek to wash them. When she was out of sight of their camp, she started running. She didn't know where she was going but anywhere was better than staying in camp with him. The area along the creek where she was running was heavy with trees and underbrush that kept hanging on her skirt. She had only gone a hundred yards or so when she heard him yelling. Fear shot through her, and she couldn't keep from crying as she ran faster, but the full riding skirt was hampering her efforts, so she pulled it up to give her more freedom and kept running. Her only hope now was to stay out of his sight until it was too dark for him to find her.

She ran until she was totally out of breath, and her legs wouldn't go anymore. She stopped and sat beside a tree, listening for any sound that would warn her of his coming. A few minutes rest was all she needed, and she was up and going again. This time she stayed at a fast walk and changed directions to throw him off her trail. When it was too dark for him to see her tracks, she changed directions again and headed back toward the trail they had come down to get here. She couldn't be sure, but she thought she was going in the right direction.

She walked until her feet hurt, and her legs were so tired she just had to sit down. Her skirt and shirt were torn, and she had blood on her arms and face from scratches she received while running through the brush. She leaned against a tree, planning to rest only a few minutes. When she opened her eyes, the sky was getting light in the east, and she knew she had slept. She jumped to her feet and almost fell. Her legs were so sore and stiff she could hardly move them, and pain shot threw her feet, and tears came to her eyes. She looked around to see if anyone was nearby. When she didn't see anything to be alarmed about, she started walking slowly at first because of the pain in her feet and legs. The farther she walked, the better her legs felt, but her feet only got worse. With the sun coming up in the east, she was able to choose the right direction. She found the trail left by their horses yesterday and followed it until she realized that is exactly what she should not be doing because that's the first place Sarg was going to look. As soon as that thought entered her mind, she looked behind her to see if he was there. He wasn't, but she expected him to show up any minute. She ran away from the trail into the trees and underbrush, hoping she wasn't leaving a trail that he could follow. She came to a thick grove of trees and lots of underbrush and settled down to rest. She could see where their trail was and was watching for Sarg when she saw movement farther down the trail in the other direction. She didn't think he would be that far ahead of her, but she unconsciously ducked behind a tree. Now she was watching in both directions.

A few minutes later, she was rested and thinking she should start moving when she saw the movement down the trail again. This time it was closer, and moving slowly toward her along the trail they left yesterday. As it got closer, her heart started pounding, and she wanted to scream. She jumped up and ran as fast as she could until she was within shouting distance, "Clay! Clay!"

Clay saw her running toward him, and he tried running toward her, but his feet wouldn't allow it. They met in a tight hug and held each other for a long time. Finally, he could speak and asked her, "Did he hurt you?"

"No, I got away last night just before dark. We need to get off this trail, I'm sure he's following me, and this is the first place he's going to look."

"I'm sure you're right, let's go."

She pointed, "I was hiding up there in those trees when I saw you coming. I didn't know who it was at first, but when I recognized you, my heart just about stopped."

Clay only wanted to sit down and never move again, but he knew Marilyn was right. So he held on to her as they struggled up the hill to the trees trying not to leave a trail. They found a secluded place where they could see the trail below and collapsed to the ground. Both were so tired they could hardly keep their eyes open, but they were so happy to be back together; they didn't want to fall asleep. They were in too much danger, and if Sarg came upon them sleeping, that would be the end of everything. Sarg had all the weapons except for the knife on Clay's belt. He didn't know why Sarg didn't take it. Apparently, he didn't see it and forgot Clay had it. Whatever the reason, Clay intended to use it to its best advantage if he got half a chance.

Marilyn asked Clay, "Have you had any rest since yesterday morning?"

"I stopped a few times for a few minutes when I couldn't go anymore, how about you?"

"I must have slept a couple hours sometime during the night." She said, "I stopped to rest and fell asleep. When I woke up, the sun was just about to come up. I've been walking ever since until just before I saw you. Why don't you lie down and rest? I'll keep watch as long as I can. I promise not to fall asleep."

"Ok, if you feel like you're getting sleepy or too tired, you wake me."

She said ok, and he lay down and was asleep within a minute. She watched the trail and looked at Clay sleeping. When she couldn't hold her eyes open any longer, she got up and walked among the trees until she was awake again. To her, it seemed like several hours, to Clay, it seemed like several minutes, when she shook him, and said, "Clay, he's coming."

Clay rolled over and looked where she was pointing. A rider was coming up the trail leading a herd of horses. They both recognized Sarg and their horses. They stayed hidden behind the trees, and brush, and watched as Sarg came closer. "You stay here. I'm gonna slip down there by the trail and try to pounce on him when he comes by."

"I have a better idea."

"What's that?"

"When he gets closer, I'll jump up and run where he can see me. When he is chasing me, you come up behind him, how about that?"

"I like that idea, but I don't like putting you in danger like that."

"He's not gonna hurt me until he gets what he wants. Just make sure you get there first."

"Ok, you can count on it."

She slipped off to the right toward the trail. When she got almost to it, Sarg saw her and let out a yell, "I got you now damn you. I'm gonna make you pay for making me chase you all night."

Marilyn was having trouble running with her sore feet, but she gave it her all. She didn't want to lead Sarg to far and make Clay chase him.

Sarg dropped the lead rope to the extra horses and spurred his horse into a run after her. With all his attention focused on her, Clay wasn't worried about being seen, and in spite of his sore feet, took off running toward them. As sore as they were, he forgot all about them when he got his sights set on the man who caused them so much pain.

Sarg raced up behind her and jumped from his horse and grabbed her by the neck and threw her to the ground. She was screaming, and kicking with all her power when suddenly Sarg went flying off her and landed on his back with clay sitting on his chest with his knife pressed to his throat.

"Hello, ole friend, good to see you again," as he put more pressure on the knife. A trickle of blood ran down Sarg's neck onto his shirt collar.

Sarg was shocked to the point of being motionless. His eyes were twice their normal size, and he couldn't get his breath. He was hyperventilating and gasping. Clay slipped the pistol from Sarg's holster and tossed it in Marilyn's direction.

"Get up, Sarg. We're gonna have a conversation, your last one because I'm gonna kill you, but you're gonna see it coming. Stand up."

When he was on his feet, Clay hit him in the jaw as hard as he could. There was a loud crack, and Sarg sank to the ground, barely moving, holding his jaw. He mumbled, "You broke my jaw."

"Oh, I'm sorry, does it hurt?" He reached down, "Here, let me help you up."

Sarg cringed away from him, "Get away from me," he mumbled.

"I'm gonna get away alright, but you're the one leaving. You're a dead man Sarg. How does it feel?"

Sarg was staring at him with big eyes, breathing heavy, and trembling.

"You know why you were so slow getting promotions, Sarg? Because you're dumb Sarg, just plain dumb. Now that stupidity is gonna get you killed. Stand up."

"I can't. My jaw is broke."

"You don't stand on your jaw, get up, or I'll shoot you where you're lying!"

Sarg finally struggled to his feet, and Clay hit him again on the other jaw. He went down and didn't move.

Clay told Marilyn, "Hold that gun on him, if he moves shoot him, I'm going to get the horses."

"No, I don't want to be alone with him again, I'll get the horses." She gave the gun to Clay and limped away. She was back in about fifteen minutes leading all fifteen horses. They were tied to trees, and the canteen was brought over to Clay to have a drink. Neither of them had had water since late yesterday, and they emptied the canteen, and got another from Sarg's saddle, and drank most of it.

Clay found his gun in the pack and dropped it into his holster and gave Sarg's gun to Marilyn.

Sarg was just starting to come around when Clay poured the last of the water in his face. He sat up, sputtering and wiping the water from his eyes, trying to focus and figure out where he was. He started to say something, stopped, and grabbed his broken jaw, and groaned.

"Get up, Sarg; it's time for you to die."

"No, Captain, don't do this, I wasn't gonna hurt her, I just wanted to get back at you, but now I see it wasn't your fault, it was all my fault. I didn't mean her any harm."

"Get up, you whining pup."

"No, I'm not getting' up, you'll kill me."

"I'm gonna kill you anyway. I'm just giving you a chance to defend yourself."

"What?"

"I'm gonna give you your gun. I can't shoot an unarmed man, even a low down skunk like you."

Clay took the gun from Marilyn, and tossed it on the ground by Sarg's hand, "Go ahead, pick it up."

Sarg looked from Clay to the gun, and back at Clay. He licked his lips and looked at the gun again.

Marilyn begged, "No, Clay, don't do it, he could shoot you, please don't."

Sarg, thinking Clay was distracted by Marilyn, grabbed the gun. He had it in his hand and pulling the hammer back when the first bullet hit him in the chest, the second hit him in the face, and he fell backward to the ground. Clay watched him until he was sure he wasn't gonna try to use the gun again. He then walked over and checked to make sure he was dead. When he was sure, he removed Sarg's gun belt, and put the gun in the holster, and turned to Marilyn. She was staring at Sarg with her hand over her mouth.

Clay walked to her and put his arms around her and hugged her tight, "It's all over now. You can relax."

She trembled and turned her back and said, "Let's get out of here."

Clay checked the gear on the horses, and saw everything in place, and tied down securely, and then helped Marilyn to her saddle. As they rode away, Clay looked back once and shook his head. "He was a good man once, not very smart, but a good man."

They rode until they came to another stream and stopped for the day. It was early, but both had had two trying days and needed the rest. They removed their boots and soaked their feet in the water. They were very sore, and the blisters had burst and were now raw sores. Clay found an extra shirt in Sarg's saddlebag, and one of his extra shirts, and made bandages and wrapped their feet. There was no way either of them could get their boots on.

They lounged around resting, sleeping when they were sleepy, and eating when they were hungry. The horses were moved to new grass and led to water several times a day. They were somewhere in north Texas or Oklahoma, they didn't know for sure, and it really didn't matter. They were just enjoying being back together, and except for the sore feet none the worse for the ordeal they had gone through.

CHAPTER

FOURTEEN

The Bar W Ranch, Cuero, Texas 1875

Ed Carter came out of the barn, and called "Hey, Carter, bring that horse over here!"

Seven-year-old Carter Wade yelled back, "Yes, Sir, coming up." He grabbed the lead rope on the colt he was working with and brought him to where Ed was waiting. "How's he coming along, Carter?"

"Just fine, Sir; he's the smartest one of the bunch. He's learning fast. I really like him."

"When do you think you'll ride him?"

Carter thought a moment, and shook his head, "I don't think he's quite ready for that yet, give him a few more days."

"Alright, keep up the good work. You're gonna make a first-class horse wrangler yet."

"You think I'll ever be as good as Lefty?"

Out of the corner of his eye, Ed saw Lefty approaching, "Hah, you're already as good as Lefty. In a couple more years, you'll be riding circles around him."

Lefty heard that last remark, "Don't let him mislead you kid, ain't nobody as good as ole Lefty when it comes to riding and training horses."

Carter laughed, "Yeah, I've seen you get thrown too many times to believe that."

"You better watch it, Kid; I'll throw you in the horse trough again."

"You can't catch me; your legs are too bowed to run faster than a turtle."

"Ah Carter, now you've done hurt my feelings."

Carter came back with, "Ha, you don't have any feelings."

Gerald Williams came up leading a horse, and asked, "Y'all ready to go?"

"Just waitin' on you, boss," Lefty said.

Lefty and Gerald mounted, and rode away, leaving Carter with Ed and the colt.

They crossed the Guadalupe River and continued for another couple miles until they came to the herd of over twenty-eight hundred longhorns. As they rode up, Luke came over to meet them. "Everybody's anxious to get moving, y'all ready?"

"Yeah, does everybody know what they're supposed to do?"

Luke answered, "They've all been told over, and over if they don't know by now, they'll never know."

"Alright, let's do it."

Gerald rode to the north side of the herd, lifted his arm over his head, pointed north, and yelled at the top of his voice, "Head 'em up and move 'em out!"

Two thousand eight hundred head of Texas longhorns were headed for market in Abilene, Kansas. Gerald had assembled a crew of eighteen men, some as young as sixteen, to make the drive. Some had been up the trail before, but for the younger ones, this was their first trip, and they were so excited they could hardly control themselves. They were yelling and waving their hats and ropes in the air to get the cattle moving and keep them going in the right direction.

Luke rode around the herd as it was getting started telling the drag riders to "Push 'em hard boys, we want 'em so tired tonight all they'll wanna do is lay down and rest. If the dust gets too thick, pull your scarf over your nose, that'll help some."

Riders were strung out along both sides every seventy yards or so and constantly rushing back and forth running strays back into the herd.

The first day on the trail was always the worst. None of the cattle wanted to be driven from their familiar grazing ground. The men and horses soon worked up a sweat and were covered with a layer of dust that mixed with the sweat and ran down their faces. The horses were worn out before noon and exchanged for fresh ones from the horse herd.

Two young men, Sam and Robert Black, were in charge of the horses. They were on the upwind side of the cattle herd to avoid the dust cloud that could be seen for miles.

The chuckwagon, driven by the cook, Wally Wallace, was traveling a mile or two ahead, and would find a spot for their camp, and have supper ready for them when they arrived.

Abilene was over seven hundred miles as the crow flies, but these cows were not crows, so the distance would be considerably farther for them. If they average ten miles a day, they would be there in about seventy-five to eighty days. They would be happy if they made it in three months.

Abilene was almost due north from Cuero, so they set a course as close to due north as they could and held to it when possible. Settlements and ranches had to be skirted, and hills, creeks, and rivers threw them off course, but they always continued in a northerly direction. It was the lead man who picked the route. He was riding in front of the herd, and after a few days, they followed his horse wherever he went. An old long-horned brindle cow took the lead, and all the others fell in behind. Every morning when the lead man rode out and yelled to get them moving, that old cow moved out and set the pace for the day. They were allowed to spread out so they could graze as they walked, but at night they were pushed into a tight bunch, and the night herders rode circles around them to keep them from straying.

They were between San Antonio and Austin when they ran into their first trouble. A group of men approached them in the middle of the afternoon. Luke saw them coming first and alerted Willie and George. Luke and George rode out to meet them before they got close enough to spook the herd. Willie and Lefty rode out, one on each side of the group, and stopped about one hundred feet away with their rifles held across their arms in front of them. A couple more of their men rode up and stopped a short distance away. When the strangers rode up to Luke and George, and stopped, the leader, a big man wearing a black hat, and sporting a thick black beard, asked, "Who's the owner of this herd?"

Luke answered, "I'm Luke Wilson, one of the owners. What can I do for you?"

"We're gonna check your herd; we got some complaints about y'all pickin' up some of the local's cattle as you passed through. We're gonna cut 'em out and charge you ten dollars a head for every one we find belonging to our neighbors. Y'all stand aside and let us do our job, and there won't be any trouble."

Luke looked at the group carefully before he answered. They all looked like a bunch of out of work cowpunchers right out of the saloon. "What is your authority Mr. ......?"

"McConnell is my name; I'm the head of the Cattleman's Association for this part of Texas."

Luke said, "Ok Mr. McConnell, give us a list of the brands we're supposed to have picked up, and my men will cut them out for you, but there will be a charge of twelve dollars a head for the trouble of rounding them up and cutting them from our herd. Is that satisfactory to you?"

"You don't seem to understand young feller. We do the cutting, and we determine which brands to cut out."

"You don't seem to understand Mr. McConnell, so I'll say it real plain for you; your men ain't cutting nothing. We've been really careful not to pick up any cattle as we pass through, and I can guarantee there are none in this herd except the ones we left home with. Now you can take your men and go about your business somewhere else."

McConnell motioned to his men, "Spread out men and do your job. If anyone tries to stop you, shoot him."

One moment Luke was sitting his saddle nice and easy; the next moment, McConnell was looking down the barrel of Luke's gun.

"Go ahead, McConnell, try and cut this herd. You'll be a dead man before the first man has gone three feet, but it's your choice, you do what you think is best."

McConnell looked at Luke a moment, and then glanced at Luke's men sitting on their flanks with rifles, and said, "Ok, Mr. Wilson, you win this round, but you ain't heard the last of us."

They slowly turned their horses and rode back the way they came. Luke and George watched them ride away. George said to Luke, "I think we are gonna have trouble with them. If not tonight, then sometime when we least expect it."

"I think you're exactly right. So we'll have to make sure we are expecting it when it comes."

Luke called for Lefty to come over. Lefty galloped over, and asked, "You want me to follow, and keep an eye on 'em, without them knowing I'm doing it?"

"You read my mind Lefty."

Lefty sat his horse waiting for McConnell and his group to go out of sight over the hill, and then he rode off at an angle and disappeared over another hill. When he was out of sight, he turned in the direction of McConnell's men, and, staying below the ridgeline, he followed until they stopped and settled down like they were going to be here a while. He pulled his horse up behind some trees and brush, tied it loosely so if he didn't come back, the horse could get loose.

With his rifle in hand, he made his way to the top of the hill to where he could see the men. The whole gang was sitting around a fire, drinking coffee, and liquor from a bottle that was being passed around. Lefty stretched out under a bush with other brush in front of him so he could see without being seen. The men down below didn't appear to be in any hurry to go anywhere, so Lefty relaxed and watched. Just before sundown, McConnell got up from where he was lounging and gave an order. The men slowly got to their feet and gathered their gear and went to their horses. A few minutes later, they rode out, headed in a direction that would put them ahead of the herd. Lefty watched until he was sure of where they were going, and then he went back and got his horse, and followed at a safe distance, always staying out of sight. When they reached the last hill between them and the herd, they stopped and dismounted, and appeared to be preparing for a long wait. Lefty watched them a few more minutes and then turned his horse and quietly rode away until he was far enough that they couldn't hear him. Then he put the spurs to his horse and hurried back to where the herd was bedded down for the night. As he got closer, he slowed his horse to a walk and circled the herd until he met the first-night rider. He explained what he had seen and told him to spread the word to the other night riders. He then rode to the chuckwagon, where he found Luke, George, Willie, and the rest of the crew. Again he explained what he had seen and what he expected to happen at any moment. The three all agreed with him, and got their heads together, and discussed their defense.

When they all agreed, they called the rest of the men together and laid the plan out for them.

Luke told them, "Ok, men, listen up. We are expecting an attack at any minute from those men who wanted to cut our herd today. My first guess is they will probably try to stampede the cattle. The second guess is they may try to sneak in between the night herders, and steel a few head at a time, and drive 'em off before we know what they're doing. Either way, we're gonna be ready for them. We need to double the men riding herd tonight, the rest of you will ride with us. George will take four men, and move off the right side; Willie will take four men, and move off to the left, I'll take four men and wait in the middle. Where ever they show up, they are gonna get a surprise welcome. First thing, when you see 'em, try to make sure it's who we are expecting. We don't wanna open fire on some innocent riders. Once you're sure, open fire. The only one I would like to see taken out of action for good is that McConnell. He's the ring leader; without him, the others will probably scatter. If they put up a fight, then all of them are fair game. Any question?"

They sat quietly for a few moments until Luke said, "Ok, Willie and George pick your men, and let's go."

The men divided into three groups and moved out.

Lefty rode to the night herders and explained to each of them what was going to happen, and then joined Luke a mile up the trail. They spread out on both sides of the route they expected McConnell to take, and waited. An hour went by with nothing happening. The men were getting anxious and tired of waiting. Another hour went by, and still nothing. It was getting close to midnight when they heard horses coming. Luke whispered, "Get ready, men. Don't fire until I give the word."

He took his binoculars from his saddlebag and focused on the riders. "That's them." He whispered. When they were within fifty feet, and easy to see in spite of the dark, Luke said, "NOW!" and all his men opened fire. They couldn't pick individual men, so they were shooting into the group. Men were screaming, and falling, horses were rearing, and bucking, and running away, some with riders, some without riders. It was all over in a few seconds. Everyone remained where they were watching the bodies on the trail. A couple of them were rolling around and groaning, while the others appeared to be dead. Luke spoke to Lefty, "Cover me while I check them, and get their weapons. Lefty covered them with his handgun while Luke picked up all the guns, and tossed them in a pile in front of Lefty. Then he checked on the wounded men and found one that may live if he got medical help soon, but the other one wouldn't last but a few minutes the way he was bleeding. Luke kneeled by the man who might live and asked him, "If I get you on a horse, can you make it to a doctor?"

The man could barely speak above a whisper, but said, "I don't know, but I guess I have to try, get me on the horse."

Luke told him, "I'll patch you up the best I can, but I'm not a doctor, and I don't have anything to bandage you with."

The man whispered, "There's a shirt in my saddlebag, use that if you want to, it looks like I won't need it."

"Which horse is yours?" Luke asked him.

"It's the sorrel with the white sock."

Lefty found the horse, and brought the saddlebags back, and found the shirt inside. The wounds were bandaged the best Luke, and Lefty could do it. The man was loaded on his horse and tied in place so he couldn't fall off. According to the man, the nearest town was over twenty miles away, so the horse was pointed in that direction and sent on his way. They never knew if he made it or not.

George and Willie heard the shooting and came running, but it was all over by the time they got there.

The next morning a three-man detail was sent out with shovels to bury the dead. By the time they finished their gruesome job, the herd was several miles up the trail.

Clay and Marilyn were still recuperating from their ordeal with the Sergeant, but they were taking their time riding south with their string of horses. They made quite a group with the ten caught from the wild herd, plus the two they were riding and their packhorse and all those left to them by the men who tried to steal them. They were in constant danger from Indians if they were seen with this many horses. They would be too much of a temptation for any Indian to pass up. He was doing everything he could to avoid them, but out here in west Texas, there isn't a whole lot you can do. The area was too open to conceal much of anything, so they tried to stay off the high ground and not skyline themselves. When they had to cross over a hilltop, Clay stopped the group before they reached the top, and went forward on foot with his binoculars and took his time looking the area over.

It was on one of those occasions when he saw several horses standing around a water hole at the bottom of the hill only a hundred yards away. He immediately dropped to the ground behind a bush and lay perfectly still, knowing that movement attracts attention. He watched a few moments before he saw the Indians lying around in the shade. He assumed they had stopped at the water hole for the same reason he would have, to give their horses a drink, and fill their water bags. It looked like there were maybe five or more men down there. He didn't know much about Indians, but since this was known Apache territory, he assumed these were Apache's. Not that it made a bit of difference because regardless of how many there were, it was more than he wanted to tangle with. He was lying under a cedar bush in the shade, and his clothing blended in with the colors, so he lay still watching, hoping they would move on soon. His main concern was the horses. If either group got wind of the other, they were likely to whinny, and then their neck would be on the line. He checked the direction of the wind and determined it was blowing from east to west. The Indians were south of Clay and Marilyn, and their bunch of horses, so unless the wind shifted, they probably wouldn't get their scent. He eased back away from the hilltop and made his way to where Marilyn was waiting with the horse and explained their situation. When he said the word Indians, she just about fainted. He told her not to worry; there's only five or six of them; We can handle them. He said it, but it was all for her sake. He wasn't at all sure that they could. They were in the middle of it now, and they had no other choice. If they tried to leave, their herd of horses would make too much noise, and they would be discovered immediately. He figured their best chance was to remain quiet and out of sight and hope they went another direction when they left the water hole.

Clay got all their weapons laid out with ammunition ready, and instructed Marilyn what to do should they be attacked. He made sure she knew how to fire and reload, and then he crawled back to the hilltop to check on the Indians. When he was in position again, he searched the area around the water in the shade but didn't see any men. The horses were still standing where he saw them last, but the men were nowhere in sight. He knew they were in serious trouble now. They must have seen him when he crawled up here the first time, and he thought he was so careful not to be seen. He watched the area in front of him, trying to decide what he should do. He had a strong feeling they were moving in on him, but he couldn't see anyone.

Marilyn was back there alone. If they got behind him, she would be vulnerable to their attack. He slowly backed down the hill until he could stand without being seen. He then ran to where Marilyn was crouched behind a tree clutching her rifle so tight her knuckles were white. He saw the relief on her face when she saw him coming. He crouched down beside her and took her hand. It was shaking so bad he doubted she would be able to fire a gun. He patted her hand and assured her everything was going to be ok. He looked around the area they had to defend and didn't like what he saw. It was too open with scattered trees and thin underbrush, which offered very little cover. After digesting the situation, he took her hand and led her as fast as she could run a short distance away. When he stopped, they were in thick brush within sight of their horses. He motioned for her to lie down beside him and be still. Knowing that motion catches the eye, he told her not to move no matter what happens. He pulled his hat down, so only his eyes showed, and laid as close to the ground as he could. Only his eyes were moving as he searched the area in front of them. The area they were in was thick with brush and no different than the rest of the area. There was nothing here to attract attention. That's why he chose this spot. The horses were off to their right, but close enough that he could see if anyone approached them, and he was hoping the Indians would be looking at the horses instead of looking for him and Marilyn. Minutes went by with nothing but flies buzzing around their faces. He wanted so bad to shew them away, but if he moved, he was afraid the Indians would see him. All he could do was blink his eyes.

After what seemed like hours, but was only ten or fifteen minutes, there was a movement in the brush on the side of the hill. He whispered to Marilyn, "There's one on the side of the hill, don't move." Soon there was another one twenty yards from the first one. Clay watched as they moved silently down the hill toward them. His eyes were sweeping from side to side, searching for the others. They were there somewhere, but he hasn't seen them yet. A few minutes later, a third one showed farther over from the first. They apparently had their eyes on the horses expecting Marilyn and Clay to be there. As they got closer, Clay slowly eased his rifle into position and sighted in on the one closest to him. He still wasn't sure how many there were, but whatever it was, it was too many. He had three of them located, but there were at least two more, and maybe three that he had not spotted yet.

He watched as they got closer to where the horses were tied. Something had to be done soon, or they would take the horses, and he wasn't going to let that happen without a fight.

They were moving very slowly and making no noise what so ever. He had to marvel at how they could move through the brush like a gentle breeze without making a sound.

Finally, he spotted the fourth one almost to the horses coming in from the other side. Just before he reached the first horse, Clay drew a bead on him and pulled the trigger. The shot sounded so loud and unexpected in the still afternoon that the horses jumped, and tried to pull away. The Indian dropped out of sight, but Clay knew his shot had been good. That eliminated one of them. He looked for the others, but they were no longer in sight. They had gone to the ground and would be almost impossible to find now. He continued to stay perfectly still.

The smoke from his rifle barrel was drifting up and was a sure giveaway. After a few moments of tense waiting, he saw a slight movement of a bush near where he had seen one of the men before his shot. He sighted in on the bush and fired three shots, one in the middle, and one to each side of the bush where he saw the movement. There was a thrashing in the bush, and then quiet. Mark one more off. There were still three or four out there somewhere. There was too much gun smoke drifting up for them not to know where they were, but he couldn't figure out why they were not attacking or at least shooting at them. While they were waiting for something to happen, he slipped more cartridges in the magazine of his rifle.

Suddenly, Marilyn screamed and rolled to the side away from Clay. He tried to turn and bring his rifle around, but a body landed on top of him, knocking the breath from him. He instinctively threw his hands and arms in front of his face knowing a knife was probably aimed for his throat. He caught the wrist just as the knife pricked the skin on his throat. It took every ounce of his energy to stop the knife and push it away. The arm was strong and slick with sweat and hard to hold. He tried to roll over, but the weight was too much. He brought his knees up under him, bringing his hips off the ground. Using the strength in his legs, he lunged to the side and rolled, bringing the Indian to the ground beside him. Clay was still holding the knife hand with his left hand, and with his right, he went for the Indians' eyes. He managed to get his thumb in one eye and shoved as hard as he could. He heard a sharp gasp, and the knife dropped to the ground. He grabbed the Indians' throat with both hands and squeezed with all his might. The Indian was struggling to break his hold, but Clay was determined not to turn loose. He tried to see what was going on around him, but he was too busy trying to stay alive. A shot exploded almost in his ear, and all he could think was, "I hope it was Marilyn doing the shooting." The man he was fighting was big, and strong, and smelled of bear grease, and sweat. He was slippery and hard to hold. Clay finally got him on his back, and applied all the pressure he could muster to his throat. The man slowly got weaker and finally relaxed. Clay looked around him and saw one Indian laying a few feet away. He assumed that was the one Marilyn had shot. He didn't see the others anywhere but knew they were still nearby. He grabbed Marilyn's hand and said, "Let's go." She was on her feet and running beside him in two seconds. Clay led them to several trees growing close together that offered more protection.

He looked to the horses, and saw they were nervous, and pulling at their rope. He suspected someone was trying to cut them loose.

"Stay right here, and don't let anyone sneak up on you." He jumped to his feet and ran to the horses. When he got there, two of them were already cut loose and running off through the trees. He charged as fast as he could, screaming at the top of his lungs with his knife in one hand and his pistol in the other. An Indian rose from the ground right in front of him. Clay fired his revolver at point-blank range and hit the man in the chest. He went down without a sound. Clay squatted to the ground looking for the others.

He had about decided there were no more when he heard Marilyn scream. He whirled around and ran to where she was lying on the ground. An Indian was standing over her with a knife in his hand. Just as he dropped to his knees beside her and grabbed her hair, Clay shot him in the head. He fell across her pinning her to the ground, but she was screaming and trying to shove him off. Clay got there a moment later and grabbed the man by the hair, pulled him off, and threw him to the side. When he was satisfied the man was dead, he turned to check on Marilyn. She was lying on her side with an arrow in her shoulder. Her face was pale and looked like she was in shock. Clay dropped to his knees beside her and told her not to move. He wasn't sure if there were any more Indians around, but all he cared about now was Marilyn.

His first instinct was to remove the arrow. He had no experience with that sort of thing, but he had treated bullet wounds, and this shouldn't be too much different. He checked the area around him and didn't see anyone, so he turned back to Marilyn. He felt of her back to see if it went all the way through, but there was no arrow there. Then he felt a lump under the skin and gently removed her shirt enough that he could see what was there. It was obvious the lump was caused by the arrowhead pushing the skin out from the inside. It had almost broken through the skin.

He checked the area again and still didn't see anyone. He told her, "Rest easy, Baby. I'm gonna get a fire started and get that arrow out of you."

He quickly scraped a pile of leaves and small limbs together and got a fire going. He filled the coffee pot with water from his canteen and put it on to heat. He dug his last shirt from his pack and ripped it into strips, all the while keeping an eye on the area around them and Marilyn. He cleaned his knife and put it in the fire to sterilize. When the water was hot, he took the pot off the fire and moved to Marilyn's side. "Marilyn, I'm gonna have to make a small cut in your back to get the arrow out. This is gonna hurt, but it's the only way. It'll be over in a minute, just try to relax."

He broke the arrow shaft off in front of her shoulder and rolled her over on her side so he could get to her back. He straddled her to hold her as still as possible with his weight. He hesitated a moment, said a silent prayer, and quickly made an incision over the lump and exposed the arrowhead. Before she could react to that pain, he shoved the arrow through and out her back. She screamed and fainted. "It's over now, you rest." From his saddlebags, he retrieved the bottle of whiskey he always carried for emergencies like this. She was still out when he returned. That was a good thing because when he poured the whiskey in the wounds, front and back, to keep her from getting an infection, it was not going to be pleasant. He pulled the wound open in front of her shoulder and poured the hole full of whiskey. The pain must have felt like fire. She came off the ground, screaming and passed out again. He rolled her over on her stomach and filled the hole in her back. This time she flinched, and groaned but then relaxed. He used the strips of shirt to bandage the wounds. She was still out when he finished, and he let her sleep.

The coffee water was boiling, so he dropped in a hand full of coffee grounds and sat back to wait for it to boil a few minutes before pouring him a cup.

While he was tending to Marilyn, he had not seen or heard any sign of Indians. He could only hope there were none still around.

He held her hand and drank his coffee. The sun went down, and it was getting dark, and she still had not come around. He checked her pulse and found it steady and strong. Her breathing was normal, and he figured the best thing he could do for her was to let her sleep.

He was still concerned that there might be more Indians around, but all he could do was stay on his toes and hope for the best. He needed to check on the horses but didn't want to leave Marilyn here alone.

He heard the horses doing their usual thing, so he wasn't too concerned. He convinced himself that there were no more Indians around, or he would have heard from them by now.

He made a meal of jerky, and coffee, and sat beside Marilyn through the night. Several times she stirred, and whimpered but never fully woke up. He knew that it was best since she wasn't hurting while she was sleeping.

The next morning he was moving like a zombie from no sleep. Just after the sun came up, Marilyn started coming around. When she was awake enough to feel the pain, she groaned and grabbed her shoulder. When she felt the bandage, she looked down to see what it was, and then remembered she had been shot. She started crying, and Clay took her hand and told her, "Hey, it's ok, just a little ole arrow high up in the shoulder. It didn't hit anything important. You're gonna be fine. Would you like some coffee?"

She took a minute to digest what Clay had just told her, "Yeah, that sounds good," she whispered.

Clay poured a cup and set it on the ground beside her while he helped her to a sitting position and leaned her against him. Her hand was shaking so bad she was spilling her coffee, so he helped her hold it steady while she took a sip. "Oh, that tasted good."

She looked down at her shoulder with the bandage and asked, "How bad is it?"

"Not as bad as you might think. The arrow went almost all the way through and was pushing the skin out in back, so I just made a small cut and shoved it on through. It didn't bleed much, and I sterilized it with whiskey, so there shouldn't be any infection. The whiskey probably hurt you more than the arrow. We'll rest up here until you feel like riding."

"I would rather move on now. I don't like being here. Those Indians must have friends around somewhere. If they come looking for these, we could be in bigger trouble."

"Alright, if you feel like riding, we'll do it."

He left her drinking her coffee and chewing on jerky while he got the horses saddled, and lined out on their lead lines. When he came back for her, she was on her feet holding to a tree. He had to help her get in the saddle, but once she was up there, she made out fine.

He was leading all the horses since he didn't want them pulling on her injured shoulder.

They traveled as fast as she could tolerate the rest of the day and made camp beside a small stream just before sundown. Clay made coffee and heated beans and jerky. When they were finished eating, he put the fire out, and they mounted up and rode for another mile in the dark before stopping for the night.

Marilyn had a restless night and kept waking Clay with her moaning every time she moved. He didn't know who was more tired the next morning.

After a quick breakfast, they were mounted and on the trail again. As far as they could see, there was nothing but grass. The land looked to be as flat as a tabletop, but Clay knew from experience that was deceiving. There were low hills that could conceal an entire tribe of Indians, or an entire village that you wouldn't know was there until it was too late. He was constantly turning his head from side to side, doing his best to keep from being surprised.

It was late afternoon when he pointed out a dust cloud directly in front of them. There were still at least two hills between them and the dust cloud. Clay was having an argument with himself about what was causing it. His first thought was Indians. But he couldn't imagine Indians stirring up that much dust. It could be a herd of buffalo or wild horses, but he soon ruled that out too.

The only thing he could think of that would cause that much dust was a large herd of cattle.

"Marilyn, I'll bet you that's a herd of cattle. Probably going to Abilene. What do you want to bet?"

She was in no mood to play his games. She was holding to the saddle horn with her good hand and slumped over like she may be asleep. Clay was riding close by her side in case she started to fall from the saddle.

It was after sundown when they topped the hill and saw the herd stretched out for almost a mile. The stopped and watched as the leaders were held up, and the rest of the herd was brought up and stopped for the night.

The chuckwagon was on the upwind side of the herd out of the dust. Clay saw a fire flicker and told Marilyn, "I'll bet we can get a couple of free meals that'll be better than anything we've had in a while." She roused up enough to understand what he was saying and looked at the herd. "I've never seen that many cows at one time in my life."

"Yeah, that's a big herd alright; it must be some big rancher driving them to Kansas to the railroad."

Let's ride down there, and bum a free meal, what do you say?"

"I'm all for that."

They rode slowly toward the chuckwagon while watching the men get the herd settled in for the night.

Clay pointed and said, "Let's swing over that way and look at their horses. I never could pass up a horse without looking at it.

The moved a little farther to their right to pass close to the horses. Before they got close enough to tell anything about them, a young wrangler came galloping toward them. Clay saw right away that he had his rifle out and ready. When he was within twenty feet, he stopped and told Clay, "You better stay away from them horses, Mister."

"We don't mean any harm. I'm just a sucker for a pretty horse, and it looks like you have a nice looking bunch there."

The rider positioned himself between them and the horses and turned with his rifle pointed in their direction. As any westerner will, Clay glanced at the brand on the rider's horse. He stared a moment and then looked toward the horses in the remuda. All were wearing the same brand. He asked, "Whose horses are these?"

"They belong to the BAR W. Why."

CHAPTER

FIFTEEN

When the cattle were all settled down for the night, Luke and Willie rode to the chuckwagon, poured a cup of coffee, and sat down leaning against a wagon wheel discussing the day's events. The rest of the men who were not riding herd came straggling in and got their coffee. They were laughing and joking, poking fun at each other when one of the men said, "Boss, riders coming, looks like a big bunch of them."

Luke and Willie jumped to their feet and looked where the man was pointing. They saw a large group of horses, but they were too far away to tell anything about them. Luke went to his saddlebags and got his binoculars. He rested them on the edge of the chuck wagon to get a better look. The men were reaching for their rifles and getting ready to mount their horses. Luke was watching the riders as they got closer, then he slowly lowered the glass, and told Willie, "You gotta see this. I don't believe what I'm seeing."

Willie looked at him with a puzzled look on his face and took the binoculars and focused on the riders.

"Well, I'll be a horn swaggled chicken. I see it, but I don't believe it either. Come on!" They made a break for their horses and took out in a full gallop racing toward the riders. The rest of the men in camp didn't know what was happening, but they had their rifles and took a defensive position. Several of them ran to their horses and mounted prepared to make a fight of it if it came to that.

Clay and Marilyn saw riders racing toward them, and stopped.

The riders were coming at breakneck speed and showed no signs of letting up. Clay dropped the lead rope, let out a rebel yell that scared Marilyn, and put the spurs to his horse and went racing toward them. They all slid to a stop a few feet away and piled off their horses. Clay came off his horse and met them in a big bear hug. They were slapping each other on the back so hard a dust cloud was making them hard to see.

Marilyn quickly realized they all must know each other. Things were starting to calm down by the time Marilyn reached them.

Luke noticed Marilyn and jerked his hat off and turned facing her and asked Clay, "Who is the beautiful lady with you, Clay?"

Clay said, "This is my wife, Marilyn. Marilyn, this is Luke Wilson and Willie Stanton. They're, or were, my partners in the ranch. I don't know if I still am since I've been gone so long."

"You sure are," Willie said, "and that herd down there is one third yours too."

"You gotta be kidding me."

"No, I'm not kidding. Nothing has changed since you left. Everything is still split three ways. We figured if you never came back, Carter would have a big nest egg when he grows up."

Clay was silent a few moments, "How is Carter? I guess he's a pretty big boy by now."

"Yeah, he's almost up to my shoulder. He's really a good kid. You'll be proud of him."

Finally, Luke butted in and said, "What're we standing around here for, come on into camp, and meet the rest of the boys."

Clay mounted, and they were all still talking at once as they slowly rode to the chuckwagon. When Wally Wallace, the cook, saw who was coming in, he dropped everything and came limping over to slap Clay on the back and said, "Welcome home, Clay."

"Thanks, Wally; this is my wife, Marilyn. She got an arrow in her shoulder a few days back. Will you see what you can do for it? I did the best I could with what I had. I know you're a pretty good trail hand doctor."

"Sure, come on over here by the fire." He brought a chair from the wagon, and sat it close to the fire, and brought a lantern out, and lit it to give him enough light to see what he was doing. Marilyn sat in the chair and unbuttoned her shirt and slid it off her shoulder. Wally removed the bandages Clay had applied and examined the wounds. After a few minutes of examining her, he said, "Everything looks like its healing good. You did a good job, Clay."

Wally had the food ready, and the men crowded around filling their plates, and stealing glances at Marilyn.

They were all sitting around eating when Lefty and George rode in. When they saw Clay sitting and eating like he had been doing it every day, they both stopped and stared. Finally, Lefty, being his usual self, said, "Wally, when did you start lettin' just any stray dog comes into camp and eat our food?"

Clay recognized the voice and jumped to his feet and piled into Lefty, giving him a big hug. "Lefty, I'm surprised you're still here. I figured you'd be married to that little gal at the diner, and have a house full of little ones by now."

"No, she had so many men after her she couldn't make up her mind which one she wanted, so we all had a meeting and decided for her."

Clay laughed and asked, "And what was that decision?"

"We decided none of us was big enough for her, and none of us wanted her bad enough to give up one of our friends, so we had another beer to celebrate and went home."

"That'll fix her."

Wally had taken Marilyn under his wing, and brought her a plate of food, and fixed a bed for her under the chuck wagon. He even hung tarps from the sides that hung to the ground, giving her some privacy. Soon after eating, she was nodding off, so he took her by the hand and led her to the bed, "You crawl in there, Missy, and get a good night's sleep." Then in a loud voice, "If these cowpokes will hold the noise down so a lady can sleep!"

The camp got quiet, and the men went to their bedrolls and turned in. Some of them would be awakened in a couple of hours to take over the night herding job.

Clay, Willie, Luke, Lefty, and George sat around the fire, catching up on what each of them had been doing since Clay rode away from home. When they asked Clay what he had been doing, he just said, "Wandering, trying to get things straight in my head. When I lost Ellen, I guess I went off the deep end. I was a deputy U.S. Marshall for a short while, a scout for the army for a year or so, I lived with some beaver trappers one winter, almost froze to death, I was a deputy sheriff in Wyoming for a while. That's where I met Marilyn, and my life just seemed to turn around and become complete again. I thought I had lost her when I saw that arrow sticking out of her. I just about lost it again until I saw she was still alive."

Luke asked, "How many Indians were there?"

"There were six that I know of. There may have been another one or two that got away, but we killed six of them."

"That must have been quite a fight."

"Yeah, I don't wanna do that again."

Lefty asked, "Where did you get all those horses? You have some beauties there."

Clay told about trapping the wild horse herd for most of them, "And the rest of them came from men trying to steal them from us. We only intended to try to capture six of the wild ones, but we ended up with ten, and couldn't decide which ones to turn loose, so we kept all of them. I think two or three of those stallions will be good for breeding on the ranch. We should be able to sell the others for some good money. What do you think?"

Lefty said, "I'll look them over in the morning and let you know."

George asked, "What are you gonna do now? We're driving this herd to Abilene, do you wanna tag along with us, or are you going on to the BAR W?"

"I haven't given that any thought. Running into y'all way out here was a big surprise. I think Marilyn needs rest, and this is a good place to camp. We may just lay up here for a day or two, and let her gain her strength back."

George turned to Luke, and Willie, and asked, "What do y'all think about letting the herd graze here for a couple of days. It'll give the men a rest too."

Both men said, "Sounds good to me. I can use the rest myself."

It wasn't long before they snuck off to their bedrolls. Clay eased in beside Marilyn without waking her and was soon asleep. He was awakened several times during the night by Marilyn groaning in her sleep, but she never fully awakened, so he knew she was getting the rest she needed.

The next day the herd was allowed to spread out and graze while the men rode circles around them to keep them from going too far. Clay and his two partners, Luke, and Willie, stayed in camp most of the day except for when they took Clay out to see the cattle.

Marilyn was up and moving around camp, helping Wally with some of his chores using her one good arm. She sat down several times to rest. When she did, Wally was right there to bring her anything she wanted.

Late in the day, the herd was brought back together in a tighter bunch and bedded down for the night.

Wally was up before the sun even thought about coming up and had the coffee brewing and breakfast ready. The men came out of their blankets complaining about having to get up before they could even see to find their horse. They all grabbed a quick breakfast, saddled up, and rode out to the herd, and relieved the night crew. By the time they finished eating, Wally had packed everything away and was hitching the mules to the wagon.

Clay had their string of horses lined out, and ready to ride when George walked over, and asked him, "Have y'all decided which way you're gonna go?"

"Yeah, we talked it over, and we think the best thing to do is go on to the BAR W. Marilyn is still hurting, and I would like to get her home as soon as I can."

"That's probably the right choice. We'll be on the trail at least another month, so we'll see you when we get back. If everything goes as planned, we'll have a big payday for you."

"Ok, y'all be careful."

"You too, you should be safe enough from here on. We ain't seen a single Indian. But you can never predict what an Indian will do."

They mounted, and each went their separate way. Clay and Marilyn sat for a long time watching the herd get underway.

Finally, Clay said, "That's a pretty sight."

Five days later, they came to the hill overlooking the BAR W. "There's your new home."

"Clay, it's beautiful. You didn't tell me it was this beautiful. Is that our house?"

"Yep, you like it?"

"Yes, it's bigger than anything I ever lived in."

They sat looking down at the place for a few more minutes when Marilyn asked, "Are you nervous after being gone so long?"

"Yeah, I didn't think I would be, but I can't help wondering what Carter's gonna think. I don't know what he's been told about me if anything."

They touched heels to their horses and walked them toward the house. When they were almost there, they heard a small voice yell, "Uncle Ed, there're a couple of riders coming with a bunch of horses. I wonder what they want."

Clay heard the reply and recognized Ed Carter's voice. He had butterflies in his stomach, thinking that the small voice he heard was probably Carter.

They rode past the house and came to the barn where they stopped and looked down at a young boy with reddish-blond hair and freckles across his nose. Clay's heart skipped a beat when he realized how much he looked like Ellen at that age.

Ed Carter stood staring a moment until he got over the shock.

Then he rushed up to Clay and just about dragged him from the saddle. They were slapping each other on the back, and both were talking at once until Ed stepped back, and looked Clay up, and down, and said, "Well, looks like you still have your hair, and you don't look like you've been mistreated too bad. Who is this pretty lady with you?"

"Marilyn Wade, this is Ed Carter, and I assume this young man is Carter Wade. Marilyn is my wife, and Ed was Ellen's brother."

"You're right, that young gentleman is Carter. Carter, come over here, I want you to meet this man. Do you remember me telling you about your Pa who used to live here, but he went away and would come back someday?"

"Yes, Sir." Carter was staring at Clay and slowly walking closer.

When he was within reach, Clay held out his hand to shake Carter's hand. Carter tentatively held out his hand and asked, "Are you my Pa?"

"Yes, I sure am, and I'm most proud to be back, and this pretty lady is your new mother. I hope we can be good friends."

"Yes, sir, I hope so too. Are you gonna be here for good?"

"I sure plan to, unless you tell me to leave."

"No, sir, I ain't gonna do that. It might be fun to have a real pa and ma."

Marilyn dismounted, and came over to meet Carter, and hugged him and kissed him on the cheek."

Carter blushed, and touched his cheek, and smiled.

"Are you really gonna be my Ma?"

"I sure am if you'll let me."

Carter smiled and said, "I'll give you a tryout and let you know."

They both laughed, and Marilyn hugged him again.

Clay said, "I'll tell you what, Carter. Since you know your way around, why don't you help me put these horses away, and feed 'em?"

"Ok, come on."

As they walked away, leading the horses to the corral, Carter looked back over his shoulder, waved to Marilyn with a big smile, and touched his cheek again.

THE END

Printed in the United States
By Bookmasters